By Brad Stucki

Copyright 2020 by Brad Stucki

Kindle Edition

Check out Brad Stucki's Author Page for occasional free downloads and click "Follow" for new release updates.

Chapter 1

Admiral J. Vance Hamblin, *Retired*, stood in the lit archway of the dingy bar he'd always heard about. In the past his personal code had made him look down on such places having foresworn any sort of stimulants. When he was young, he'd dreamed of getting into the Naval Academy and serving in the Imperium Fleet. That would take discipline. Now he realized he'd probably gone overboard but he'd always held to his youthful promise, that he'd not touch that stuff ever . . . Until now. It was late at night and he didn't know what else to do with himself.

He felt as if the bar entrance was swallowing him. That didn't seem such a bad thing. Someone brushed by and he moved to the side. Argon lights and syncopated music prattled over the din of blended voices. A green recruit on his first voyage would be less nervous. What should he do? How should he act? He probably stood out like a sore thumb. The drab brown "civvies" he wore had a razor-sharp crease in his shirt and trousers folded fit over his 38-year-old frame. The spit shine on his boots insured he would be distinctly out of place from all the scuffed shoes and equally scuffed people he observed inside.

His hand extended up and unconsciously brushed back his bright blond hair still standing stiff in its military crew, lost without his ship's cap -- and his uniform too for that matter. That's what had brought him here. To drown his sorrows like he'd heard others did, but he wasn't sure how to go about it.

Taking a deep breath, he stepped inside and found an open table. A waitress appeared, a look of bored indifference on her green tinted face. Face tinting was all the rage now in these places. Vance stared for a moment then ordered, trying to keep his voice quiet. "Water please."

The waitress continued to stand as if waiting for the joke to be over and the real order to come. "That's all? You want water?"

Vance glanced around. He was sure everyone in the place had heard. He nodded when no one appeared to notice. "Just water . . . For now."

The waitress committed a deep sigh and walked away. Vance turned to watch the crowd in the bar. Always a keen observer, this place was a veritable wonder of different types. Free spacers milled in roguish wares, almost a parody of swashbuckling pirates in the hollo novels. Business beings were in prim, slender dark colors with blue or red piping, as if it were a uniform. Dirt Siders were arrayed in varied forms of dress, almost comical at how they were trying to impress their importance on others. That was their way and it marked them more surely because of their desire to blend in. He'd run into them all countless times in the service.

Thinking of the service brought a twinge. The waitress sauntered up and snapped down his water bulb and moved off. Vance clutched it between his hands and began nursing it like an old friend. After his first pull and his throat was wet, he sat back, one hand on the table around the bulb, the other in his lap. He pursed his lips and rehearsed again his decision to retire from the admiralty.

He'd just turned 36 standard when he was the youngest Admiral ever to make rank in the history of the service, in spite of the best efforts of those above to put him down. That had been the hardest part to take. He knew he came out of the academy naive, but when he'd started to push to fulfill his assignments, rather than praise he got criticism. His superiors had told him not to be so spit-and-polish, not to be so danged diligent, not to be so "conscientious". They'd spat the words as if they were slimy. To him, those were things he'd always thought the service represented. Instead, his superiors were hard, jaded, and to him, represented all the things the service was against; complacency, mediocrity, and yes, even corruption.

When he'd reported these items to their superiors, they'd told him to relax, go with the flow. Rules and regulations were for brass in the ivory tower not for scrunchies out on patrol. Vance knew lack of discipline was dangerous, especially in the vacuum of space. When he'd pressed the point trying not to be too obnoxious, he found himself assigned to more and more remote duty; then more and more dangerous assignments. The problem for his critics was even in these assignments he'd performed well -- officer material. He not only completed every task, every dangerous duty, every monotonous assignment with fervor and outstanding character, they'd had no choice but to give promotions. If they couldn't get him to buy in, bore him, or get him killed, the only way to get him off their back was to recommend promotion and move him on.

Vance had quickly grown disgusted. It was only his belief in the nobility of his chosen calling that made him press on. Somewhere in the service, especially in the ranks of the highest officers of the fleet, there had to be men and women who felt as he did. For the most part he'd been mistaken.

Each time he'd been moved or promoted, he found pretty much the same environment. There were a few exceptions, of course, and those who recognized what Vance was trying to do in bringing some Naval Order to whatever task he'd been assigned, they quickly maneuvered to serve under him. Their rank leaders were only too happy to oblige. After all, it solved their problems as well.

This went on for some time. Each time he was promoted, he took with him as many of those who'd believed as he did as possible. It became almost two different divisions of the same service. There had been "Hamblin's" service, and then the rest. Whenever something critical needed to get done there was no doubt who'd pull the assignment. Vance didn't mind. That's what he, and those who followed him, had signed up for.

Then it came: The final promotion. When he made admiral, he'd vowed he'd clean up the service. Surely others in senior command felt as he did. Again, he'd been wrong. Whenever he'd proposed action to begin the clean-up, he found himself blocked by all the other senior command officers; up to and including the Chairman of the Joint Chiefs. That's when he'd had enough. He knew he was fighting a losing battle. No matter what he said -- and he was quite frank in what he said to the others -- he met with a stone wall. At last he'd been boxed into a position he couldn't act on his own as he'd done in the past. Even as a lowly scrunchie, he'd had some authority to act on his own within the scope of his own assignments. Even there he had made a difference. Now he couldn't. Who would have thought the rank of Admiral would be a place where someone could be kept out of the way? That's just what he realized had happened. His assigned duties amounted to nothing. He couldn't enact anything of substance without the concurrence of others, and that protected the status quo.

Then the real frustration began. He was pointedly ignored in joint meetings. His assignments were parsed even further to just overseeing construction, maintenance and repair of fleet ships, a duty at which he excelled and even those deep in the corruption appreciated his work. To everything else, he was just there, a figurehead, a name on a faceplate and an office. He had those who'd moved to serve under him working well, so even things which would normally occupy attention were delegated to capable people. There was nothing for him to do, nothing at which he could make a difference, nothing that meant anything. When he realized how fully he'd been immobilized was when he'd made the fateful decision to retire.

There was a huge fanfare, a military bash like no other. Vance knew it was a party celebrating his removal. The senior officers had shown genuine joy at his farewell party, *the only thing genuine about them,* Vance had thought at the time.

He'd cleaned out his quarters, started his pension, located new surroundings, and quickly became bored. The more he thought about it, the more he fumed. He'd surrendered! That made him madder than anything. He'd surrendered to the very things he'd sworn to fight. That's what had led him to the star port bar tonight. He'd heard about those who went on a whopping drunk after some sad episode in their lives. Vance didn't think it would help - in fact he knew it wouldn't, but what the heck. He didn't have anything better to do.

He was still nursing his tube of water gazing blankly into the dancing lights on the crowded dance floor when a few spacers sauntered in. They glanced in Vance's direction. One nudged the other, tilted his head in Vance's direction and led the way to the furthest corner. Just behind came a diminutive woman dressed in a plain blue coverall snug enough to leave no question of her gender. Her brown, curly hair was trimmed short with enough bounce to be attractive in a teasing way. She moved up to the bar next to a bruiser dressed like he was a handler from the ports and waved for a drink.

The big man slugged back his drink. He turned his head to gawk, a big smile growing at the corners of his beefy jowls.

"What have we here? A vision before my eyes. You picked the perfect spot to meet a real man, you have."

The woman turned a look on the man that would have withered anyone with an IQ above three. The man hesitated a moment, then the smile returned.

"Buy you a drink, lady?"

"No thank you," ice dripped from the words.

Again, the man smiled apparently relishing a challenge.

"Sure, you want a drink. I'm buying."

"I said no thank you. I'm not in the habit of letting strange men buy me anything." She regarded him with a long, scornful look. "From what I see, you're about as strange as they come."

Smiling, Vance focused on the exchange.

"Come on lady, that's not a nice thing to say. You don't even know me. I can be real friendly, you know." The beefy man leaned down and took hold of her hand. "Now let me buy you that drink." His tone left no room for argument.

The lady tried to pull away but couldn't break from the man's grasp. "Ouch! You're hurting me. Let go." She beat at the man with her other fist. The man laughed.

"You got spirit. I like that in a woman."

People began moving away not wanting to get involved. "Come on lady, just one little drink. Then we can go over to my place . . ."

"Why don't you leave the lady alone?" Vance had moved over from his table to stand behind the man. More people moved out of the vicinity. "I don't think she likes you."

"You stay out of this." The big man placed a hand on Vance's chest and gave him a shove, sprawling him into a nearby table.

"Hey! Watch what you're doing." The patrons at the overturned table moved off to the side, trying to salvage their drinks and keep a good view of what would come next.

Vance got up, straightening his shirt and brushing himself off. The man was stronger than he looked. That wasn't about to stop Vance. The man had a rough arm around the squirming woman and was calling the bar tender to bring another drink.

Vance moved up and tapped him on the shoulder. The man looked back over his shoulder. "Don't you know enough to go away when you ain't wanted?" The woman was still squirming under his grip.

"You really should let her go."

"Or what?" the man turned and put his other arm around the woman, pulling her tight against him while leering at Hamblin.

"This!" Hamblin drove his fist into the man's midsection as hard as he could. It felt as if he'd hit a rock. The man laughed.

"That all you got?" The man swung his right arm in a roundhouse. Vance ducked under and stomped on the man's instep with his heavy boot. The man howled and stumbled in pain. Vance followed with a right to the temple with a clenched fist. He could feel his knuckles split from the force. The big man roared in anger. He released the woman and lifted Vance off his feet in a bear hug. Feeling his ribs popping as if he were about to be squashed like a bug, Vance kicked out with both feet, catching the bruiser on the kneecaps, and drove the top of his forehead into the man's nose.

A grunt escaped the man's lips and a gush of blood started pouring from his mashed nose. Vance was dropped and the man held his hands up, trying to stem the flow of blood. The woman quickly darted out of the bar. Vance turned to follow when, again, he was grabbed by the arm and spun around. The bruiser had brought his right arm back and was about to deliver a blow Vance was sure would put him in a med unit. Quickly, he stepped inside the swing and felt the fist whistle past his ear. He brought his knee up sharply and heard a satisfying gasp of pain. Stepping back, Vance watched as the man fell to the floor, clutching himself. He looked around feeling the stares of the bar patrons. Suddenly two dark ship-suit dressed men stepped forward. One flashed identification too quickly for Vance to make it out.

"Come with me, please."

Vance blinked. There was something familiar about this man.

"Wait. I haven't done anything. I was just helping the lady."

"What lady?" the man asked. His companion was staring pointedly at the other bar patrons who started moving back to their tables or turned back to face the bar. They didn't want any trouble with these officials, whoever they were.

"She just left." Vance looked at the man still on the floor. He was still groaning. "Look, I don't want any trouble. I was just making sure this guy wouldn't force himself on her." Vance looked back at the stranger struggling to place where he knew him.

"Doesn't look like he'll force himself on anyone now. Please come along."

"I don't think I will." Vance was starting to get angry. He hadn't done anything wrong. "If there're damages, I'll settle them with the owner. I'll be hanged if I'll be railroaded for helping a woman in trouble."

The man stepped closer as his friend continued to watch the crowd as if expecting trouble. "Vance, please. It's not safe here. We need to get you away." His voice was pitched so only Vance could hear.

Hamblin was shocked the man had used his name. He stared hard, still trying to place his familiar face. The stranger noticed his gaze.

"We went to school together, way back. I'm a bit different, but you knew me as Mycal Petrs."

It was true. Vance could see it now. "What? ---"

"You just have to trust me. We have to leave now."

He remembered Mycal, had often wondered about him. They'd been friends, always in the same group all through his teens. They'd talked about the future many times. Vance had kept trying to get him to enlist with him in the service. Mycal always demurred. Had always said he was needed in the family business though he was never specific about what that business was. Vance had never figured it out. Mycal had disappeared upon graduation from secondary school. Vance had gone to his house and found it vacant. He'd checked with the neighbors on either side. All they knew was that movers had come in early without so much as a word and they were gone. No, they didn't know where or why. They'd been pleasant enough neighbors, though private.

"Vance? You have to decide. There are people after you and you need to leave with us now if you're going to." Mycal gave him a look that Vance remembered. It was a serious look, one of great concern. Mycal had been a caring person though not vocal about it. He'd only seen that look one other time. It was when one of their friends had gotten injured and Mycal was trying to keep him calm while administering first aid. That made up Vance's mind.

"I'll go."

Mycal nodded to his associate and they both started toward the door, Vance in between as if they were his honor guard . . . or bodyguard.

***

As soon as they left the bar, the big man rolled off the floor as if nothing had happened and slipped out behind them dabbing at his bloody nose with a rag he'd pulled from his pocket. He left just enough space to keep them in sight, but not enough they could easily look back and notice.

Chapter 2

Mycal led them out onto the northbound slideway for 30 seconds, then nodded to his partner and they grasped Vance's arms and said, "This is where we get off." Mycal indicated an intersection with his free hand.

Vance didn't know whether to be irritated that they were helping him like some old man, or worried they were now trying to restrain him. If they were trying to restrain, they'd be disappointed. He'd decided to go with them, so he thought he'd play it through at least until he knew what was really going on.

"One . . . two . . . three." They stepped in unison off the slideway and went down a ramp into the darker allies of the space port.

They moved along at a brisk pace. They'd dropped Vance's arms and he was moving freely beside them. Both Mycal and his partner kept their eyes moving, watching. They turned down another alley and Vance realized they were heading toward the private hangers. The commercial port was the opposite direction. This was getting more interesting all the time. He stayed silent. They continued moving quickly down the alley for several hundred meters. Both Mycal and his associated kept their eyes moving and occasionally glancing back as if seeing if they were being followed. Vance felt he would have to wait to get answers anyway. He trusted Mycal. At least he trusted who Mycal had been when he knew him years earlier.

Without a word, Mycal grasped his arm, bringing them all to a stop in front of a dark, silent hanger. Vance had noticed when they entered this section the lights in the alleyway had been blackened. There was enough dim light to see their steps but not enough for anyone to get a real visual on anything that could possibly happen in the alley. There was no talking. Mycal's associate pulled out a palmcorder and touched a few buttons. A man-door slid back in the metal sided hanger and Mycal ducked inside. Vance followed with the associated close behind. He heard the door slide shut again in the pitch black he had stepped into. As soon as the door had snicked shut a blue, hazy light grew slowly, allowing their eyes to adjust. Mycal was standing facing him. A smile of relief appeared. "I still don't have time to give you a full briefing, but at least here I can give you a quick rundown while we prep for takeoff." Mycal's associated nodded at Mycal and ducked past them, moving further into the hanger.

The blue light grew in intensity showing the interior of the hanger. Vance could now make out the bulk of the ship within. It had sleek lines and appeared built for speed. The size indicated a 10-man cruiser. It looked private, but even in the dim light he could make out the curved nacelles on the sides indicating weapon placements. Private ships never had those. The associate was again punching buttons on the palmcorder and a seam of light appeared as the hatch seal opened and a gangway hinged down. He hustled up the stairs lit by dim amber lights with the rest of the ship's interior still dark. They were being very careful. Vance was sure the warehouse was shielded from allowing any light to bleed out.

Mycal touched his arm and moved forward taking the steps up into the dark interior. Vance shrugged and followed, resting his hand on the bulkhead, as if touching it he could determine its intent, its destination. They were going off world for sure. This was no puddle jumper. It was an interstellar capable craft. He thought of turning back. If he stepped on this ship, he was making a commitment and there was no information on which to make this decision. All he had was the sudden appearance of a friend he hadn't seen in years. Vance hesitated on the ramp.

He recalled what he'd known of this youth so many years back. When they were young, Mycal had never been one to act like a kid, even then. He never did a practical joke, never teased. Mycal had been happy, good natured, and never got angry – except for one time they'd seen a small kid being bullied. Mycal had torn into the bigger kid before the group knew what was going on. When it was over, Mycal was embarrassed. He'd taken the bully apart. At the time Vance had been amazed at the ferocity of the attack, and it had made him a bit nervous for several weeks after. There was something about what Mycal had done that, now he thought about it, had spoken of some hand to hand training. Odd he should recognize that now. The memory had been buried along with the years. Calling it up now didn't give him any distinct comfort.

Underlying, though, Mycal had always been a good kid. He hadn't tried to run things, hadn't ever tried to impose his will on the group. He was just always there with them, happy to go along. They were a good group. Good kids; idealistic and expecting to impact mankind in their lives, especially Vance with his dreams of being in the fleet.

Thinking of the fleet and recalling his bitter disappointment in that institution made him grit his teeth. That decided it. There was nothing for him here. The memory of the *good kid* Mycal had been tipped the scale. A man can change, yes. But he'd sensed that kid still inside when the recognition had finally dawned.

Vance dropped his hand off the bulkhead and stepped inside.

Mycal was waiting for him at the top of the stairs as if understanding and respecting the decision Vance had just made.

"The bridge is this way, Admiral."

Vance caught the use of his rank though he really didn't hold it any longer. He nodded and followed. The bridge wasn't far. Backlit consoles provided the only light. Two others were on the bridge. One was Vance's colleague. Vance was taken aback as the woman at the Comms board turned towards him and nodded. It was the woman from the bar. He turned to Mycal.

"I see you remember Cassie," he said.

Vance started to feel set up.

"It was necessary to get you away quickly and provide a diversion at the same time," Mycal continued. "You've got an active, open contract on your head and there was no time for a polite invitation."

Vance's mind started to churn. "And maybe you're filling it?" He didn't question about the contract, though that seemed preposterous. Who would want him dead? He was ineffectual in about every way now that he was out of the service: No command, no influence, no followers, nothing.

"You know . . . knew . . . me better than that or your instincts wouldn't have let you come with me. The contract is about *what* you know – and *who* you know is doing what, and where. Those at the top don't want you publishing any memoirs."

Vance's mind was still reeling.

"We got you out, so you'd have a choice as to what to do next."

"How would you know about any contract?" Vance was starting to put things together. "You're plugged in yourself, and now I want to know who and what you are."

"Gomy's aboard," Mycal's colleague said, turning from his navigation station. "Hatch is sealed and we're ready for lift."

"Proceed," Mycal said and then held out his identification to Vance. This time he didn't take it away. Even in the dim light Vance could make out the shield and the crest of Imperial Security blazoned on it. "I was sent by the highest levels. We've been watching you for some time, just waiting until we could *talk* to you."

"You can bet we're going to be talking," Vance said then turned as a hulking man entered the bridge still holding a rag to his nose and took up what Vance recognized as the weapons station. It didn't surprise him it was the same man he'd taken out at the bar. Vance shook his head. "I feel like a green recruit. You had me."

"I knew you couldn't resist a damsel in distress. Besides, it was the only thing I could come up with as a diversion on such short notice. Candidly I was shocked when you made for the bar. That's not like you."

Vance was watching the view screen as the hanger door raised and the navigator touched sensors and the ship slid silently out of the hanger without lights. The view changed as the ship inclined and drove for atmosphere.

"Where are we going and why?" Things were happening fast, and he knew he didn't have time for subtle questions.

"I'll answer the second question first. We need to get you out of the sites of every hit man who can hold a weapon. The contract on you is big and has excited a few thugs. We also wanted to speak with you, to make you an offer of service. We know you're disappointed – no frustrated - with the service. Maybe we can give you a chance to finally make a real difference. As to where we're going, you name the destination. We'll take you there. Right now, we need to get you off planet and away from anyone with ill intent."

Vance thought a moment. "Take me out into a deserted portion of space where we can sit, and you can answer all my questions without interruption."

"Fair enough." Mycal turned to the navigator / pilot. "Take her out atmosphere and follow a random course until we're ready to hit hyper. Make sure no one gets a tracer on us. Find us a big empty space and go there."

"Understood." The navigator smiled quickly at Vance then turned to his board and began dancing his fingers over the console. Vance turned his attention to the view screen. The darkness began to form into little pinpricks of light as the atmosphere died away and the darkness of night resolved into the blackness of space with the light of stars beginning to show brighter without any atmosphere haze.

"Sir, we're being hailed," Cassie said from the Comms station. "It's military."

"They're moving to intercept," the navigator added. "We can't get a run up to hyper because they're blocking the way."

"Put it onscreen," Mycal said and moved to the center chair, leaving Vance back in the shadows of the bridge.

An officious looking Captain appeared onscreen. "Heave to and stand by for boarding."

"This is a private vessel," Mycal said. "I believe you have to state a reason for stopping us. It's the law."

"I'm stopping you for an inspection. We have reason to believe you have a fugitive on board."

"Just your belief is not sufficient if I recall the law correctly," Mycal countered. "You have probable cause?"

"You some kind of attorney?" the Captain spat. "I don't need probable cause. You will comply or you will be shot down."

Vance moved forward into the visual pickup. He couldn't take the arrogance. He'd had to put up with it too many years, and he wasn't going to stomach it now.

"This is Admiral J. Vance Hamblin, recently retired. This ship is going about in a legal and lawful fashion. You have no cause for detaining us unless there has been a system wide band broadcast, warning all ships they must stop for inspection. You have also not stated a probable cause. There has been no broadcast. You will remove yourself from our flight path and allow us to pass."

The captain's eyes went wide. He looked to the side and made a cutting motion across his neck. The transmission went blank.

"Sir, they're powering up weapons." This came from the hulking brute at the weapons console. Gomy was his name, Vance absently remembered. It was an old habit of remembering all the names of those you worked with. Had he unconsciously decided he was working with these people?

"Shields up!" Mycal turned to Vance. "Looks like you're the fugitive they're looking for." Mycal turned to Cassie. "Any other transmission?"

"None, sir," she replied.

"I wonder if that Captain is looking to cash in on your contract. No more warnings."

"They're preparing to fire." Gomy said.

"Evasive! Take her down and under. They have less gun coverage there. Then start defensive pattern Delta. This class of cruiser has speed on us, but we can out jinx their weapons lock for a while."

"You know your ships," Vance commented. He had been about to suggest the same thing. Mycal was far more knowledgeable than any civilian should be. Of course, he wasn't a civilian. His ID had pegged him as Imperial Security. Still, it was unusual to have a non-military man know so much about the strengths and weaknesses of a military vessel just off the fly.

"These used to be your guys. We can't outrun them, and we can't outgun that big of ship. Looks like they want you dead. Need any more proof?" Mycal said, his eyes intense.

The little ship rocked with a glancing hit from a laser pulse. "Their gunner is good. Did you train him?" Mycal asked.

"Screens were phased by that hit," Gomy said, fingers dancing over his screens. Shields are holding for now. I'm bringing them back up to full." There was a pause. "Another shot off. Clean miss. We won't be lucky forever."

Mycal looked at Vance. "No offense but we're trying to save your butt. Any suggestions?"

Vance grit his teeth, hardly believing what he was about to do. He was about to fight against the service he'd sworn to serve. Yet this captain had broken all procedure, ignored the law. There had been only a half-hearted attempt to apprehend. The shots they were firing were not to disable, but to destroy. It was no better than piracy.

He moved over to the weapons console. "You mind?" he asked.

Gomy looked at Mycal, who nodded. Gomy hesitated, then moved just far enough for Vance to stand at station, glancing down at the console.

Vance noted the console was top of the line. It would be high-end for a battleship to have this sophisticated of station, much less in this small spitkick. He absently wondered again about Mycal and his connections.

Satisfied he could do what he wanted, he turned, noticing Gormy hovering beside him like a mother hen guarding eggs.

"If you don't mind," Vance jerked his head for Gomy to move further back. He didn't want anyone to see what he was going to do. Security was a hard habit to break and he still wasn't sure what was going on.

Gomy hesitated. "Do it." Mycal ordered. Gomy moved, clearly not wanting to.

Vance's hands danced over the console adjusting the phasing of the weapons systems. When he was over the maintenance on the fleet's ships, he'd come across a weakness in all the shield's defenses. It had been a fluke that he'd caught it. Running a diagnostic on a weapons simulator he'd hit a frequency that was half between bands that shouldn't exist but could be modulated by holding the dial halfway between settings on a weapons frequency unit then moving it back and forth while firing. It was just a silly thing he did, trying to see if he could cause the system to crash so he could take his frustrations out on something. What he found was that the simulator actually found the half frequency and fired, and it slipped right through the shields of the simulated battlecruiser. Curious, he'd tried it again, and again. Then he'd set up a test with two ships in the yard for maintenance.

The simulator hadn't been wrong. There was a way to breach the fleet's shields; every one of them, every time. He immediately classified his findings and sent a report to the builders and the rest of the Joint Chiefs. He'd brought it up in their meetings. As usual, he'd been ignored. *Time to find out if they were paying attention after all.*

Vance turned to Mycal. "Plot a course back directly underneath. I'm going to take out their engines."

Gomy chuckled and shook his head, as if humoring a stupid kid. Vance's anger started to flare. Mycal turned to the navigator. "Do it."

His hands danced across his console then turned back to Mycal and nodded. Mycal turned back to Vance, who also nodded his readiness. "Execute."

The star scape on the viewscreen whirled. Vance considered the tremendous gravities they were going through which would crush them all if the inertial dampeners weren't working. The Imperium cruiser came back onto the screen. He could just imagine what the captain must be wondering. Vance was about to suggest they take evasive going in, but the screen zigged, and he realized the navigator had already assumed such. Good.

Vance turned back to his console and locked on to the rear portion of the ship he wanted to target. He hoped targeting was as advanced as the rest of this equipment. He'd be too busy with the modulation to worry about targeting. If it was off and hit a vital station, people would die. Even though they were trying to kill him, he wasn't sure he wanted deaths on his head, especially those he knew were innocent, just following orders, not knowing what situation they were called to Combat Stations for.

On the view screen the ship grew closer, sliding from side to side, weapons fire sliding past them as the navigator continued the deadly dance. Then Vance's hand began tweaking the control knob, hand poised over the firing stud, watching as a mini screen on the console showing a tactical display and firing solution came closer . . . "Now." he said to himself while touching the stud.

A beam lanced out from their little ship and as expected, sliced through the cruiser's shields as if they were non-existent.

"Direct hit!" Gomy shouted. Vance turned to see he was again hovering over the console staring at the tactical with him. So much for secrets. He should have noticed Gomy had moved closer, but with his focused concentration, he hadn't. What to do about it? He'd figure that out later. For now, he wanted to know if that hit had done what he wanted.

"Sir, the cruiser is dead in space. Their engines took a hit," the navigator reported.

"Good shooting, Admiral," Mycal said. "How did you get through their shields?"

Vance turned to Gomy who'd moved back, eyeing him with a blank face. "That hole in the shields is classified." He put emphasis in that last word while looking directly at Gomy. Gomy nodded.

"Any damage other than engines?" Vance asked, anxious.

"None, sir." The navigator responded back directly to him. That was out of order, but Vance ignored it. It was a sign of his acceptance of Vance's authority, though being retired, he technically had none.

Mycal turned back to the view screen now showing empty space. "Put us back on your original heading, Ben. Jump for some empty space that, hopefully, will be peaceful and quiet." Mycal turned back to Vance.

He nodded acceptance.

The view screen shifted to the star streaks of jumping, then the gray swirls of hyperspace.

"Ten light minutes out?" the navigator asked.

"That should do it," Mycal said. "Rig us in stealth mode." This he said to Gomy, who moved back to his console. Vance got out of the way and went to stand by Mycal.

"Dropping out, now," the navigator said. The view screen streaked with light from stars red-shifting then normal space returned. "Scanning . . . All clear sir."

"Stealth mode engaged," Gomy announced.

"No chatter," Cassie said from communications.

They were well trained, Vance observed now the heat was off. Better than any crew he'd seen, except those he'd trained, Vance thought. Definitely not civilian.

Mycal turned to Vance. "Now to answer your questions." He glanced over his shoulder. "Ben, you have the con, we'll be back in the conference room."

Mycal lead the way off the bridge, down the narrow hall and turned at the second door on the right, hitting the open toggle. The door snicked open.

Vance followed him inside the room. Lights came on. Vance saw It was decked with a dark wood table, six cushioned leather chairs surrounding and dark wood paneled walls giving it the appearance of a miniature board room.

"Nice," Vance said as he took the proffered seat at the head of the table. Mycal took a seat on the right corner chair next and touched a toggle in a keyboard he'd slid out from under the table.

The door snicked shut, the lights went dim and a hollo pixilated into view from the center of the table. Vance leaned back in the chair and watched the visual form into the head and shoulders of the Empress of the Imperium seemingly staring straight at him. This was a shock. Of all the things he could have expected, this was not one of them. The image began to speak.

"Admiral Vance. I'm sorry to have interrupted your retirement but you are needed. I know you have every right to say no. I know you have worked tirelessly to fix the problems you saw in the service. I saw them too, but because of reasons I won't go into now, couldn't fix them from where I sit. You have learned from experience that sometimes the position isn't all it's cracked up to be, and your hands can be tied."

Vance knew what she was saying all too well. The anger inside him flared anew and all the thoughts he'd had about giving up came rushing back.

"What I can offer you is a chance to fight back, but this time with some real teeth. I'm asking you to join me in a serious operation to clean up the service. It needs to be done and quickly. There are other concerns which, again, I won't go into here, but necessitate a cleaning up of the service in short order. I trust you are the man who can do it. I need you. I hope you accept. That's all I can say now.

"Major Petrs knows how to contact me with your decision, and once made, he will either see you to any destination you choose, or he will bring you to me, where we can meet in person and I can brief you more fully.

"I don't have to tell you regarding the security of this conversation. However, you can trust Major Petrs implicitly. He has my full confidence, and should, I think, have yours. After all, you were schoolmates at one time. Think about the strength of his character from before. I can assure you he hasn't changed. I hope to see you soon. If not, good luck with your retirement and I'm sorry to have misjudged you."

The hologram faded. Vance heard another toggle being touched on the keyboard and the lights came back up. He turned to see Mycal watching him. That didn't bother him. He was thinking, his mind turning over what he'd just heard.

There was plenty under the surface, he could tell. Something big was up. He wondered just how the Empress could use him to clean up the service. How could he do it with so many in top leadership positions complacent or on the take? What types of powers would he be granted which would allow him to do what needed to be done? Was it constitutional? Heck with that, would it be supported by the actual troopies? That's what mattered most. They would either support him or turn on him. Either way, it would be far from easy.

It was then he realized he wasn't considering whether or not to accept. He was thinking about *how* he could make it work. He was back in the fight.

He looked at Mycal.

Mycal touched another toggle on the keyboard and spoke. "Ben, set course for the pre-programmed location. We just got ourselves a new recruit."

Chapter 3

"So where are we going?" Vance asked

"I could tell you, but it's only designation is the coordinates, which I doubt you'd recognize. It's an area that has been blacked out of the maps for years for *special meetings* known only to a few of the most trusted in the government. It's what you'd call an extra-large Situation Room.

"Suffice it to say, it's in about a dead a place in space as we could find close to the heart of the Imperium. And the way we'll take to get there is a classified route also, even while we're rigged for stealth running."

Mycal held up his hands to show he was not trying to be evasive. "If you want, I'll show you the coordinates and the route. You heard the Empress. She is trusting you, so that gives you the highest clearance there is."

Vance took a deep breath, taking time to let things settle in a bit. The way to this moment had been pretty charged. Time to take stock now and let things catch up.

"How long will we be traveling?"

"By the route we'll take, about 72 standard hours."

Vance sat a moment, thinking.

"Okay," he finally said. "Talk to me. Tell me about you and why I find myself sitting in this ship heading for . . . wherever it is we're heading."

"Fair enough," Mycal said. "I'll inform you about me and about this ship – and all it represents. Some of this, the Empress needs to address. I don't want to steal her thunder. It would be bad for my career prospects."

Vance nodded.

"How about we continue this over some physical activity?" Mycal said. "I need to blow off a little tension, and I think you do too. Besides, we'll consider it part of a demonstration of sorts."

"A demonstration? Of what?"

"You'll see," Mycal said, and stood, moving to the door of the conference room. Vance followed.

They moved further down the corridor, then down a branching set of steps to a lower deck.

Vance was impressed by the ship's design. It was compact but seemed to have a high level of quality and amenities based on the materials and finish on the bulkheads.

"This looks like a cross between a diplomatic ship and a raider," Vance remarked remembering the bridge set up, the weapons console, the sleek lines he'd seen from outside and now the elegant lines of the interior. ". . . or a spy ship that covers as a private vessel."

"That's an astute observation," Mycal said. "You're pretty close to it, as you'll soon realize." Mycal turned right into another corridor toward the center of the ship. He stepped through a bulkhead that was dressed up to look like a wood panel door if you ignored the atmosphere seals – pretty heavy duty to boot.

"And this is a real tight ship," Vance observed, trying to draw more information out. "Looks like the designers had an eye for quality but expected heavy action."

"Thanks," Mycal said, stepping into a broad room with a higher ceiling than the companionway they'd just stepped from. "I appreciate the compliment. I was actually the designer – or the main one anyway."

The lights flicked on via sensors in the walls illuminating a small-scale gymnasium. It was about 30 feet across and along the far wall was a series of exercise equipment set into the wall and fastened down in case of inertial failure. The center of the room was covered in a layer of matting Vance recognized was situated for sparring and calisthenics. The room wasn't large by gym standards, but large enough for about 4 people to use the room comfortably at one time.

"All the comforts of home," Mycal said watching as Vance turned about the room, taking it all in. on the right were a wall of mirrors so one could observe their own movements, like a ballet studio, which made Vance wonder if the room doubled for dance practice too. He smiled and Mycal caught it.

"Don't judge until you see my demonstration. That's why we're here. That and to knock some kinks out from the abrupt exit we had to make. I always need to relax a bit after a tense situation where we have to hold back. Let's me vent my spleen in more productive ways than snapping at my crew."

Mycal pointed to a doorway on the left. "Through there is the showers and locker room. You'll find a locker there with some workout gear that will stretch to fit the stature you've attained." Mycal smiled as Vance realized they'd settled into the same humor they'd had as school children years gone by. "My gear is over here." Mycal pointed to another door on the other side. "Captain's prerogative. I get my own locker and shower. Can't have the brass messing about with the enlisted, you know."

Vance smiled, nodded then turned to the doorway. "I'll meet you back out here." He could have pulled rank, and was tempted to do so, based on *old times* but decided for now, the gear he'd need was in a spare locker anyway. Seemed part of Mycal's *demonstration* would include a bit of sparring. That was good for him. He was just now realizing how tense he was.

Inside he found a small locker room and shower. Enough for 5 people – mainly the crew in shifts, he suspected. Three lockers appeared taken. He opened the door on a spare locker and found a workout suit typical of the Service. It was truly 'one size fits all,' and donned the gear. It felt good to wear something familiar again, something he loved and had dedicated his life to serving. It was the ideal of the Service, and he was surprised something so simple could stir such feelings in him again. There appeared moisture in the corners of his eyes, and he again was surprised at his emotions. "Doddering sentimental fool," he said out loud as he pushed the locker shut and stretched, letting the garment material adjust itself to a more comfortable fit.

Back out in the main room, Vance noted Mycal on the mats going through stretches and warm-ups. Vance started his own regimen, not saying anything, instead, centering himself as he always did prior to a practice session. It was part of the physical training, geared to relaxing the mind as well as the body in preparation for peak performance in both. Mycal had been right, this did feel good to get the tension out. It would make what he would learn sink in easier and allow him to evaluate it better. But what was he going to learn? Time to be about it, Vance decided and stood up and moved to the center of the mat as Mycal did the same.

"Ready old man?" Mycal said, smiling. He stood casually, like he was just standing on a street somewhere talking to an old friend.

"Last I remembered," Vance said as he assumed a ready stance, "you were a month older than me, boy."

With that, Vance launched into a throw which always worked. It was something he'd mastered and used on Junior Officers as a means of breaking the ice and humbling them at the same time.

Going through the motions without thought, Vance grasped hold of what he thought would be a surprised Mycal, but instead, he felt himself being gripped on the outside arm as Mycal dodged beneath him and using his own motion against him, Vance found himself thrown in the only counter to the move he'd ever experienced. He landed hard on the mat but used his momentum to carry him quickly back to his feet, turning and back on guard.

Mycal had already turned, facing him, and standing again, like nothing had happened.

He was quick. Vance remembered. As kids, Mycal had not really shown off, nor had he demonstrated much physical ability other than what a normal lanky kid would do, except the one time Vance had already remembered. The image surfaced again of Mycal tearing into a bully picking on a smaller boy. It had been over almost as soon as it had started and the bully was on the ground, groaning and Mycal helping the small boy up.

"You wool gathering, old man?" Mycal said, raising his eyebrows. "Or are you wondering what just happened? Looks like the Admiralty didn't require you to keep up on hand-to-hand."

Vance grinned. This was going to be fun, no matter how it came out. It felt good to hit something hard, even if it was his body hitting the mat.

"We'll see, boy," Vance said as he moved in again, slower this time and with more deliberation. What would work? He'd already used his surprise gambit that had never failed. Let's see how sheer grit and determination worked – along with a bit of finesse.

This time Mycal was the one moving forward, grasping Vance by the left arm, his movements faster than Vance thought possible in a human, but Vance thought he was ready. He stepped into Mycal and ducked under and pulled on the arm he'd grabbed, moving into a throw over his right shoulder. He was gratified this seemed to be working, and Mycal went with the throw, then a surprised Vance realized Mycal was again using his own momentum to follow through with the throw and pulling Vance into a counter throw as Mycal went to the mat, pulling Vance and sending him partway across the room, slamming again, hard into the mat. This time Vance didn't roll out of it as fast, though he came to his feet as fast as anyone else could have after that kind of impact. Mycal had some deeply hidden surprises, it seemed.

Mycal was on his feet again facing him, still in that nonchalant stance. It almost looked belligerent this time, though Mycal didn't show that in his face.

"I seem to be behind a bit on my advanced hand-to-hand workouts," Vance said, warily moving forward. "Where did you learn those moves?"

"This is part of the briefing, but if you'll excuse me Admiral, I'd rather show than tell. In a bit, I think you'll be able to surmise some things, which will be more effective than me just telling. And I'm doing this in a most respectful manner, I assure you." Mycal grinned again in an expression Vance remembered as Mycal's *sincere* look.

"As you wish," Vance said. This time he punched out with his left fist. If grappling wouldn't work, he'd try another tack on the hand-to-hand. Mycal casually swatted the punch aside, but Vance had quickly followed it with a right roundhouse while stepping forward. Mycal ducked under the right, barely evading it, but counter punching with a short jab with his own left into Vance's kidney, then stepped around behind Vance, moving away, and leaving Vance wondering, again, what had happened.

Vance had been a championship boxer in the early days of his enlistment and had been undefeated until he'd grown in rank to where it was no longer *politic* to box anymore.

He felt the sting of pain in the kidney but forced himself to stand up straight and come to a guard position in case Mycal moved forward on the attack. Instead, he was standing back, casual as you please with a stupid grin on his face.

"You move faster than anyone should be able," Vance said.

"See, the demonstration is working, and you're starting to think about this. Why do you suppose that is? And who do you think I work for?"

Those questions caught Vance off guard, but it slid his mind into a direction it had started to drift in.

"I surmise," Vance said, "A special security service I'm not familiar with, which would be very rare, given my clearance. That denotes Imperial level. Court status, and by the way of the special training, which I detect, and by the communication we just had with the Empress, I would gather you are with a special branch of Her security known only to a very few, since I don't know anything about it."

"Bingo." Mycal said.

Vance laughed. "You always used to say that when someone got something right. I never asked then, but now I want to know. What does, 'Bingo.' mean?"

"It's a real old reference, way before intersystem travel. It means, 'you hit the nail on the head.'"

Vance shook his head. "And what does that mean?" Vance hadn't a clue what a 'nail' was unless it referred to his fingernail, but that didn't make sense.

"For an old man, your education is sorely lacking." This time Mycal started to move forward, his hand moving faster than Vance could register and he felt slaps on both sides of his face, both sides of his arms, then felt himself being pulled forward as Mycal fell back, and Vance was again flying over and slamming onto the mat. Mycal didn't give him time to regain his feet, which he would have done even slower this time, but instead followed him over and was now holding him in a choke hold he wasn't familiar with. He couldn't breath and was about to black out when Mycal loosened the hold.

"Any other observations?"

Vance's vision came back and found himself staring up at Mycal's ridiculously grinning face.

"Advanced training wouldn't account for all the speed. You have Augmentation?" That was supposed to be illegal in all the treaties.

"You now have Top/Top security clearance and know all my secrets save one . . . well, maybe two," Mycal stood and helped Vance to his feet. "I'm the Empress' brother. That's one secret."

Vance felt he could have been knocked over by a feather. "The Empress' brother? I didn't know she had any family. Why keep that a secret?"

"Vance, think about it. Again, I'm not being flippant. I know things sink in better when you discover them yourself. Answer your own question."

Vance thought, his mind moving rapidly, and the physical exertion – no, punishment – helped his mind to slip rapidly into the easiest solutions.

"Security. For her, as well as you – and any other family. And the special training and augmentation means it's a personal, closely guarded thing. Hardly anyone knows. It's a *secret weapon* to assist when things get really bad."

"You went deeper than I thought you would," Mycal said, this time his face gravely serious. It's not a look Vance had seen Mycal ever have when younger – except that one time. "Think about what that means and why you're here."

Vance was silent a moment, thinking. "Oh Crap." he said.

"You're right," Mycal said. "On all counts. I'm part of a special branch of security that's personally responsible for the safety of the Empress. It goes beyond that of her Security Service everyone knows about. This is only for certain members of her family . . . and now you."

Vance was startled a bit he'd been right. But it made sense. And then the last comment . . . "Wait a minute . . ." then he stopped. Yes, he supposed he had agreed to meet with the Empress and go along with Mycal, so . . . he could be considered what Mycal had termed a *Recruit*.

"Never mind," Vance finished.

Mycal continued smiling as if he was reading Vance's thoughts. "Wipe that stupid grin off your face," Vance said, moving forward and reigning a combination of punches as fast as he could muster, hoping to catch Mycal by surprise. And he did.

Mycal stepped back, then back again, ducking, blocking, swaying and finally one punch connected to Mycal's jaw. Vance had held back just enough it wouldn't cause damage, but the punch swirled Mycal around. It felt good to finally connect, and Vance's frustration started to find a release. Which was short lived. Vance should have known better.

Mycal went with the punch, then dropped lower as he swung around and swept out with a leg, catching Vance unaware it was so fast, and Vance slammed to mat yet again. This time he stayed down. Not because he was hurt, but because something had just occurred to him.

Vance held up his hands, calling for a break as he slowly got to his feet. Mycal stood by, waiting. Vance was a bit gratified to find a red mark rising on Mycal's jaw, but still he was grinning.

"Pretty good old man. No one has touched me like that in years. You're better than you realize."

Vance ignored the compliment. "Tell me what's going on in the Imperium. If you're coming to me, this is something more than just rot in the navy. The Empress could always fire her top people and find others to fill the spots who would clean things up. And you aren't just a bodyguard. There's more to this, and it goes beyond the service."

"I told you finding your own answers were better. And if you think about it, you've already stated the answer to what you didn't ask. You are correct. Absolutely and unequivocally. However, as to what's really going on, that's why you're being recruited. You and I are going to find that out and fix it. But there I go. You've twigged out of me what the Empress was going to talk to you about. Well, at least you'll have some time to think about it so you can give her your answer immediately. Sis hates to be kept waiting when an answer is obvious." Mycal rubbed his jaw. "But you'll have to swear I didn't tell you a thing – which if you recall honestly, I didn't say a word. You just figured it all out yourself. That will impress the heck out of her – but I can't imagine why. I would have wondered about you if you hadn't figured it out for yourself."

This time Vance laughed.

"Let's hit the showers," Mycal said, "and then get some chow. The crew is waiting to meet you formally. They seem to be in awe of your record, though I can't imagine why." Mycal smiled. "However, since you were able to catch me one on the kisser, I think they may be a bit right."

"They aren't augmented are they. Just you. And they are part of your "Service" but not dialed in fully. They don't know you're the Empress' brother." Vance was starting to see things falling into place. It had been a gift of his, his *tactical ability* others had called it. But whatever it was, Vance found he could string things together based on small threads of information and extrapolate to find what he needed to gain an edge.

"Your reputation is well earned," Mycal nodded. "And remember, I didn't tell you any of this. But please keep it to yourself. I don't want to blow my deeper cover even with my crew. It's not for me. It's for them. It helps them stay a bit innocent and safer if they don't know, and if others don't know. I don't want them to be taken for any supposed leverage bad guys may feel they can get on me – and hence the Empress."

Vance nodded. "No worries. I won't say anything. I agree with the limits. Makes sense, especially if others knew, your effectiveness in what you're doing would be severely compromised and you'd have to be pulled from the front lines of – whatever it is you do."

"You know very well what I do . . . and what you'll be doing shortly." The grin was back.

Chapter 4

After a sonic shower and more time for thinking, Vance dressed in ships livery he'd found placed inside his locker by a crew member. His other clothing had been removed. His personal effects where still there. He met Mycal and they went back up the stairs to the main companionway and strode farther back into the ship, though not far, until they turned right into another, smaller room, the galley and dining room.

It was brightly lit, well-appointed and appeared like what one would expect as a simple, fine dining restaurant, though more compact. There was one table, large enough to fit about 8 people in one seating. Two of the chairs were filled. Another crew member was standing, serving.

Vance was surprised the server was the hulking brute, Gomy.

He saw Mycal and Vance, stopped mid service, and nodded. "Welcome Captain, Admiral. You're just in time for Breakfast. I presume you want your normal omelet with hash browns and sour dough toast?"

Mycal, nodded. "It is Thursday," he said. "Thank you." He gestured for Vance to take a seat as he took a seat at the head of the table around which the others had centered. It left half the table empty.

"Admiral?" Gomy asked as Vance sat in a chair next to the woman, Cassie, he'd *rescued* in the bar. She turned a radiant smile on him. "My gallant Admiral," she touched a hand to his arm. She seemed sincere in her gratitude even though it wasn't called for. Vance wondered if she was as good at hand-to-hand as Mycal had been – though probably not augmented. He thought this whole crew would be sufficient in that area, given their captain and the branch of service they were in.

"I'll have the same as the Captain," Vance stammered as Gomy waited respectfully. Gomy nodded again, put a plate in front of the Cassie and another in front of Ben, the pilot, then turned back to the appliance wall on the far side situated as a kitchen.

"Let's formally introduce you to the crew now things have settled down a bit and we're all here," Mycal said. "Cassie, why don't you start. And bear in mind, Vance has the *highest* of clearances so no need to hold anything back."

Cassie nodded. "Admiral, I'm Cassandra Rutledge. Call me Cassie. First, I'm married to the brute you saved me from." At that, Gomy turned and winked leeringly at her, to which she smiled and blew a kiss. "I handle comms, cryptology and small weapons. My rank is Lieutenant. I've been with Imperial Service for 8 years. I was recruited from the Navy. Prior I had been a scrunchy midshipman on the Excalibur when you were XO under Captain Ballard. I was drafted by Mycal after you left, and I was thinking of leaving the service.

"I was impressed by your example. I joined the service to *serve* and you exemplified that. But Captain Ballard – and the rest of his crew . . . well, you know.

"I was glad when Mycal came along and told me about a *special assignment* I was uniquely qualified for."

Vance looked at her closely. Her hair was a bit longer, her face fuller, and she had aged a bit, yes, but now he recognized her. They'd hardly had any contact during his Excalibur assignment, but he remembered her. He'd been impressed with her. Had often given her section head assignments for her, specifically.

"I remember you," Vance said. It's all he could think of to say.

She smiled radiantly again and patted his arm. "You're sweet," she said.

Gomy came over and put a plate in front of Mycal and Vance then stood straight. Vance could see his nose was still red and bruised and his eyes were starting to blacken as well. Vance winced, having been the unwitting cause.

"I'm Gomy Potrassic. Ship's engineer, weapons officer and counter-intelligence." He was resting his large hands on Cassie's shoulders as she reached back and placed a hand on top of one of his. "Also, resident science officer when needed. That just means I run the computer better than the others so I can find things quicker." He smiled and Vance could tell his lip was a bit swollen too.

"Sorry about that," Vance said. I didn't realize . . ."

"No need to apologize, sir." Gomy said. "I'm glad there's someone who'll still stand up for a lady even if she can throw me – or any man except Mycal – six ways from Sunday." Gomy squeezed Cassie's shoulders and came to the other side of the table and sat down.

"Gomy isn't joking," Mycal said. "Cassie has her small weapons assignment for a reason. Her hands and feet are her best weapons. In fact, she'll be putting you through your paces during training," Mycal winked at Vance.

"Gomy served under you as Engineering Mate on the Excalibur at the same time as me," Cassie said. "Mycal got us both in the same net as we were just starting to see each other back then."

Vance was surprised. The service frowned on enlisted getting together, especially on the same ship. It was just too hard. Apparently Imperial Security, or whatever ultra-secret branch this was, didn't have the same standard. The relationship seemed to be working in this case, anyway.

Cassie continued. "Gomy's also our unofficial chef. We started out taking turns, but Gomy loved it, so decided to add it to his duties."

"And not one person ever complains," Mycal said, gesturing to Vance's plate. He looked down and could see a perfect omelet, hash browns with a side of sour dough toast staring back at him. It was complete with a sprig of green and a garnish of fruit.

"My definite compliments," Vance said, impressed. "Smells great. And much better than any ship's rations I've ever seen."

"Thank you, Admiral," Gomy said, and started into his own meal consisting of a bowl of what looked like oatmeal and juice. Vance surprised such a big man would have so little an apparent appetite.

"Now for you, Ben," Mycal said. "We have to keep reminding him to speak on occasion or we'll forget he's here."

Ben chuckled and wiped his mouth with a cloth napkin. "I'm Ben Sprague. Navigator, pilot and infil/exfil specialist. I also second Cassie on Coms, Gomy on Weapons, and XO to Captain Petrs."

Vance was a bit surprised at his position. He didn't mention any military rank and neither had Gomy. He'd file that as a question for later. It was more about his relative age to the others and holding second seat.

"Ben is also my *cousin*," Mycal said. Vance noted that Ben caught the reference and stole a quick glance at Mycal, who nodded back imperceptibly. He'd just let Ben know Vance was in on the *double secret* portion of what that meant. Apparently, none of the others knew this, again confirming Vance's original supposition. It was also Mycal's way of letting Vance know where everyone stood without having to go into any detail.

"I came up through the service and served on a number of ships. There were a couple where we'd just missed each other," Ben said, smiling at Vance.

"You made quite an impression in each posting. Some were sad you left. Others were relieved the 'SOB' had finally been punted upstairs where you could no longer give them any grief."

"That's a respectful quote sir," Ben hastened to add, but it was clear to Vance, he was enjoying this.

"Ben, as you can see is quiet, though direct."

"Which is why we love him," Cassie said. "He's the best pilot I've ever seen, and he leaves no room for doubt in his communications."

"Miscommunication kills, sir," he said to Vance. There was still a small smile on his face. "Myself, I was sad to have missed serving under you. I think now I'm going to get my chance."

Vance could see a small resemblance to Mycal and believed they were real *family*.

Vance could also tell Ben was sincere in his words. It made Vance unaccountably choke up, and he had to concentrate on breathing evenly to keep from betraying his emotions. He was startled he should feel this way, though he realized rationally it was because he was receiving validation of how he'd served and why. Others felt the same way he did. It felt good to be reminded of that, especially now. It almost made him regret he'd given up the fight and retired. But had he? Here he was, enlisted in a cause he only guessed at, but about to dive into serving again, though in a different way.

Ben interrupted his ruminations. "I was recruited by Mycal about 3 years ago. Took him long enough. I'd been waiting . . ."

"It's a requirement you start shaving before you can join Imperial Security," Gomy teased. "Besides, it built character to serve under all those *officers*."

"That's not what I'd call it," Ben said, then went back to eating. Apparently, he was done speaking.

"There you have it," Mycal said. "Our own little family."

"You forgot one," Ben said, looking up, clearly a bit indignant. "You forgot Lula. She's as much family as anyone."

"Lula?" Vance asked.

Mycal laughed. "You're right, Ben. Sorry." Vance could tell he meant it.

"Lula is short for *Little Nebula*, our ship. She's the most advanced craft ever assembled. We've been testing her out for the last couple of months, and with her performance, we have ordered a few more for other teams like ours."

"We're going to need them," Ben said, then clamped his mouth shut, like he'd misspoke.

"That's okay," Mycal said to Ben. "Vance has pretty much guessed what we're all about."

Ben nodded and then went back to focus on his eating.

The rest of the meal drifted to small talk about common people they'd served with and how good the food tasted. Vance mostly listened, occasionally commented and observed. He knew Mycal sensed what he was doing . . . sizing up the crew. He didn't mind. He knew what Vance would find.

And Vance was impressed.

Chapter 5

The hours went by rapidly. Vance started each day in a session with Cassie in the fitness room. Mycal had been right. Cassie was deadly with her hands and feet. Vance never got close to landing a blow or throw, and he was sure Cassie was not augmented like Mycal, she was that good. She gave him tips and started him on a regimen of exercises that would limber him up, get him in shape and fit him for a higher level of hand-to hand methods she said he'd probably want to learn.

Vance wasn't so sure he'd be able to ever learn what Cassie was trying to teach, but she assured him, he would, and in not that much time. There were other training methods they would employ when they got to a place with the proper equipment. Vance had looked at her askew and she'd smiled and shook her head. "No augmentation" she'd said. "Just some new ways of learning that haven't been introduced into the general populace – or other branches of service just yet."

Those two-hour sessions helped him more than just physically. They helped him get back in touch with his life. It felt good to work hard on something. And it helped him center his mind too. He was preparing for his meeting with the Empress, after all. That was mainly done through his daily one-hour briefings with Mycal. Though those were more Vance asking questions and Mycal doing his best to answer. Most of the 'what will I be doing' questions were deflected with, "That is up to the Empress and you. I have no knowledge or direction on that. My job was to bring you -- if you wanted to come. Beyond that, I'm just guessing, so I won't say anything."

No amount of cajoling on Mycal's *guesses* would elicit anything. When Vance asked about what Mycal had been doing, he wasn't evasive at all – directly. Instead, he would answer but very broadly.

Mycal, it seemed, had left school upon graduation and entered into the Imperial Security Services. He'd been assigned to various postings and assignments, getting experience and proving himself until the Empress had drafted him into the Personal Security ring of Imperial Security. Such an assignment had the role of ensuring the personal safety of the Empress. Though Vance had the impression that *Personal Security* had a broad interpretation.

When Vance had voiced that suspicion, Mycal had only smiled and said, "You're right. But she *is* the Empress. Rest assured, we stay within Constitutional Authority and do nothing illegal – strictly."

Given that Mycal had picked him up and was bringing Vance to a personal meeting with the Empress, Mycal couldn't deny his duties were more than just being a bodyguard to the Monarch of the Galaxy.

Mycal was pretty open about his other assignments and experiences, though didn't go into specifics. There was one in particular where Mycal had been posted to a place where there had been some unusual explosions surgically taking out some anarchists who had openly declared war on the Empress, threatening terrorist acts until certain demands were met.

Vance, and everyone else, had openly speculated about the *accidental explosions* of the heating elements of the building in which the Anarchists had taken over and were holding hostages. However, the hostages had been miraculously saved just prior to the explosions by a small group that only identified themselves as Hostage Rescue Specialists, and then they'd disappeared.

No one in local government or local detachment of military services had taken credit for the rescue. They each had assumed the other had taken that role, and all were left a bit confused.

Vance had wondered about it himself at the time. Many had surmised the Empress' government had a hand in the rescue and resulting explosion.

It had sent a message to would-be terrorists then the event had faded into the background as other news of the Imperium superseded it, and life in the sprawling cavalcade of aligned systems had pressed on.

There were a couple of other incidents Vance remembered in places where Mycal indicated he'd been posted. The sparkle in Mycal's eyes when he named the places he'd served told Vance all he needed to know, realizing that Mycal would never claim credit for the spectacular events which had occurred, leaving many scratching their heads as to *who* had performed that rescue, or arrested those subversives . . .

The rest of the time Vance had to himself. His stateroom had full access to an advanced suite of entertainment and news programs. He could pull news and information from the farthest reaches of the Imperium and had access to all the most up to date publications and reports. There were also tie-ins with all the major universities and laboratories that required expensive subscriptions for access. All were at his fingertips. He spent a lot of time reviewing things he'd let slide while he'd been away sulking. He started seeing a pattern he hadn't seen before. A disturbing pattern. And wondered if it had anything to do with his meeting with the Empress. But what could he do about such things?

That got him thinking of the Empress herself. She'd ascended the throne after her parents had been killed in what was touted as a tragic accident. A rupture in the anti-matter containment on the ship they were taking to a State Event, caused an explosion destroying the ship and the loss of all hands. The investigation had been thorough. No culprit or fault was ever laid at anyone's feet.

Empress Serena had only been 23 years old at the time, however, she'd been trained all her life to rule, and she'd passed all the psychological, physical, mental and aptitude tests required of the Monarch by the Imperial Constitution. The Imperium was at peace and the Parliament voted to confirm her as Empress. It was that or have a Constitutional Crisis in the Imperium. It had been the wish of her parents, and it was not contested by the only other person in line to take the throne, her uncle Jules Mattock, who was serving as

Chamberlain and Chief Advisor, and who continued to serve in that capacity even now.

At first the Imperium watched closely. There were political squabbles with parliament thinking she would be easy to manipulate, but when the populace saw, surprisingly, that she could hold her own with the swags in parliament, she quickly won them over, and even gained the grudging respect of parliament.

That had been 12 years ago. Vance remembered being extremely impressed himself and had paid close attention to her astute political and social moves over the intervening time. He'd even met her once, though not personally. She'd come to a ceremony with the Joint Chiefs of Staff and the Admiralty to commission the navy's newest and most advanced flagship, the *Imperator*. Vance had stood in front of her, bowed as his name was announced, then he moved on down the line. That had been the extent of it.

During times when he needed to rest his mind, Vance spent voyage time exploring the *Lula*, always ending up on the bridge. Mycal had given him full access to anything, and the crew cooperated. Ben was ecstatic about showing him her capabilities. It was clear Ben was in love with the ship. Vance had been equally awestruck, the craft being outfitted as she was.

Tactical, communications, navigation, propulsion and even weapons were top of the line. Cassie told him during one of their workout sessions they were going to get a weapons targeting upgrade during their stop at the rendezvous. The unnamed system had the capability to be a refit outpost they'd used before.

Vance had been surprised because from what he'd seen *Lula* already had the most advanced target acquisition systems he'd seen in the navy – and he would know.

"You know those eggheads," she'd said. "Always tweaking, trying to make things better." And then she'd slammed him to the mats yet again.

***

Finally, they arrived. Vance was on the bridge with the full crew as the non-descript world swam onto the viewscreen.

"Time to get you dressed for the Prom," Mycal had said, standing from his captain's chair and turning to lead Vance back to his stateroom. Vance could tell he wanted some private time with him.

They walked down the corridor.

Mycal stood aside and let Vance palm open the door. Inside, Vance noted on the bunk laid a new uniform. It had his admiral's rank insignia and the decorations he'd been awarded, but it was different from the regulation navy uniform he'd worn before. There were subtle differences, and it was a shade darker in color. Vance had no doubt it had been custom fit to his measurements.

"Now you know why I've pushed you into those exercise sessions with Cassie," Mycal said, a mischievous smile playing across his lips, but his eyes held a sharp, searching gaze. "I wanted to make sure you'd fit into your new uniform." Vance could tell the words were just a façade and Mycal was really seeking to learn what Vance thought about all this.

What did he think about all this? Seeing the uniform make his throat constrict and his eyes water a bit. He missed the service, though he'd only been gone a short time. But this uniform was different, and he knew from Mycal his *service* would also be different.

"I'll be honest," Vance said – and he meant it. He'd decided that Mycal was someone he could – and should – trust. Vance realized, whatever was happening, he would need to have someone on which he could truly trust and rely. "I like the uniform, but with the design and color, I see I'm not going back into the normal chain of command. With the way this ship is outfitted, and with you . . . being who you are and finding and bringing me here . . .

"And with the news and reports I've pieced together I'm really interested to see what the Empress has in store. Whatever it is, I'm ready. Truly ready, if it's anything close to what I'm thinking she wants . . ."

"You always were one to see the main current from small trickles of information. And for what it's worth, I think the Empress has made the right choice. Like I said, I don't know entirely what it's about, but I've seen the same things as you. Once things are settled, we'll talk more."

"Then I guess ought to put on this monkey suit and keep my appointment with the Empress." Vance moved over to hold the uniform up.

"You need help with the buttons, old man?"

Vance laughed. Then Mycal got serious.

"Thanks. Thanks for being here. Thanks for caring. You really are needed."

With that Mycal turned and strode out the door. Vance was sure Mycal had gotten choked up at the end.

"What have I gotten myself into?" he asked aloud, starting to change into his *new* uniform, realizing once he put it on, he was taking whatever assignment was coming, sight unseen.

It *felt* right though.

Chapter 6

Vance and Mycal left the ship sitting on the immense landing pad. They'd been met at the bottom of Lula's ramp by an escort of silent, somber guards who were in the livery of the Imperial Security. Mycal had not really ignored them but played along with their stoic nature. He could see Mycal's natural irreverence made it hard for him not to make some silly remark just to jab at the seriousness of it all.

Mycal hadn't been loud in their youth, but he'd never been the somber type either. Just the opposite in fact, and it made Vance smile at the memory. No wonder Mycal had been detached for *special duties* in his service. He never would have survived the serious nature of it otherwise.

It was bright daylight and Vance took in the natural alpine beauty of the lush surroundings. The landing field was in the center of a natural valley surrounded by tall craggy peaks capped with snow and covered in lush green pine-like forest. It reminded him of ancient postcard views he'd seen of a place called Switzerland on old earth.

There was one building in the far distance at the edge of the broad field. There was only one other ship standing a far distance away from where Lula had landed. It was a much bigger ship and Vance recognized it as one of the Empress' personal vessels; Sleek, bright, armored and deadly.

They got into the waiting ground car and sped off in the direction of the distant building. The closer they got the larger the building loomed. The distance had hidden its size. The building was classically built with elegant, though not gaudy lines. It was three stories tall and was several lengths long with manicured landscaping of grass and small shrubbery making it look elegant, though not thick enough to provide cover for anyone trying to sneak up from a distance.

Vance thought it must be tough having to live so security conscious, even in the most private of places. He started to get a picture of how the Empress had to live and felt a bit sorry for her. They got out of the ground car and walked up the broad walkway to the entrance. The two guards stayed with the vehicle, which surprised Vance, though they were met at the entrance by another two guards.

Mycal nodded and presented his identification. They didn't ask Vance for his, which surprised him. They were beckoned through the door, and met again by two guards, this time more pleasantly.

"Hello, Mycal," came a voice from behind them. Vance turned and saw a dignified, elderly man striding up. Then he looked more closely. It was the Imperial Chamberlain. It surprised Vance he wasn't dressed in the ceremonial robes of his office, though maybe he shouldn't be. This was *off stage* so to speak, and obviously, informal. But why had he needed to get dressed in this new uniform?

"Uncle Jules." Mycal said, stepping forward and embracing the older man.

"It's good to see you," the Chamberlain replied, hugging Mycal back. "Admiral, may I call you Vance?" he held out a hand to shake in a casual greeting as equals. "I'm so glad you came."

"Yes, and thank you sir," Vance said, not sure how he should address the Chamberlain since he wasn't in his formal robes.

"Let me introduce myself. I'm Jules Mattock. You will, no doubt, recognize me as the Chamberlain, however, I really am this rascal's uncle." He smiled at Mycal. "And while we're here and in private, call me Jules," the man continued. "At least when we're alone. You'll learn when to use the proper titles and all that, but since it's just us here on *Home* as we call this place, we like to keep it less formal."

Vance took quick note of the man, whose face and bearing most people knew, but never really *noticed*. He was always overshadowed by the Empress, and he never, ever, was in the spotlight or carried any political power for himself. Though being in his presence, Vance could definitely feel a personal power and confidence which radiated from the man.

He appeared to be in his early 60's though obviously very healthy and hale. He wasn't a large man. Slighter in build than Vance himself, and shorter by a few inches than Mycal. His hair was white-gray and cut short, but still relatively full. He was dressed in tan slacks, loafers and a casual silk shirt of black. Very understated, but carried clear, though casual authority in his bearing.

"Certainly . . . Jules," Vance said as he allowed the man to lead them down the wide, brightly lit corridor. Then Vance was surprised again. The two guards had bowed to the Chamberlain, who had apparently given some sign that they be left alone, because the guards had moved off back to their previous stations, leaving Mycal and he alone with the Chamberlain.

"Is there a problem?" Mycal asked, noting Vance's concern.

"Security seems a bit lax here. I know you are close to the Empress, but still, I haven't been asked for my ID and I'm walking with you and the Chamberlain alone, with no guard. I could pose any number of threats to the Empress . . . or to the Chamberlain. I get that you are a known quantity here," Vance said to Mycal, "but I'm a stranger, really. An outsider, and I should have been searched, asked for my ID, vetted more thoroughly.

"Not to put too fine a point on it, but they should have searched you, too, Mycal."

"I told you," Mycal said to Jules, who was smiling.

Before Vance could protest, Mycal held up his hands. "We were scanned and provided the proper clearance ID and signals coming into this sector, and then again when we entered orbit.

"We were scanned for weapons when we got into the ground car, though you didn't notice it. The car has a built-in weapons detection system. And then when you came through the front door, we were scanned again on a DNA level by the embedded scanner in the door. We both passed as our DNA is on file. It had to rise to a high enough amount present that can't be faked by an imposter. And by the way, we also had your DNA scanned while you were aboard Lula just to make certain of who you were. It's been a long time since we last met, after all."

"And the final level of security was more personal," the Chamberlain interrupted. "Mycal embracing me and calling me *Uncle* was the final all-clear sign. Any intruder wouldn't possibly anticipate that grievous informality, but it let me know – and those watching via hidden monitors with laser emplacements hidden in the walls above," he swept his hand around the hallway, "that everything was, indeed, clear. Oh, and by the way, even if that wasn't enough, your uniform has embedded microscopic trackers. If anything is amiss, it helps the hidden lasers home in on you – and something in your uniform can also be quickly triggered to give you a lethal jolt – Well, I'm just kidding about the lethal jolt stuff. The uniform really does have sensors to help with targeting, though."

Vance thought a moment, then nodded, chuckling. "My apologies. Sorry to overstep. And I'm sorry I asked."

"Not at all," Jules responded warmly. "Mycal warned us you wouldn't be afraid to speak your mind, especially where something regarding performance was concerned. And I'm certainly glad you are concerned about the Empress' safety and security. It further confirms the Empress' choice of you – and Mycal's recommendation.

"But come," the Chamberlain continued, now taking a slightly more formal tone. "The Empress is waiting," and they continued down the corridor.

Vance looked around as they walked. He was tempted to shuck out of the uniform jacket he was wearing but thought that wouldn't look good right now.

The place was bright, inviting, like a luxury residence more than the high-end office building it had appeared from outside. The ceiling was high, at least two stories. At the top outside wall were skylight panes of glass letting in light that illuminated the hall with natural warmth. Along the corridor, on the inside, were doors evenly spaced to interior rooms. The outside wall was spaced with art décor and an occasional furniture piece on which sat sculptures or there were chairs arranged for visitors to sit and causally wait to be invited into one of the interior rooms.

At the end of the hallway, they came to another alcove and a recessed doorway that had more ornate trim than the rest. There was a larger seating area situated in the small anteroom created by the recess. "We'll wait here," the Chamberlain said, bowing to Vance, and gesturing at the door. It was clear Vance was just supposed to walk in by himself. He nodded his head and walked to the door, took hold of the knob, opened it and strode into the room.

Vance didn't know what he expected, but when stepping into the room beyond the door, it wasn't at all what he thought.

The room was brightly lit from skylights in the domed ceiling high overhead and bright light sconces inset on the walls of the circular room. The room was completely devoid of décor. The walls were white and smooth and there were no windows other than the skylights above. The flooring was a smooth white polished marble with slight grey veins and there were only two plainly elegant chairs facing each other sitting in the center of the room. Standing beside one of the chairs, facing him and resting a hand on the back of the chair stood the Empress of the Known Worlds, smiling and holding out her other hand, beckoning him forward.

"Come, sit." Her voice was melodic, light, crisp and clear. She was used to speaking in large rooms where she needed to project to be heard without seeming to strain or raise her voice. That wouldn't be regal. And of course, that's exactly what she was.

She was dressed in a simple, flowing white gown that draped while conforming enough to her trim figure it left no doubt, she was female – very much so. Her thick blond tresses were hanging casually long, draped over one shoulder as if she'd been positioned just so to give the right effect to inspire awe and majesty in her simple stature.

Vance had to concentrate on walking normally while he strode over and took her proffered hand, gently in his own, leaned over and kissed it. Executing a bow along with the kiss.

"Empress, I am honored you would invite me here."

"It is I who am honored," The Empress responded, and gestured for Vance to sit as she took a seat in the simple chair opposite. Vance couldn't help looking at her deep blue eyes and clear, healthy, almost ruddy-looking skin as he looked at her more closely. And now that he looked closely, he could see a resemblance of Mycal's facial structure and slight mannerisms with the tiniest quirk in the smile she directed at him, as if she found all this profoundly absurd, but had to play along.

This made Vance smile back and feel much more at ease. And he realized this all . . . the lack of formality, the lack of elegant surroundings, her simple dress, even the lack of make-up on her face, all were geared to send him a message. She was being completely open, honest and inviting. She was not going to hold anything back. Of course, all of this could have been a ruse, a set piece designed to reel him in, but he didn't think so. And in return he would show her the same trust as she was apparently showing him.

No one else was in the room. Undoubtedly, there were people watching closely, and of course the monitoring of his new uniform would ensure deadly aim if he made any sudden moves that would endanger the Empress, but still, this was unprecedented trust and openness being shown.

"I know you are curious as to why you are here," the Empress began after, apparently waiting for Vance to make his assessment as she had intended. She was very smart, this Empress. Vance was becoming more and more impressed just being around her. Normally, he would think she was being calculating, but in this instance, it was more that Vance was being observed, tested and measured.

In most cases, Vance didn't worry about such things. Either he was good enough or he wasn't. This time, though, he found himself very much wanting to measure up, and he wondered within himself as to why?

The Empress was still watching him, and Vance knew then, what she was waiting for.

"I understand, Empress, and I think I have some inkling of why you have asked me here, though certainly not the specifics."

"Ah," she said, that smile again surfacing, this time with more mischief than he'd seen before. She was clearly enjoying this and had come to a conclusion.

Here it comes, Vance thought.

"Then let me skip right to the end," She held out her hand, and Vance instinctively took it in his.

She looked directly into his eyes, and he saw nothing but sincerity. "I want you to Marry Me."

Chapter 7

"Well?" The Empress asked, still holding Vance's hand in hers. Her smile was dazzling, and she was clearly struggling to keep from laughing.

Vance found he wasn't breathing, wasn't thinking, just sitting there numb, his mind and body frozen. Then it kicked in, his wits came back, and he realized something . . .

"Yes," he said. "I will marry you. If that's what you have in mind, and if that's the tack we'll need to take."

At that point, the Empress leaned back and did laugh, a loud uncontrolled belly laugh. "Mycal said you were good. And you really are. I'm serious of course, as you realize, but I truly didn't think you would get it. I was going to have some fun with you first before explaining. I see, though, that I don't have to explain, do I?"

"No, Empress. You don't," Vance said, smiling back. "Though I always thought when I married – if I married – I would do it for love. Not an assignment." And then it sunk in further. The new uniform. The subtle differences. It wasn't just for the hidden sensors inside. He was beginning to wonder if there really were hidden sensors at all, or if it was a result of Mycal's sense of humor, which closely matched that of the Empress, it seemed. No, the uniform would be his new uniform, in his new role as official Consort to the Empress, which held the ceremonial role of being Commander-In-Chief of all the military.

"You don't mean my new role to be ceremonial, do you." It wasn't a question, and Vance knew the answer.

"My, but you are better than I'd hoped." the Empress said, and this time she leaned forward and hugged him.

Vance didn't mind returning the hug, though it felt a bit awkward hugging the Empress of the Known Worlds. And she would soon be his wife. That raised all sorts of other questions, which he would never assume . . . This was going to be strictly for the benefit of the government. Nothing more, he was sure.

"Now that you've accepted my proposal," The Empress pulled back and sat easy in her chair and raised her hand. It was clearly a signal. "We'll move to more comfortable surroundings and we'll all give you a full briefing. My, but you are refreshing, and just what I . . . *we* need."

The door burst open. Mycal and Jules strode in. Mycal's face was a large question mark. The Empress saw it and laughed. "Of course, he accepted. I didn't have to tell him a thing. He sussed it out as soon as I asked him."

"Sussed what out?" Mycal asked.

Jules nudged him. "You mean you didn't know what was going to happen?"

"No." Mycal said. "I knew she was going to ask him to help with all that's going on, but I didn't know specifically what . . ." and then his face grew beet red. "You mean . . . No. You didn't."

"I did," the Empress said. "And he foolishly agreed."

Vance chuckled and shook his head. "Is your family all like this?"

"Yes." Jules, Mycal and the Empress all said together.

Chapter 8

They all moved back out of the larger chamber, through the door and back down the hallway to the next door and entered. Here was set a small table draped in white linen surrounded by four chairs. There was food set on a side table. The room was still accented white, brilliantly lit with crystal chandeliers and crystal covered wall sconces. The carpeting was a lush white and the chairs and artwork surrounding the room were elegantly appointed. Here was a room for serious entertaining, Vance thought.

The Empress gestured for him to be seated while she sat next to him. Mycal and Jules sat in the other chairs at the round table. Two attendants came into the room and began to serve them food. It was then Vance realized he was hungry. He hadn't eaten prior to leaving the ship and he could smell the breakfast.

"Mycal let us know your breakfast preferences," the Empress began, smiling. "Breakfast is my favorite meal of the day. It's usually the only one I get to eat informally."

Vance could only imagine with all the people wanting to meet with her, to have her ear on thousands of requests. Again, He was glad he wasn't her . . . and then he caught himself. Soon he would be part of all this, and he shuddered. He hated politics.

"I see it has finally sunk in what you have accepted." The Empress put a gentle hand on his arm and Vance was embarrassed at not guarding his reaction, then he relaxed. He had decided to trust these people completely. The Empress had revealed herself to him completely, so he must return the honor. The attendants had finished serving them and left the room. Vance felt it was safe to talk.

"I'm sorry," he said. "But you must understand, I have never been known for my tactfulness." Then he caught himself again. "Of course, you know all that and still chose me. So, you realize you need a bull in a china closet and not a politician." Vance was still reeling a bit as all the pieces continued to slide together for him even more than before.

"You're expecting me to wreak havoc in the Service, and not be politic about it at all."

"We're expecting you to do what you know is right. And do it in the way it needs to be done," the Empress said, still with her hand on his arm.

"I should tell you, though," Vance said. "I think it's more than just the Service. I think it's widespread throughout the Imperium, and it's coordinated. It's organized by a central group, based on what I saw in the patterns." Vance's mind was thrashing through the information he'd gleaned during the passage here. A pattern had shown itself and he couldn't stop from blurting it out as it suddenly solidified in his mind. All the unrest and the laxness in the military seemed of a set piece, showing coordination and organization . . . and a goal. The final piece sliding into place was how hard someone had tried to stop him from even getting here.

"They know what you're doing and want to stop it." Vance concluded. "They were going to capture or kill me before I ever arrived."

"Well," the Chamberlain sat back and threw his hands in the air. "That's deeper than the briefing we were going to give him. It's deeper than we've even discussed," he was saying this to the Empress. It seemed he was irritated and thinking Vance even a bit eccentric for his leaps of logic.

"And it's just what I've been suspecting for some time," the Empress said. Vance caught a faint look of surprise cross the Chamberlain's face, which he quickly hid. She continued, apparently ignoring it. "This isn't just a general rot in an Imperium which has been prosperous far too long without any trials to strengthen or awaken a lethargic people. This is a systematic attack on us. It's something more."

Mycal was staring back and forth between Vance and the Empress.

"Hold on. Aren't you two taking this a bit deep? There are problems, yes, but I thought we were just talking about cleaning up the Service so we could keep the Imperium on track, and so we could wake up some of the politicians who were starting to openly act subversively."

"It's much more than that, and Vance has just confirmed it," The Empress said. Her eyes were now flashing with fire. "You said Vance was smart and could connect things together no one else could and be right. You didn't realize just how dead on you were in your assessment. I've spent a year studying this, looking at every scrap of intelligence, hoping I was wrong, but to see how Vance connected it all with a few reports and seemingly unconnected events. He's right and you both sense it if you will be honest with yourselves."

Mycal and the Chamberlain were silent, then Mycal slowly nodded his head. The Chamberlain inclined his head slightly. It may not have been agreement, just acquiescence. Vance couldn't tell. The Chamberlain was more guarded than he liked, but he didn't know him. And clearly, he was protective of his niece – the Empress.

The silence hung for a moment, then the Empress said. "Look, we're getting intense here. Let's finish eating and talk more. We're going to plan a wedding, after all."

Mycal chuckled at that, and the Chamberlain seemed to relax a bit also, but not by much. Vance had to continue. And he was sorry to do it.

"There's going to be a problem with that," he said. "Since . . . whoever . . . knows what you're planning, they are going to try and block it. They put out a contract on my head." He turned to Mycal, a fork halfway to his mouth filled with eggs.

"Since they didn't succeed, the next thing they'll do is try to discredit me, to make me look highly unsuitable for you to marry. They will begin spreading rumors of my incompetence and being a lawbreaker and a bar-room brawler," Vance winced at how he'd been drawn so easily into Mycal's quickly conceived net. "They will also make a case that I fired on an Imperium ship going about its lawful duties."

Everyone stopped. Vance continued. "If we want this to work, and I agree with your plan, Empress," Vance nodded to her. "We need to immediately put out a charge against the captain of the ship who tried to board us against all regulation and laws. We have the recording from our ship?" he looked at Mycal, who nodded. We characterize this as a respected Imperial citizen going about his lawful business and make that charge before the Navy can get anything out. Knowing them, they'll only just be thinking about this now, so we can get in front of them. They'll look foolish if we put out the charge and the recording all at the same time, the Navy won't be able to dispute it. They'll probably have to demote the captain and transfer him to some far-flung post. We'll also need to get with the owner of the bar and make a generous contribution, so he'll say he was treated completely fairly and testify that I was only defending a helpless woman being accosted. We should put that out immediately also, so that my image is of a person who only breaks things in defense of helpless ladies." Vance smiled at that.

Mycal started laughing as did the Empress. The Chamberlain held a hand to his face to cover a demur smile. "We've already paid off the bar owner," Mycal said, "but we'll get with him again with more to *help* his memory of what really happened and get some video testimony from him and some of the other *witnesses* in the bar so they can't be swayed later." Mycal stood up. "I believe this is something needing immediate attention?" The Empress nodded. "Uncle," Mycal bowed to Jules, smiling, then he slapped Vance on the back. "You come here, expecting to marry my sister and get everything riled up. I knew it was going to be fun being around you again." He went around and kissed his sister on the cheek and left, whistling."

The Empress shook her head, then turned back to Vance and the Chamberlain. "Can we please now start planning my wedding?"

At this, the Chamberlain chuckled, and Vance nodded. "Whatever you command," he said.

Chapter 9

Mycal was finishing an extremely long and busy day. And now he sat in the dim recesses of the Astrolabe bar. It was in the early hours of the morning, and he was seated in a nondescript booth in the far back corner. Dim light, and despite all the health regulations in the Imperium, a smoky haze hung in the air. "Good thing they cured cancer," Mycal thought, as he watched the crowd, albeit thinner than a couple of hours ago. All the semi-honest people had left. All who remained were the drunks or crooks. Just the people he was looking for.

Mycal had taken it upon himself to do some investigation surrounding the corruption seeming to surge within the Imperium. Vance and Serena were handling the military and government for their aspects, so he decided to look where he was best suited, among the criminal element, to see what he could dig up. And he thought it best to start with the source of the contract put out on Vance.

Mycal was dressed in his, 'somber gray business attire', as he called it. Gray slacks, gray silk shirt, thin black tie and gray suit jacket, eminently suitable for the criminal element. Mycal chuckled under his breath at the longevity of both the tie and the crisp white silk pocket square in his jacket pocket. Those things had survived centuries of non-essential and nonsensical use. Still, he wore them to blend in.

He also wore them for the thin shock panels in the jacket and pants, though he hoped they wouldn't be needed. "If hope were fleas," he thought, "I'd be disease-ridden."

"Ah, there," he thought, the customer he'd been waiting for had just arrived. A gangster by the name of Moe Gorwin. He went by the epithet, Mighty Moe. Originality is not a strong suit of criminals, Mycal thought. The description and vid pic matched. Shaved head, thick neck, two meters tall, one meter wide, and a broken, flattened nose.

Mycal had tracked down Mighty Moe through the various electronic, sneaky, and semi-legal sources at his command. As the advertiser of the contract on Vance, if anyone would know the originator, Mighty Moe would.

Mycal got up from the booth, strode to the bar, and as he approached Moe, seated at the bar, a drink having been placed in front of him, two large mountains of men wearing suits very similar to Mycal's, blocked him. They didn't bother to hide the blaster bulges underneath their suit jackets.

Loud enough for Moe to hear behind them, Mycal said, "I need a word with your boss, in private. Gustafa sent me. It's about the offer." It was cryptic enough for those not in the know, but it did the trick. Mighty Moe swiveled on his bar stool.

"Open." He said. The two mountains in front of Mycal adjusted slightly, allowing a sliver of view to open between them so Mighty Moe could look Mycal up and down. "I don't know you," he said.

"Probably a good thing." Mycal said. "But that's about to change."

"What do you want?"

"You heard," Mycal said. "But in private, at the booth over here. Your . . . ah . . . men can stand guard as long as they're outside the privacy screen."

"Gustafa sent you?"

Mycal didn't answer.

"Which booth?" Moe finally said.

Mycal sensed, more than saw, the two bodyguards in front of him relax just slightly. It wasn't in their stance; it was more in their aura. Mycal almost smiled to himself.

"You know the booth and you know why," Mycal said. Then he turned to stroll back to the booth he had just exited.

This was a special booth, one reserved for the most discreet business, maintained by the proprietor. Only those who were supposed to know knew it had sweepers for bugs, mics, weapons, and bombs. It also had security shielding.

Mycal was taking his seat just as Moe, flanked by 'Larry' and 'Curly', Mycal labeled them, harkening back to some of his favorite ancient vids he collected of the three stooges. Serena would just shake her head when he tried to describe them to her, though the two men certainly didn't resemble the real Larry and Curly.

Moe took a seat opposite. He was dressed in brown, drab, dirtside-garb, with a silk collarless shirt of a tan color underneath his jacket. The clothes were somewhat rumpled, which Mycal thought apropos, given the person wearing them.

"Do you want to do the honors?" Mycal asked.

Moe glared at him for a second, then the light dawned, and Moe reached to the side wall and hit a nondescript button, activating all the security devices within the booth, including the security screen.

"I'll make this brief. We're both busy men." Mycal leaned slightly across the table, staring directly at Mighty Moe, and smiled. "My needs are simple. If you want to leave this booth without serious injury, you'll tell me now who originated the contract on Admiral Vance Hamblin." Moe's eyes widened. He tilted his head, his mouth gaped open.

Mycal chuckled and watched Moe's thoughts dance across his face. It was then Mycal watched as two other men, not quite as large, also moved near the booth. So, he had four men with him. Others in the bar started leaving. They sensed something was happening. All to the good.

"Gustafa sent you? I don't believe that. Who are you?"

"I'm the guy asking the questions. And I don't have any more time. I've got another visit to make before heading home, and she's a lot prettier than you."

"You come here and threaten me? You won't make it out of here alive. I don't care who you are, or who sent you?"

"You forget," Mycal said. "We're in here, and they're out there." Mycal reached over and flicked a finger against the security shield, watching it shimmer slightly. "In here, it's just you and me."

Moe's predicament dawned on him. Predictably, he reached his hand out to hit the button that dropped the shielding.

Mycal darted his hand forward, barely using his augmentation and snatched Mighty Moe's wrist in a vice-like clamp just before he touched the button dropping the booth's shielding. He did use augmentation to squeeze enough to cause Mighty Moe some pain.

"Ow," he said, "what are you doing?"

Just then, Mycal heard the spat and sizzle of blaster fire hitting the screens still up on the booth.

"I asked you a question," Mycal said, "and I want an answer."

The blaster fire ceased as the four goons realized their shots couldn't get through. All they could do is watch their boss squirm at Mycal's mercy. Mycal darted a quick glance at them and smiled as he also noticed the bar had completely emptied now save for those four and, Mycal noted with a wry grin, the bartender who was just watching, he had seen things like this before, obviously.

He even looked a bit curious. Had he called somebody? Mycal didn't think so. He'd probably wait and see. Maybe Mycal was a bigger dog than Mighty Moe and would cause him problems if he did call the authorities. Good.

"I can't tell you that," Mighty Moe said, trying to wrench his hand away to no avail. Mycal squeezed harder.

"Hey, you'll break my wrist!"

"Yes, yes I will, unless you answer my question."

"Others will do a lot worse if they find out I squealed. It's not good for business."

"Your business isn't my concern and right now I'm here and *Others* aren't. Now spill." Mycal tightened his grip even further, not sure how much pressure would indeed break the wrist, but he was willing to do it. He was sure Mighty Moe had done worse to others. It was time the old-fashioned notion of karma circled back around to this thug.

"Ohh," Moe groaned with the increased pain. He was writhing and pounding the table with his other fist. Mycal glanced back out the security screen. One of the goons had gone to the bartender probably asking if there was some way to switch off the security screen other than from inside the booth. The bartender was shaking his head. Mycal knew he was lying. He was still on the fence. Good. Mycal thought.

"I'll start with the wrist," Mycal said, "but I can do fingers more easily and then arms, and what do you think it would do to your face if I punched it a couple of times while holding you? Your nose isn't so pretty now. Maybe it'll become even more famous if I flatten it more."

"Okay. Okay. I'll tell you what I know, but it ain't much."

Mycal waited. Then squeezed slightly more, prodding.

"There was this guy that came to me, told me about the contract, asked me to spread the word, but he was disguised . . . wait, wait," he said before Mycal could squeeze harder.

"I don't got a name, but I'll tell you what I know. I swear."

Mycal kept the pressure up. "Tell me what you know, and I'll see if it's worth it."

"He didn't give a name and he was disguised, like I said, but he was tall and thin. You can't disguise that. And he hadn't disguised his hair."

"What about his hair?"

"Well, it was dark, black. Something about the cut made me think military. And something about the way he talked. Military. A high up. Someone in charge. That's all I got. I swear. Please don't tell anybody you got that from me. Now let me go. I told you everything."

"No, you didn't," Mycal said and squeezed again. "Tell me when and where you met him."

"Ow. Okay, okay. Lighten up."

Mighty Moe told him the date.

It was just before Mycal had heard about it himself, and just as Serena and he were deciding upon a plan to bring Vance in to get his help.

"Now where?"

"Right here in this booth. I gotta change this up," Moe groaned. "That's probably how you found me, isn't it?"

Mycal didn't answer. He was thinking he could hack into the exterior cameras around this place, but he doubted he'd get anything. Any true professional would know how to counter that much as Mycal had, with the distortion scrambler built into his collar. Its electronic field left a fuzzy blur on any camera that happened to catch his head from any angle. Still, he'd check the feeds just to be sure. There were obviously no cameras inside the bar. They never wanted evidence of anything happening inside.

Military. That made sense. Vance had never worried about making enemies or the consequences it would bring. So, this was probably just related to the enemies Vance had made in the military. Though why would they act now. Vance had retired.

Mycal thought a moment and realized he was done here.

Now to see if he could get out of this bar without blaster burns ruining his good gangster suit.

"Okay, Minnie Moe," Mycal said "you've been very helpful. I'll make sure everyone knows just how helpful you've been."

"No, please."

"Oh, don't worry," Mycal said, "I'm sure everyone will be pleased to work with you again since you were so helpful to me."

"Now here's what we're going to do." Mycal drew a blaster out of his shoulder holster. It was small, easily concealed under his jacket, but very recognizable, especially at close range.

He held the nozzle a short space from Moe's forehead. "You're going to lower the shielding, and then you're going to tell your help not to do anything stupid, and to put their blasters on the floor in that corner." Mycal nodded with his head behind him.

"Then you'll tell them to stand against the opposite wall where I can see them."

"You ain't getting outta here alive." Moe said, Mycal squeezed his wrist again where he'd lightened the grip but hadn't let go his hold. "Hey, I told you everything."

"I don't respond well to threats, and you should know *I* never threaten, I keep my word." Mycal gestured with the small blaster. Moe looked at him, saw the seriousness in Mycal's eyes.

Mycal let Moe reach out with his other hand, awkwardly to touch the button and the screen shimmered off.

"Okay boys," Moe began, and Mycal nodded as he repeated his instructions.

"How do I know you're not gonna kill me anyway?" Moe said once he'd finished.

"I won't kill my ticket out of here unless you or your boys try something." Mycal watched as the four bodyguards moved and placed their blasters on the floor, then moved against the far wall.

Mycal watched closely as they walked, particularly their legs.

"You," Mycal called "you with the blaster in an ankle holster. Take it out and slide it over with the others. Do it now." And he squeezed Mighty Moe's wrist, eliciting a sharp cry from the man.

"Do it!" Moe ordered. One of the goons stooped, pulled out a blaster from the holster around his ankle and slid it across the floor. It was far enough away, if not quite with the others.

"Here's the plan," Mycal said, loud enough for them all to hear.

"I'll have this blaster on your boss at all times. You've already failed him once. Don't make it worse." And then he looked pointedly at the bartender who nodded slowly.

"Any sudden moves and Minnie Moe gets one in the head, and then you all follow. Every one of you." Again, he glanced at the bartender who got his meaning.

"I'm fast and accurate. Moe and I are going to walk out of here and you're all going to stay inside, no calls on com links. You'll wait here for three ticks. I have people outside ready to kill anyone who steps out that door before time is up.

"Once I'm outside, I'll leave your boss there, and he better not move for three ticks either." He looked at Moe, who nodded. There were tears of pain in his eyes. Mycal realized he had not let go his grip. Well, now was the time.

Mycal had been serious about the other visit he wanted to make before heading back to his quarters. He needed to make sure she was all right and let her know he was going to be busy for the foreseeable future.

"Okay, Moe. Let's go."

Everything went according to Mycal's plan, which surprised and disappointed him a little. Mycal nodded to the bartender on his way out. "I'll send a big tip," Mycal said, "large enough you'll know it's from me. You don't want mess with me or my bosses." The bartender nodded.

Outside the bar Mycal listened. There was no movement. "Well, thanks again, Moe. It's been a pleasure." And with that, Mycal tapped him on the nose with a slightly augmented fist. He went out like a light and slumped to the pavement.

No one had been called that he could see, and his distortion scrambler would obscure his features. He'd remain anonymous. His work here was done though, it had only confirmed what he already surmised. He'd continue this line of search, but it would most likely lead to the joint chiefs or someone with a grudge.

With word getting around what Mycal had done to Mighty Moe, and how easily he'd been handled, perhaps the heat on Vance would cool. Of course, the bartender would talk. Moe was out of business at the very least.

Now to make that visit. It will be pleasant but bittersweet.

Chapter 10

Empress Serena sat on her throne in the state audience chamber back on Zyzeen, the Capital World of the Imperium from which she governed. Having left her little retreat, with Vance in tow, it was time to get back to work.

Here first appointment, and most important of the day, was stepping forward with his own retinue of sycophants. It was the 1st Minister, Head of the Imperial Parliament, and a frequent visitor to her court.

Henri Wallach was tall, lithe and muscular. He was known as a mean brawler and frequent and as yet, unbeaten dueler. His hair was at present jet black and perfectly coifed to match the exacting style of the moment, which was short and plastered flat against his skull. His stride was stately, sufficiently slow to show his dignity and to convey he wasn't anxious to all those who attended court as clerks and records keepers, not to mention the media reps who constantly streamed views to an Imperium-wide audience that totaled in the billions any given second court was in session.

Serina suppressed a laugh. All this ceremony was starting to get to her now that she had a definite plan of action. Her strategy session with Vance, the Chamberlain and Mycal when he'd returned from setting things in motion had been gratifying. Sure, she planned her wedding, but it ended up being more in the vein of a war conference than picking out flowers.

Just the way she liked it.

This meeting would be the first salvo in the upcoming war. She had no illusions that what she had started would be a war, but one for the benefit of her people and preserving their freedoms. She hoped it would be political, and hence relatively bloodless. But blood had been spilt to build what they had. If blood needed to be spilt to preserve it, then that would be the cost. She had to be willing to see it paid.

True to what she'd hoped, and even beyond, Vance had proven to be quite astute in their planning as he gained further information. But his first impressions blurted out had been dead on in her opinion, much to the consternation of Uncle Jules and to the amusement of Mycal.

Vance truly intrigued her. And he'd opened up to them all – especially to her, showing that he was *all in* on their plans. Also, that he was truly putting his life in her hands. It scared her a bit as well. She'd have to think about that a bit more later. For now, she had this meeting to get through. The wildfire this announcement would cause would be fun to watch.

Henri had made his way the last several steps to just below the dais, his retainers being left the requisite steps behind. He bowed low in easy respect, but in a demeanor that spoke of casual deference, not sincere, following the formalities, almost as if to say that he was doing this for appearance's sake. For those watching near and far.

"I have come as you summoned," he said, his tones cultured, smooth with practiced diction.

"My thanks for your coming so quickly," Serina said. She carefully modulated her tone of voice to neutrality, though her words indicated just barely that his quick appearance before her was a sign of his anxiousness to please her. It was a touch demeaning, though it couldn't be completely construed as such. She smiled. This was the appropriate response to his casualness in her presence. Such was the way of Court. Appearance and posturing to no end, seeking to curry or give favors and slights to obtain the smallest edge. Well, she hadn't risen to become Empress on her lineage alone. And she was a natural at this. She had a sixth sense when it came to such matters. She wasn't afraid to use every tool at her disposal, especially when it came to men like the 1st Minister.

She noted with satisfaction his eyes narrowed a bit at her words, and he inclined his head slightly to acknowledge her admonishment. Henri was an adept at this subtle court language himself. He hadn't risen to his lofty position on money alone as Serina well knew.

Time to get this bit going, Serina thought and stood from her throne to give her words the proper solemnity and power. This surprised everyone in the room, especially the 1st Minister whose eyes widened, and his posture stiffened just barely.

Good, Serina thought. She wanted to make an impression, so here goes . . .

"1st Minister," she began using the formal tone of state announcements – which this was going to be. "I invited you here to inform you of my desire to follow some particular counsel you have given me of late." She noted Henri's eyes widen slightly, and then as her words sunk in and understanding dawned, he began to smile.

Got him. Serina thought. He realizes what I'm going to say but will be miles off the mark just the same. This is going to be good.

"You recall encouraging me to seek a Consort such that I could be assisted in all matters military and be able to more fully direct my considerable wisdom to the act of governing our diverse Imperium?"

"I do, Majesty." Serena noted the 1st Minister now stood taller, more open in his stance. It was clear he expected to be invited to *be* that Consort, for such was his reason for suggesting it in the first place. Indeed, Serina thought, it had been Henri that had given her the first kernel of this idea, though it's actual implementation would be far from what Henri was angling for.

"I have decided, after thinking on it at great length, that I wish to be married."

There was an audible gasp in the expansive room. She could just feel the recorders zooming in close on her face and then panning back out to include the 1st Minister. Here was true drama coming from the court.

Serina continued as though her announcement was just an ordinary proclamation.

"I thank you 1st Minister for such wise counsel and want to congratulate you . . ." This was going to be delicious, Serina thought as she watched Henri all but starting to preen. ". . . on your good and wise judgement." She continued to watch him carefully, she had other reasons for his close observation than just the sheer joy of taunting him. It appeared clear that Henri hadn't heard that her Consort would not be him. It let her know two things: First that Henri was either a very good actor – which very well could be the case -- or second, that Henri was not part of the group trying to have Vance killed prior to his meeting with her. It was clear that group had an inkling of what she'd been planning, as Vance had surmised and clearly assessed during their meeting. It was a bit disappointing that Henri reacted the way he did. She was almost certain he would have been part of that group. Now she had to re-think things a bit. Nevertheless, she continued.

"I wished you to be here for the official announcement and introduction of my new husband to be."

At this point she caught the first sign of Henri's beginning surprise. This wasn't going as he'd hoped. Time to insert the dagger a bit further before the twist, Serina thought.

"Since you represent the Assembly, it is only fitting you be here to witness and be first to congratulate my fiancé and soon to be Consort of the Realm, the Commander-in-Chief of all the Armed Forces of the Imperium." She smiled broadly as she watched Henri's face pale, though he was covering it well. The size of this announcement . . . the impact of it . . . and what it meant for him, who had sought the *honor* and power. Mostly the power.

"I want to present Admiral J. Vance Hamblin, retired. Formerly of the Admiralty. His career has been exemplary and his honors and distinctions many."

At that point, Serina held out a hand and from the far side of the chamber strode Vance in his new military uniform, the one Mycal had designed for him complete with all his insignia, medals and commendation ribbons. He was an impressive sight even as the spots of the podium swung from hidden controllers to highlight him stepping up and taking her outstretched hand in his. She was a bit surprised at the thrill it gave her to touch his hand. It was warm and gentle.

So seldom had she any physical contact with anyone, it was a bit of a novelty to be holding this man's hand and realizing they would soon be doing this more often, if only during state events and formal occasions. Still . . . it felt pleasant.

Got to stop this. She told herself. Need to focus.

Vance bowed over her hand and gently pressed it to his lips. This sent another chill through her body. His lips felt . . . soft on the back of her hand. He had no idea what he was doing to her. It made him all the more captivating – his unassuming nature. His shock of blond hair highlighted by the bright light, and when he looked up, the light caught his face and piercing blue eyes . . . and then he smiled.

"I am honored, Empress. I pledge myself to your service solely and completely. I accept you as Empress and as my lead and my heart. I am also humbled to be considered Husband." Vance said, sticking with the script they had settled on. It seemed he was totally at ease, which amazed her. This was the first time he was being introduced to the Imperium, and he was looking directly at her, as if she were the only one in the room. And his tone of voice and demeanor indicated he meant every word, every gesture, and was wholeheartedly devoting himself to her. That was heady. And his gaze seemed electric.

Serina stared back, captivated.

"I congratulate you, most heartily," the 1st Minister intoned. He was being formal, completely controlled and using his stentorian administrator tone. She recognized it as a defense mechanism. It was what Henri fell back on when he was at a loss. And clearly, he was at a loss. She tore her gaze from Vance, who was still smiling in that dazzling way and turned to acknowledge the 1st Minister.

"Our thanks to you, 1st Minister." She nodded in acknowledgement. "I also wanted to inform you of a small matter which came to my attention as I was requesting Admiral Vance's attendance some days ago. It concerns what must have been a rogue faction of the military from where Admiral Vance hails." Serina was speaking the set piece they had decided to get the advanced truth out on what had happened in Vance's attempted abduction via the military, but she was also very conscious of Vance still holding her hand. It hadn't been necessary, but it felt right. It felt good, if she were being honest with herself. Somehow it lent her strength – a strength that clearly was emanating from Vance himself. She hadn't ever expected to need something like this. And she still didn't . . . but it felt good.

"We have released all pertinent facts to your office and to the relevant media outlets. I wanted you to know of this so you can truly see that your advice was timely." She smiled at Henri, again noting his minute confusion and discomfiture. It was clear, he had no knowledge of this as she had broached the same subject from a different direction and he still was seeming clueless. "From this it is apparent some closer oversight of the military is needed, which will now be seen to," she inclined her head to Vance and acknowledged his deference – while still holding her hand lightly. She liked that Vance was doing this. It added great effect and showed complete solidarity. He appeared to be a natural at court as well. Or maybe he just wanted to hold her hand. She knew she was just being silly, now. Of course, Vance was doing this for effect.

"As you say, Empress," Henri bowed, which surprised Serina. It wasn't required, but it further indicated just how rattled poor Henri was at this point. He clearly was not expecting any of this. "My hearty congratulations . . . to you both," this time Henri looked at Vance, and she detected a subtle undercurrent of . . . anger now. His surprise and discomfiture disappearing and being replaced by that.

When anger started to surface, it meant she had learned all she was going to.

"My thanks for your coming, 1st Minister. We will send you all of the information regarding the upcoming wedding celebrations. Of course, you and your family are invited as my honored guests."

"It will be our supreme honor to attend," Henri said, bowing for the final time, as required, stiff with formality, the mask of his professional politician façade now firmly back in place.

Now, Serina thought. Time to watch closely for the fallout.
That would be telling. She hoped.

Chapter 11

Henri Wallach found himself standing in the center of a round room about 30 feet across, dimly lit and deserted. It was empty except for many small alcoves surrounding the plain concrete walls with the exception of the entrance through which he'd been escorted and told to wait.

He wasn't used to waiting. However, the invitation had been intriguing enough he would grant a bit of patience. It had come from one who's impeccable qualifications made him agree to the meeting. Those qualifications, if he were honest with himself, had been this person's having amassed an enormous fortune over a relatively short life. That and the man had always been a substantial donor to his political campaigns and causes.

The invitation had also come with a promise of something only hinted at, but again, intriguing. The man had mentioned the upcoming wedding of the Empress to the much-celebrated Vance Hamblin, and how that honor should have gone to Henri. Indeed, that was how *they* had planned for it to occur.

The intriguing part was that Henri wasn't aware of any group who was working on such a level as to try and affect the Empress' choice in consort. Henri had thought it only *his* idea. Though in thinking about it, he wasn't entirely sure where the thought of a consort had come from within himself.

It had only been a day since his meeting with the Empress, and Henri was still reeling with the impact of what it meant. Henri had plans for himself, and they had just been set back a great deal. And then there was this supposed attempt on Hamblin's life. The court had clearly shown it came from the military at a high level, but information got obscured from there. Of course, it all could have been fabricated to engender sympathy and support for this Hamblin character. Designed to smooth the way for what the Empress was undertaking -- whatever that was. After all, Henri had fabricated some *threats* before to advance a particular agenda that suited him.

Henri had hoped to be the one pulling the strings, but clearly, the Empress saw and forestalled it by making her own choice.

Then there were these *others*. The group his benefactor had hinted at. It was most unusual that Henri didn't have all the factions known to him. That was another reason he had agreed to this secluded and secret meeting which his inviter had assured him would accrue greatly to his benefit.

His thoughts were interrupted by lights winking on in each alcove – save one -- being filled with holographic images purposely blurred to obscure identity, sex, weight, height, anything which would enable a clear description. The final alcove was slightly larger and indicated a *head* of the circular room. It was immediately across from the entrance from which he'd come, but the door had been securely closed and bolted after he'd come in.

They were being very careful. Henri smiled. This was going to be interesting. All the empty alcoves became filled with the projections and a spot from the ceiling beamed down on him, putting him at the center of attention.

Again, Henri smiled at this amateurish attempt to intimidate or awe him as he noticed the larger alcove had finally filled with a projection.

"Thank you for coming 1st Minister," the image spoke. It was a sexless tone, though pleasant and clear so there would be no misunderstanding of what was spoken. "We will not bandy words, nor waste your time. We have invited you here as it appears we are working for the same thing. Not that we want to lead, but we want someone to lead with whom we can work."

Henri paused at what the head of this group said sank in. Henri wasn't positive it was even a *he* but preferred to think of him that way. And there was a clear sense that the person speaking was in charge. Henri could bridle at the assumption that he would allow himself to be subservient to them. It wasn't presented specifically that way, but it was clearly implied. Or he could simply wait and hear what they have to say. How to respond? How to find out what they wanted without giving anything away himself?

"No need to reply and commit yourself," the image spoke again. "as I said before, we will not try to trick you nor mince words. We had intended for you to be the Consort of the Empress. That plan has been delayed. Admiral Hamblin has proven to be more of an opponent than we had supposed. We just wanted to meet and let you know we stand behind you. We also wanted to let you know you need not take any action on your own. We will remedy things. Although Hamblin has proven wily, we will not underestimate him further."

At this point Henry was starting to get worried. These people were talking treason. At the very least, interfering with the government and kidnapping. No, not kidnapping. Murder. Clearly, these were the ones who had put out a contract on Admiral Hamblin. He was about to speak, to protest, if nothing else than to cover himself then he was interrupted.

"you need say nothing. You need to do nothing. This meeting was just to let you know we are behind you. We support you. We are your friends."

"who are you?" Henry asked.

"we are the *Council.*"

There was silence for a time. Finally, Henri asked, "Just who is the *Council*?"

"you have learned all you need to know. You may go now but remember, do nothing."

Henry cocked his head to one side. He wasn't used to being treated this way, being ordered around. Who did this *Council* think they were? Then again, Henry realized there was no one in the room he could protest to that would do anything other than making him look foolish. The last thing he needed was to look foolish in front of these people. He quickly thought through his words. There was no exposure. He had said nothing incriminating. Then Henri heard the bolt of the door behind him unlock and the doors swung open. Without saying anything further, Henri strode from the room. He had a lot of thinking to do. He also needed to check all his sources and learn who this *Council* was.

The room remained silent until Henri left and the door swung shut. The projections in each alcove were still present. Finally, one of the projections nearest the door spoke. "He is gone."

"Why don't we just make him one of us?" came from another of the projections on the other side of the room. It was addressed to the leader.

"He is sufficiently malleable as is. The 1st Minister will do our bidding as long as it's in his interest. And it will leave him untraceable to us." This came from the leader. "We may yet have need of a scapegoat. Henri fits the bill nicely."

"What of our plans? Hamblin has set us back and our people are getting anxious to come over."

"Vance, through his release of the recordings has forestalled a smear campaign for now. We must adjust our plan. Perhaps this allows us to speed up the Crossing," said the leader.

"How?" This came from another of the projections.

"We will take Vance and Mycal and make them one of us -- or we will kill them. If they join us, we'll have what we need and can discard the 1st Minister.

"If we are forced to kill them," the leader continued, "the imperium will suffer a blow and the people will be stressed, worried and fearful. More susceptible to us and our plans. The Empress will be disconsolate also. Perfect for our purposes. Either way our plan advances."

There were murmurs of agreement throughout the room.

"Are we all agreed?"

"Yes."

"the *Council* is adjourned."

The leader faded from view. Then the rest of the projections followed. The room fell into the darkness.

Chapter 12

Serena sat at the head of the small table. Surrounding it was the Chamberlain, Vance and Mycal. "Quite a small group for such big plans," She said, smiling. She relished the fact that they were finally moving on something significant, something that would make a difference. The more she had been thinking over the observations Vance had made, the more she agreed. The unrest and restiveness they had been seeing in the Imperium was more of a pattern than just a general malaise in the populace and military. She had gone back and studied the reports again and could now see clearly the pattern that Vance had quickly seen. And she had gathered even more information that seemed to further verify this. If you had sufficient clarity you could see it. It was faint, but there.

Vance and Mycal had come in together, their hair wet and their faces having a bright glow from obvious exercise they had just finished. This had given Serena an idea but held it for later. She had watched as they'd gathered breakfast food from the buffet then set their plates at places on either side of her. Before sitting, Vance had bowed over her outstretched hand and kissed the back of her knuckle. She was embarrassed but a little thrilled at the attention Vance always paid her. In every situation they met, he offered her the utmost deference and kindness. It was a bit weird, but she also didn't discourage it for some reason. She kind of liked it. Mycal had given her a lopsided grin and plopped down in his seat after making her a quick bow in respect to her rank. It was a mockery at what Vance was doing to tease her and Vance, but Vance ignored it.

The Chamberlain had taken up his seat opposite her with his customary cup of Caff and dry toast. Serena had filled a plate and she was picking through the fruit as she began.

"Now that we've gotten through the official announcement, we can plan in earnest. Let's have this wedding so we can start making the changes we've discussed.

"Uncle Jules," she looked at the Chamberlain. "You said you had worked up a schedule for important events to precede the wedding and the timeline of when we can formally get married."

She turned a smile to Vance who returned it with his startling blue eyes. He didn't seem smug, and he didn't seem possessive or self-conscious as she felt when discussing her wedding in such a casual and strategic fashion. Instead, he seemed . . . earnest, sincere . . . trustworthy. She chuckled and Vance tilted his head in question.

"Something funny?" he asked, not angry, just interested.

"I never thought planning my wedding would turn out to be so . . . "

"Like planning a war campaign?" Mycal offered. She could tell he was trying to make a joke to ease her mind a bit. They had always been able to read the other's feelings even if they didn't spend much time together. She had to admit, this wasn't quite the way she'd always dreamed of getting married, but the needs of the Imperium were more important.

"Yes, Empress," Jules had said, interrupting the banter. "You can see on your pads." he indicated the inset pads at each of their places coming active and displaying a schedule of events. He didn't go over the events, just let each of them read it for themselves.

"This looks too long," Serena said. And indeed, there did seem to be more formal events than would absolutely be necessary. "I think we do the absolute minimum and then get the wedding over with," She smiled at Vance. "Sorry to say it that way," and she was. This was sad treating her wedding as something to get out of the way so they could get on with the real work they intended.

"Remember, that in doing this," Vance said quietly, "you should still enjoy the event and try and make it all you wanted. Even the Empress can celebrate for herself as well as her people."

Serena looked at Vance. He was truly concerned about her feelings. She could tell it wasn't for himself he was bringing this up. "The people will be able to tell when their Empress isn't truly celebrating. And I will know." His words melted her heart a bit.

"If you're going to be one, be a big blue one," said Mycal. "Sis, we know this is political, but have fun with it at least."

"Okay," she smiled at Vance and Mycal. "But I still think it's too long. I promise we'll all have fun, but cut it back to the bare minimum," she said to Jules, who seemed a bit perturbed, but nodded and started striking events off the list as she watched.

"The minimum it is," Jules said. "The constitution requires certain things for the investiture of Vance, which had been intended to be ceremonial, but the actual wording gives him real authority if he chooses to take it – and is supported by the Empress."

The Empress nodded. "He is."

"Okay," Mycal said. "But at least the parties will be fun, right?"

"Jules," the Empress said. "Make sure the parties are fun."

"All business today, I see," Mycal said.

"I want to get to the real business about what we'll be doing *after* the wedding. That's the main reason we're doing all this – no offense meant, Vance."

"None taken, Empress."

"Call me Serena in private, remember?"

"Yes . . . Serena," Vance said softly. She could tell it was hard for him to be informal with her. Well, she had a plan to fix that. But for now, she had more important work to get done. Something which would hopefully start to yield results.

"Jules, are you done with the schedule?" She glanced down and noted that more than half the events had been scratched off the display. Quickly glancing she saw he had done as she requested.

"Yes," Jules said, nodding. "I can tell you have something on your mind."

"Yes," she said. "I've had some analysts pouring over the reports they've been sending, specifically asking them to see if there was any geographic pattern to the symptoms we've been discussing. Since Vance indicated he saw a larger, more organized hand behind the general malaise in the Imperium, I thought perhaps there might be some indication of a localized point that was hidden within the data. No matter how much someone wants to obscure something, sometimes things are missed, and they have a slight concentration in certain areas located around a nexus."

"And obviously you found something, from the predatory look in your eyes," Mycal jibed.

Serena ignored it and continued. "Yes, they found a slight pattern centering around the Obdure 4 Cluster. It wasn't prominent but statistically significant. More incidents, and earlier reports are centered around that area than any other. It seems to *almost* randomly move outward from there."

"That's not a lot to go on," Mycal said. Vance was studying the data points she'd pulled up on their displays. Jules was doing the same.

"It's not," Serena continued. "But then I correlated it with military discipline reports."

Vance raised his head and stared at her. "What did you find?" he asked.

Serena smiled, seeing the light of comprehension dawning on him. "I found that there was a corresponding *lack* of normal disciplinary actions flowing outward from that same area."

"Meaning . . ." Mycal prompted as he stared at Serena and then at Vance who was nodding his head.

"Meaning something is occurring in that sector which is stirring the malaise *and* relaxing military discipline," Vance said. "Brilliant insight." he continued. "You realized that military discipline should have increased with the increased troubles they had to maintain, but instead, they reduced, indicating the military is part of it." Vance tilted his head in acknowledgement.

"That's a large assumption based on slight data trends," Jules said. "It could also be that the increased activity required has made the service cadre busier and less able to get into their normal troubles."

"Is that your experience?" Serena turned to Vance. "Sometimes . . ." Vance said. "But not in such direct correlation and with such a dramatic drop in disciplinary actions. There were almost none reported at the very heart of the sector. That is highly unusual on such a populated world. Those stats are way below what they should be regardless of troubles they have to handle."

"Good catch, Sis," Mycal said. "So, I suppose that means me and my merry little band have a trip in store? You want us to go poke our noses in quietly and see if we can find the culprits?"

Serena smiled. "Yes. But be sure you're back for the wedding and at least some of the parties. I want to see who you bring as a date."

Mycal choked on the drink he was taking and looked at her suspiciously. "You been spying on me?"

"You have a secret I should know about?

Mycal laughed. "Not from you, dear Sis." Serena caught a slight hesitation in her brother's cavalier attitude. It was enough that she marked it. Then Mycal continued on. "I'll prep the crew and be off. I'll work with Jules on the normal reporting schedule and channels. I'm assuming our usual stealth mode?"

"Yes," Serena said. "But don't go just yet. There's something more I want your input on."

"What's that?" Mycal said, settling back down in his chair. He seemed anxious to leave for some reason – more than his normal hyperactivity and needing to always be doing something.

"I want you to weigh in on our overall strategy. We've talked about the problems facing the Imperium. I think we need to agree on an overall approach to take. We'll have Vance cleaning up the service, but we need to figure out a way to address what is happening with the government and populace. I know Jules and I have spoken about it with our usual advisors, but I want your and Vance's take on it."

"That's political," Mycal said. "I'm not political. You know that. It's why I opted for the Service and the sneaky side of things, remember?"

"I still need your devious mind," Serena said.

"Actually, we don't," Vance said. This startled Serena. This was the first time Vance had ever contradicted her, and she realized Vance was immediately abashed.

"With respect . . . Serena."

"Explain," Serena said. She was intrigued. She could tell Vance just had one of his flashes of insight.

"We'll be anything but be devious," Vance said. "We'll do something quite revolutionary. We'll approach them with something completely unexpected." Everyone was watching Vance closely.

"Let's give them the truth, and only the truth."

Chapter 13

"The truth!" Mycal said. "What a novel idea for a government."

"But exactly the right approach," Vance said. "Let me explain."

Serena gestured for him to continue.

"We all agree we're fighting an unknown organized foe?" They all nodded, though Serena noted Jules was watching Vance closely, not sure he was agreeing with his supposition. Vance continued.

"We need the support of the populace. We need them to be on our side. The problem is the population and their sense of malaise. We need to jolt them, to enlist them, make them aware of the problem and then enlist them in the fight."

"And that's where the truth comes in?" Mycal said. "How does that help us? I've never known Serena to lie to the public, and we still have the problems we're talking about."

"It's not only about truth. It's also about trust." Vance said. "We'll use truth to build trust. Trust brings loyalty and love. Loyalty and love are the strongest forces within a populace. If we have the loyalty and love of even a small, active portion of the populace they can accomplish amazing things."

"And what is this truth you are talking about?" Jules spoke up. It was clear to Serena he was dubious. He had been in government service the longest of them all. "You can't trust the population to do anything rational. Look at history. Populations invariably panic and do irrational things. We have to protect them from a truth that would cause them to panic. What do you think would happen if we announced we suspected some invisible group was seeking to subvert the government and cause them to all be lazy, stupid and dissatisfied with their lives? That wouldn't engender this *trust* you're talking about. It would sound self-serving and condescending."

"I disagree," Vance said calmly. "Populations do irrational things when frightened. When they don't feel they have the full story, or when they feel they have lost control. Then a mob gathers and that causes irrational behavior. But when people know the truth, and they know it in time to affect their own lives and decisions, the majority will be rational and make decision in the self-interest of their families and themselves.

"What you are referring to, Jules, is Serena sharing our *opinion* and *thoughts* about what we see happening. I wouldn't call that *truth*. Too often people share their opinion, thoughts or desires as *truth*. In very ancient times, a mystic defined truth as, '. . .*knowledge* of things as they were, as they are, and as they are to come.'"

"What on earth are you talking about?" Jules said, clearly annoyed.

"I think I get this," Serena said. She needed to be cautious but something about it resonated.

Serena continued, looking directly at Vance.

"We will use the truth, and the truth only. We will state facts, not our opinions or interpretations of the facts – unless we state them as such.

"We will level with the people. We will tell them the facts even when we worry whether or not they can handle it. And we will not tell them something is the *truth* when it is our *interpretation*. We will give them information and *request* their help in what we think is best to do but let them decide themselves. In other words, we will *trust* the people, and hope they, in turn, will *trust* and allow us to serve them."

"Exactly," Vance said.

"That will end in disaster." Jules said. "The whole reason we have leadership in government is so that smart people with all the facts can make the right decision and not be swayed by emotions or crowds being rabble-roused by special interests who stand to profit from one thing or another."

"Like we don't have that now?" Mycal said, laughing. "The leaders the people have elected are obviously self-serving most of the time, so they aren't looking out for the benefit of the people, and the people know it. That's been the biggest part of the malaise, in my opinion, is that the people are cynical whenever they hear promises from the *government*."

"We can't clean up the bureaucracy like we can the military," Vance said. "Those changes will have to come from our own example, by being completely open and honest about what is the *truth*. And in our holding those in government accountable to the people they serve.

"When the people see we trust them to do the right thing, they will trust us to do the right thing for them."

"This is juvenile," Jules said. "It is simplistic and naïve. It will cause your reign to be a disaster, Empress."

"Don't judge too hastily, Jules," Vance said. "Why don't we test it out a bit as we go around to the events we have to be at anyway. We can start small, and if we see positive benefits, we can expand what I'm saying. If it hurts, we can pull back. What have we got to lose?"

"What we've been doing to this point hasn't changed things," Serena said. "If you want different results, you must use different methods."

Jules just shook his head.

Serena was nervous, but the feeling of trying something completely different, and actually letting the burdens of her people's lives slip back to the people themselves. It seemed the right thing to do. She would *lead* and *enable*. Give her people the truth and let them rule themselves, within the law, of course. It was worth a test at least. It felt right.

"Can I go now?" Mycal asked. "All this political talk is making me antsy. I want a straight-forward spy mission to keep myself feeling clean."

"Tell the truth. You're just bored by sitting still for more than 5 minutes," Serena smiled and punched him on the arm.

"That too," Mycal smiled and stood, nodding at Vance and Jules and leaning down for a quick hug from his sister. Then he strode from the room. Serena looked down at his breakfast plate. It had been scoured clean.

"How does he eat so fast?" she glanced after Mycal incredulously.

Vance chuckled. Serena liked his smile, especially directed at her.

"Well, I've got some speeches to write and it looks like our first party is in a few days." She turned to Vance. I'll draft some ideas, but I want you and Jules to review them. I think you should prepare some talking point ideas as well. This is your idea after all. You have command of the pertinent *truth* you think we should speak of?"

"I do," Vance nodded. "And I will."

Serena hesitated a bit more, wondering if she should do this . . . then decided she should. She had to get to know Vance better, especially if he was going to be her husband.

"I noticed you and Mycal have been working out together?"

"Yes, though it's more like Mycal is mopping up the mats with me. He's trying to teach me some of his special hand to hand training. It's intriguing, though it's hard for me to pick it up working with such a . . . master of the art." Serena could tell Vance was hesitant to say anything about Mycal's augmentations. It was clear he didn't know who knew and didn't want to betray anything.

"You should know I've had the same training," Serena said, "though I'm not quite as expert at it. You want to continue your instruction?"

Vance looked at her, his eyes startled. "With you?"

"Of course," Serena said, smiling. I need to work out also. I do so every day and would enjoy a more challenging partner. Maybe I can bring you up to speed so you can keep up."

"It would be my honor," Vance said. Serena could tell he was being guarded, not quite sure whether to accept or not. After all, one didn't just wrestle with an Empress. Well, she'd just have to get him used to treating her like a normal personal, even if she had to kick the stuffing out of him to do it. Looking more closely at him, she wondered if she could.

Serena smiled. "I look forward to it. I'll send the time and place to your personal comm. In the meantime, work up some ideas and we'll discuss them tomorrow morning. I can see from Jules' expression that our allotted time for breakfast and planning is over and I have other meetings."

Vance stood and bowed, kissing her hand again and waited as she stood. Again, the brush of his lips against the back of her hand did something to her. This is going to be interesting, she thought as she left the room with Jules in tow. Her mind wasn't on her next meeting, but looking forward to tomorrow morning, for more physical contact with her fiancé.

Chapter 14

Vance stepped into his allotted quarters in the palace. These were much larger digs than he'd ever had, even as an admiral. Guess it was a step up being the Consort of the Empress.

The thought of his being the actual husband of the Empress made him shake his head as he sat behind the polished mahogany desk situated in an alcove of his quarters. Actually it was a suite with a bedroom, fresher, sitting / dining room and an office area, all richly appointed and complete with a food dispenser and attendant who would clean the room, make his bed (which he hadn't allowed yet – still retaining the discipline of making his own bed military style), and a laundry service. The attendant, uniformed in palace livery, was always interrupting him and asking if he could set out his clothing, get him a drink, arrange any meetings or send any messages.

Vance was used to having an attendant, but this time, he thought to be very careful. Something told him, since he hadn't picked this attendant as he'd always done in the past, he likely reported to someone else besides him.

Perhaps he was being a bit paranoid, but with the stakes being what they were, and the Empress being involved with politics at the very highest level, best to keep everything close to the vest.

Mycal had helped him get set up with an ultra-secure workstation so he had no worries about that, but he never left anything sitting out, nor did he talk to himself while musing. He also had Mycal scan the room with his spy equipment, which made Mycal smile until he found a listening device and a camera focused on the workstation. They'd decided not to say anything and just wait to see who seemed perturbed – if ever, when both had been destroyed. Mycal had left him a spare sensing device so he could sweep the room whenever he liked. He also brought Vance a small jammer which would interrupt any signal being sent or received within the room.

Palace intrigue went deep no matter how beloved the Empress was. Even during his short time in the Palace, Vance noted everyone seemed angling for some sort of political gain. It made Vance grateful for his time in the military, especially the times when he'd been assigned out in the hinterland of the cosmos, mostly acting on his own and keeping his own counsel.

Rather than take the time to do a sweep, Vance switched on the jammer and sat at the workstation. He wanted to get down a few ideas of what the Empress could speak about regarding their new *Truth* campaign and how it should be approached. The ideas came pretty easily, because he worked first in concepts then developed the practical applications. The same he'd always used with any command. People who served with him always knew the situation and where they stood. It was why certain people maneuvered to serve under him in his various assignments. He wasn't being arrogant, he told himself. Just assessing the situation.

As an admiral, he'd a key cadre whom he'd trained and brought with him as his administrative staff. They were good people –

excellent people – who believed and served just as dutifully as he. That's why he'd been successful. Because of the trust and dedication he'd shared with those with whom he'd served.

Before his retirement he'd made sure his people had been assigned out in choice assignments, and as he had pondered over the changes he was going to make with the military after the wedding, he realized he'd unconsciously put his people in very favorable posts who could step up and be people he could trust and rely on to carry out the true mission of the military. There wasn't near enough of them, but he had served far and wide and had a good group of contacts he could consult with in just about every sector and leadership level.

He was looking forward to being the aggravator for a bit. However, as he'd considered it, and had spoken with Mycal, Jules and the Empress about it, they all agreed, though Jules was a bit reluctant, doing it quickly and harshly was the best way to go. Finally, Vance would have the authority to make the sweeping changes to leadership and discipline he'd always thought needed to be done.

Vance also realized, doing so would earn him a great many enemies. He'd already seen the extent to which they would go even before the Empress' plans were announced. Somehow that had leaked out – which was another reason Vance was being hyper vigilant even in his own quarters.

The ideas jotted down and saved, Vance sat back and started to wonder if there were any other ideas concepts he could suggest. It made his thoughts wander to Serena and how intelligent and observant she was for a young woman. Young . . . he realized she really wasn't that much younger than he. Only three years. In fact, he was still considered quite young for the rank he'd achieved, but somehow, he always *felt* older when he was around Serena.

He admired her and recognized her leadership skills every time he was around her. Her presence, her knowledge, her wit and canny observation made her perfectly suited for her present position. Of course, she'd been groomed and trained for it her entire life. True, it had come earlier than expected when her parents had been in that tragic accident that had shaken the Imperium, but she'd stepped up, no one could deny, and now firmly held the reins of government.

Serena wasn't just a place holder, she was an active Empress, one who cared about her people and their circumstances. One he could serve whole-heartedly. To top it off, she was beautiful, inside and out.

Vance caught himself at that thought. Beautiful? Well of course. She was beautiful, and he had a right to think of her that way, didn't he? He was going to be her husband.

No. Best not to think about that. He was becoming her husband purely for political reasons. He needed to keep his focus on that. To do what he was being asked to do – and do it to the best of his ability. That was all he could – and should – expect.

Still, when she looked at him . . . was there something else he had begun to sense? When they were married, what would their relationship be like? Would they share a wing in the Empress' personal residence?

A sudden thought sprang to his mind. Would she want children?

"Come on." Vance growled out loud. "I have to keep focused here. I have a job to do and that's it."

Vance couldn't help himself. He'd never wondered about children before. Never really thought of having a wife and a family.

He'd always been single mindedly focused on his military career. And not necessarily his career, but in what it represented. Vance had always wanted to make a difference. To serve people and help them so they'd never have to suffer as he'd suffered. His mind shut off that memory pathway.

Instead he came back to the realization he'd never considered pairing off with someone, knowing there would never be anything *normal* about the life he'd chosen. It wouldn't have been fair to any woman . . . or child.

Of course, with his new arrangement a chance at a normal life was gone for good. He had to stop thinking about it. He was merely doing his duty. And this was a good way for him to do what he'd always dreamed of doing. Vance would finally be able to make a *real* difference.

His thoughts were interrupted by a distinct 'bling.' on his communicator. He picked it up and looked at the message. It was from the ultra-private app recently downloaded into his unit.

"Tomorrow 0700 hours. My quarters. The attendant will show you to my private gym. Be ready for a heavy-duty whooping. Serena."

This jolted Vance right back into his unwanted thoughts about he and Serena's relationship. Or lack thereof.

He guessed she was serious about her offer to train with him. No . . . to train *him* more like. After all, what wife doesn't want to *train* her husband. Vance chuckled and shook his head, not sure whether he was looking forward to tomorrow morning or not.

Chapter 15

Mycal put the last piece of personal gear into his ruck sack. He'd already commed his crew and gave them a countdown to departure. They were used to that, always being on call for a new mission. He figured that since they'd been on planet more than a week, they were all as antsy as he was to get moving again. To be doing something.

The Lula would already be rationed, fueled, and refitted. She was topped off every time they set down at any base, so she'd be ready for the next mission.

He wondered if he had time to send a message to Adriana before he left. Then he wondered if he'd given anything away to Serena when she was teasing him about bringing a date to the parties. No one knew about Adriana – nor could they.

Mycal wished he could bring her to those parties . . . and started composing the secretive message to the woman he loved, but whom he'd had to hide away for her own safety.

Switching his comm to the shielded and camouflaged commercial band he'd established for their secret communications, he dictated, "Dearest: Will be away on one of my jaunts. Don't know for how long. Will touch base when I return." They'd miss their regular comm talk on the secure band, but it couldn't be helped. They were both used to it.

When this was all over, they both hoped Adriana could come out of hiding and they could be together openly. It truly was a dangerous time.

Adriana was the Chamberlain's stepdaughter. The Chamberlain's first wife had died of a wasting disease many year's previous, and then he'd remarried Estella Portine 15 years ago, bringing her daughter Adriana into the family. She had been a young 10-year-old precocious girl that had wrapped Jules' heart around her little finger.

Jules had doted on her and loved her as much as if she were his own. This, of course, brought Adriane into Mycal's orbit at fancy parties (those he'd been forced to attend) and more often – and more pleasantly – secret family gatherings, which were informal. It was then Mycal and Adriana had hit it off, though discreetly. It wouldn't do to have even more court intrigue, especially when Mycal was supposed to be considered a nobody at court, and just a mere security functionary at best. This was so Mycal could easily and openly slip around the Imperium being the candid eyes and ears of the Empress, as well as her secret, and very effective Hand when a particular need arose.

And speaking of intrigue, an assassination attempt had been made on the Chamberlain three years ago, which The Chamberlain had barely escaped, but had caught his wife, Estella in the rooms of the luxury resort they'd been vacationing at ostensibly for a rest, but really for high level meetings the Chamberlain was holding with certain factions of industry seeking to bolster some trade deals or some such.

The Chamberlain had been at those secret meetings when the bomb had gone off at the resort. Nothing had been left of the wing the Chamberlain's wife and stepdaughter had been staying at. Estella had been in the room. Adriana was not. She had snuck away and was spending time surreptitiously and most inappropriately with Mycal at a nearby beach, incognito and very plainly in public.

Mycal had not been part of the security detail. He had broken away from his duties to spend a little time on the vacation world with Adriana as occasion secretly permitted. And it was good he had. As soon as the explosion had occurred, Mycal realized what had happened, and where the explosion had occurred.

Rather than taking Adriana back to *official* safety, Mycal had second thoughts. If the Chamberlain and his family had been a target, his stepdaughter would still be a target. Since Adriana didn't like life in the limelight, and since her mother was already certainly dead, they both decided it would be best for her to be assumed dead also. It was for her safety, as much for her not wanting to continue her stratified life under such public scrutiny. She and Mycal were alike in their desire for the non-descript life. That's one of the things which had drawn them together.

So it was that Mycal had secreted Adriana away with one of his extensive contacts, ensuring her safety until the culprits were found, and this all calmed down. Then they could have the life together they wanted.

As Serena and Vance had noticed something deeper going on in the Imperium, Mycal had seen it too, but sooner and in his own personal way. Along with his current missions, he was gathering evidence on who would be seeking the Chamberlain's life – or at least that specific threat which had gone so far as to kill his wife and tried to kill his stepdaughter. Working with Vance and Serena was helping him do this. The deeper in he got, the more he sensed it was all part of the same thing. Serena wasn't the only one trained in hyper observation, after all. And now Vance had joined the team, he was more confident than ever they would soon find those behind this and put a stop to it. The sooner they did that, the sooner Mycal could let his little sister know he was retiring to the quiet life to get married and raise a family . . . in peace and quiet.

Mycal put his comm away, picked up his bag and sealed his personal quarters in that special way he always did. He was such a security nerd. He smiled, hefted the bag over his shoulder and headed for the private garage where the Lula waited along with his crew.

Chapter 16

"Good morning Vance," Serena said, looking up from stretching on the mat, warming up and loosening her muscles for the coming training. She was a bit excited . . . and nervous at the same time. She had to admit she'd been looking forward to getting closer to this unique man. She'd been observing him and was increasingly impressed. Now was time to get an even better measure.

Vance strode into the room in his palace-issue workout suit, matching Serena's, but definitely fitting him quite well, Serena observed. He set the grab bag and towel he'd brought with him down on the bench off the side of the mat and strode over and knelt beside her, not too close, but still closer than anyone had been to her in without others close by.

No one else was in the room, but on Jules' insistence, there were watchers. Serena knew they wouldn't be able to get to her in time if there was any serious threat, but even Jules wasn't fully aware of her capabilities. She wasn't nervous about the training, especially since speaking with Mycal just before he left and learned how good Vance was. He wouldn't be a threat to her physically, even if he wanted to be. Though she trusted Vance not to be a threat. It was more she was nervous about being in close proximity to someone she was about to marry. They really didn't know each other at all, other than their numerous work meetings and, of course, their respective reputations. She had to figure a way to break the ice, and to get below the surface to the real person beneath.

Serena wanted to know Vance, the man. And she hoped he would get a favorable glimmer of Serena . . . the woman. Thinking of this, she felt a flush come to her cheeks and she bowed her head, ostensibly stretching more, so he wouldn't see.

She needn't have bothered as she glanced up to see Vance doing his own stretching routine, and obviously just as nervous as she. It made her glad, and then had an idea.

"Look, I know you might be as nervous as I am, so I'm going to come right out and talk about it openly. I've not really been around a man, alone, except Uncle Jules, my father and Mycal, much less physically working out with one. All my sparring partners have been excellently trained women. But I figured we're going to have to get used to being around each other more than just in formal meetings."

She stopped speaking, watching Vance closely, and seeing a touch of relief cross his features. "Well, that is a good thing, since we're going to be married and all." He smiled. She waited for him to say more. It seemed as if he were about to ask something. She figured she might know what it was, and she dreaded talking about it too. Instead, he said something else.

"I will admit, I'm pretty nervous sparring with the Empress of the Known Worlds. I've sparred with women before, but in the course of training, or duty drills. This is a bit different." She waited for him to say more. He didn't, and then because he couldn't think of what else to say, he commenced stretching again. Serena laughed.

They had both been stretching far longer than was normal for a workout. They were both delaying.

"Do you have a warmup Kata?" She asked, searching for something to talk about to get this going. It was turning out to be as awkward as she'd feared. It was clear neither one of them knew what to talk about when it wasn't related to their shared goal of saving the Imperium.

"I do," Vance said, sitting up and plainly wondering whether he should stand up or not. It was clear he was waiting on her. "If I recall, you were the one who invited me to train with you. How about I follow your lead?" He chuckled. "I need to get used to that, anyway, don't I?"

At least he was trying to lighten the mood, Serena saw, and started to push herself a bit.

"You show me yours I'll show you mine." She stood and held out her hand offering to assist Vance to his feet. The gesture was a small payback for the comment about following her lead.

Vance chuckled and shook his head. "I can tell you have Mycal's sense of humor. Next you're going to call me 'old man.'" He reached out his hand, took Serena's and then, suddenly pulled her back, rolling with it and pulling her into a throw.

It took Serena by surprise, then her training kicked in, and she went with it, flowing with the throw, but adjusted her body's motion into a roll, contacting the mat smoothly, using that momentum to come back to her feet and spinning to face Vance, smiling. This was more like it.

She was surprised again by Vance being on the attack, as if he expected her recovery and was going on to the next throw before she could defend against it. And he was right.

Stepping in close, he reached at arm around her waist, pulling her over his swiveling hip and using the leverage of his foot moving behind hers to try and throw her a second time. This time something other than her training kicked in and she grasped Vance, and not trying to avoid falling, instead she went with it again, and with her grasp around his waist, pulled him with her.

Her body maneuvered like a cat and she, again contacted the mat but lightly as she curved and rolled out of the throw, while using her own leverage to pull Vance with her and throwing him instead. It had a bit more heat in it than she had intended and was worried when Vance sailed over her.

She needn't have worried as Vance, though thrown, curved into a roll of his own and came back to his feet smoothly, turned and faced her, smiling.

"I was right," Vance said. "Not only did you have the same hand-to-hand trainer as Mycal, but you must have the same physical trainer as well."

Serena chanced a slight glance at the spy-eyes she knew had watchers. Had they caught Vance's meaning? She knew Vance would catch that glance no matter how slight.

"And I can tell you've been training with Mycal, as you've anticipated my moves and developed some counters of your own.

No one else I've trained with has been able to twig to my moves like you. And no one has ever caught me off guard."

She watched Vance closely, willing him to get the message. Vance nodded. He had.

"I can tell you're going to be quite a partner. Mycal continually mopped the mats with me, but I'm a quick learner. So, it would be odd if I wasn't able to at least keep up a bit, no matter how good your training."

Serena cocked her head a bit, and then got the message herself. She hadn't realized it and that was why Vance had come out so strongly. He was giving her a deeper message. If her augmentation was supposed to be a secret, then she couldn't be seen to beat him overly badly. It would seem strange and raise eyebrows of those watchers. They may not realize what was happening, and gossip about the fine joke of the Empress humiliating her new fiancé but others, more astute, would ask *how* she'd been able to do that, and then her augmentation would no longer be a matter of a surprise defense if it were ever needed.

Her respect and even awe of Vance's awareness and insight grew even deeper. She should have realized that herself. Instead, she was focused, like a silly schoolgirl on getting close to this man. Still, as she looked at him, he *was* quite a man. And she was going to marry him.

Without stopping herself, she allowed herself a smile. And not just any smile. It wasn't the polite smile of court. But a smile of enjoyment. Enjoyment of the situation, and the person she was with. Vance surely would catch that.

He did. And smiled just as genuinely.

They had finally connected. But how deep would that connection go? How deep did she want it to go? How deep did Vance want it to go? There was still a lot to figure out.

Chapter 17

Vance Stepped into the atrium of the Empress' private quarters. He'd been here several times now for morning workouts and meetings with Serena and Jules in preparing for tonight's event. It was the first of the galas to announce the pending nuptials of the Empress to her new Consort, who it was also rumored would be further invested as Commander-in-Chief of all the Military.

That was causing quite a row with many political and gossip vid shows. And of course, unnamed advisors to the Joint Chiefs had also commented anonymously, for those same vid shows, that they didn't think the Empress surely meant for it to be real. It had always been a symbolic position, more for ornamentation and ceremony than for actual leadership.

Vance smiled at this. From those comments, he could tell it was exactly what the Joint Chiefs were afraid of. They were putting this veiled notice out there to let the Empress know they wouldn't take this lying down. The Joint Chiefs knew Vance, and further, they knew Vance's opinion of them. They could see what was coming, though they were, true to his knowledge of them, burying their heads in the sand and hoping it would go away rather than do what was necessary to make it so Vance wouldn't have had to be called in at all.

He stood, waiting in his new dress uniform, the one Mycal had given him earlier on. It had the insignia of his Admiral's rank, but it was also subtly changed so that one more insignia could be added after the wedding and his swearing in as Commander-in-Chief. Then it would be official, and it would be high time.

Vance was chomping at the bit to get moving. All this planning was driving him a bit crazy. He knew what he was going to do, and how he was going to do it – in spite of the trepidation of the Chamberlain – and to the glee of Serena.

She truly did have Mycal's perverse sense of humor when it came to stuffy bureaucrats. Funny thing for an Empress to have when being surrounded by stuffy bureaucrats all day long. Maybe it was *because* of being surrounded all day long. Her sense of humor was a defense mechanism. He was just glad he didn't have to put up with it.

"I see I have kept you waiting a fashionable length of time," Serena said as she strode from her private quarters into the atrium.

She was stunning.

Vance about choked when he saw how beautiful she looked. Her dress was a shimmering silver that cascaded down her lean figure while accenting in appropriately *Empress* fashion her curves to give her an undeniable female shape. There was enough skin showing to be considered exotic in the right places, but modest enough to maintain dignity and grace. What a combination. Vance thought.

It was accented by an ornately jeweled hairpiece woven into her long hair, held up and coiffed in a way that also glistened and swayed, catching light in such a way as to draw attention to . . .

The radiant glow of her countenance. She practically beamed as she smiled at him. Vance thought it must be a trick of the light in the atrium, but as he gazed at her, could tell it was mostly a glow from within. It radiated beauty, grace, warmth, health and vitality, and just a touch of . . . mischief.

Vance smiled back. He was a very lucky man. Then he caught himself. They still had not addressed anything about how *personal* their marriage was going to be, and Vance certainly wasn't going to be the first one to bring it up. They had gotten more comfortable with each other, more in a friendship sort of way. They had continued to spar and train together each morning for the past several days and had gotten really easy in each other's physical presence. Vance knew Serena was still holding back with her augmented muscles and bones, though she was continuing to give Vance the benefit of the deep training Mycal had started. It was a very effective form of fighting he didn't know existed.

"You look . . . Amazing. Even those words don't do it justice," Vance stammered.

"This little thing?" Serena joked posing for a moment and then twirling around for Vance to get the full effect.

"The dress, yes, but it only accents the beauty that's already there," Vance said, then blushed as he realized this was a very personal comment. They were friendly, yes, but she was still the Empress.

"Why thank you," Serena said, her voice more subdued. "I didn't realize you could be such a flatterer."

"I'm sorry," Vance said. "I didn't mean to be so presumptuous. It just came out before I realized how forward that must sound."

"Don't worry about it. You really meant it didn't you?" Serena looked closely at Vance.

"Every word," Vance admitted. "I'm afraid they don't teach courses on flattery at the Academy. I just said what I felt – without thinking of how it must sound. I'm sorry if it didn't seem sincere. I . . ." Vance didn't know what else to say.

"Look," he finally continued. "I'm really new at this court stuff. Can we just agree that I'm going to be putting my foot in my mouth quite often? But it never will be meant in any inappropriate way. I truly do . . . care . . . about what you think and feel. As well as wanting to succeed at the task we've set."

Serena paused a moment, continuing to look at Vance. He didn't know what she was thinking. Had he overstepped? He should have shut up when he was already on the rails instead of jumping headlong in front of the grav train.

Finally, she spoke, and her humor had returned. "Why my good man. I do believe you have made even me speechless. And that's no small feat." Her cheeks seemed slightly flushed, but he wasn't sure whether it was from anger or . . . something else. Embarrassment?

"Shall we proceed?" She said, taking his proffered arm. "I have a speech to give and a new boyfriend to show off."

Vance was glad of stepping out of the awkward situation. Still, he wondered if she meant something by using the word 'boyfriend.'

This was getting sillier all the time. He was acting the teenager analyzing any word or hint to see if the girl he had a crush on *liked* him or not. Puberty was far in the past, but you couldn't tell it by what kept going through his mind at the stupidest of times. Wisely, Vance kept his mouth shut as they got onto the lift on the far side of the atrium and took it down to the audience chamber where those invited dignitaries would be graced by their presence and a closer look at himself.

***

The door swept open and a cacophony of sound reached his ears. Vance clamped down his trepidation. He'd ran headlong into a firefight and felt less nervous. Music surrounded his senses as did the murmur of voices, which quickly died with their entrance into the middle of the gathering. Now it was the quickly settling silence which made him even more self- conscious. What if he tripped and pulled the Empress down with him? Best not to think about that. Suddenly his feet felt like lead weights and his legs dragged as though walking through molasses. Outwardly Vance kept his calm as he led Serena across the room and sat her on the dais and ornately gilded throne.

She settled herself, then smiled up at him, as if realizing how he must feel, and trying to silently give him encouragement. It worked. Whenever she smiled at him in that way, it just . . . warmed him all over. He smiled back and finally realized he should start breathing again. Then she turned to the audience who had bowed as she strode across the room.

"Ladies and Gentle sirs," she began, hidden amplifiers picking up her soft and melodious voice. "I welcome you to this first official gala announcing our engagement. Let me introduce you all to Admiral J. Vance Hamblin who has agreed to be my husband, Consort and," there was the slightest of hesitations, "Commander-in-Chief of all the Military of the Imperium."

She paused and let the slight jumble of noises which had come out at the way she had announced Vance die down.

"Let me put to rest any and all speculation which we have heard concerning a certain matter." Silence hushed over the gathering. The crowd was hearing something they hadn't expected.

Vance smiled to himself and realized that Serena must certainly be enjoying herself given her sense of humor. She was quite the dramatic artist and adept at playing a crowd. Tonight, would be a memorable performance.

"When Vance is confirmed as my consort and Commander-in-Chief, the role will *not* be ceremonial. You have all seen his illustrious and honored career at such a young age and will undoubtedly realize his qualifications make him the obvious choice for such a position.

"I further confirm tonight that we have seen reasons this course is made necessary . . ."

There was a murmuring in the room. Vance watched as Serena paused and let her words sink in. This was turning into a gathering of intense interest for more than one reason. The ornately dressed guests, civilian and military dignitaries of the first rank with their partners were looking at each other, wondering if they heard right? Small exclamations of surprise and astonishment stirred through the gathering.

Then Vance noticed Jules, the Chamberlain standing below the dais at his traditional station, standing stiffly alert, his eyes carefully scanning the crowd gauging their reactions for later analysis and discussion.

Vance realized he should do the same thing, but knew Serena was much more adept at this than either of them. Lightyears ahead of them both, actually. What he was watching for was any indication of threat, anger, sudden danger. That was what he was adept at seeing. He knew there were others in the room for that purpose as well, along with spy eyes and hidden laser emplacements, but Vance was still closest and felt a strong desire to protect this brave young woman.

He needn't have worried. The people were so astonished they were standing docilely, amazed and waiting for the next words to issue forth, for they realized from Serena's bearing, more was coming, and these wouldn't be the trivialities they were expecting at this type of gathering.

Now it was going to come. The first shot in their war against whatever it was affecting the Imperium.

Serena held up her hand to still the voices.

"I have some words to say which aren't typical for an occasion such as this, but since it concerns many of you here, I thought I should speak to you directly."

Vance knew Serena was speaking to those invited here, the cream of society, the leaders in military, government, commerce, legal and social. But she was also speaking to the home audience. The billions who were tuning in on the vids watching to catch the latest gossip about the Empress' new husband to be.

All of them, Vance thought, were surely getting their credit's worth tonight.

"The changes I'm making to my personal life, are just the tip of the iceberg to the changes which must be made throughout the Imperium.

"Those changes are starting tonight with me and will be spread to every corner of the Known Worlds under which I hold sway. Those changes I'm talking about concern TRUTH.

"Although I have always spoken the truth to each of you, there have been times, on counsel of my advisors, I have not spoken *all* the truth, nor spoken frankly of my concerns.

"Tonight, that changes. From now on, I will trust each of you, and all those at home, to know the truth for yourselves, and then to act upon that truth for the benefit of yourselves, your families and your communities."

Vance continued to look around the room. There wasn't any threat. Instead what he saw was confusion. People looking at one another, shrugging, like they didn't grasp what the Empress was getting at. Well, they may not understand tonight, but they soon will. Especially if they are on the wrong side of truth.

"I desire an Imperium full of people who love and seek Truth wherever they find it. Truth brings freedom. And as servants of Truth, we are servants of freedom and help all people to be free. Free to *act* for themselves and not be *acted upon*.

Serena paused to let all that sink in, knowing it was being recorded and would be dissected by thousands of analysts and talking heads of the media. But Vance hoped, the real people of the Imperium were listening most closely.

"I hereby promise each of you tonight, I will always tell you the truth. I also will demand this from each who serve in my government at all levels down to the very lowest ranking civil servant.

"To begin my *Truth Initiative*, you have all heard and seen the reports of unprecedented job growth, employment and economic advances throughout the Imperium. This is all wonderful news, and I applaud each of those who work hard to make these strides possible.

"But what you have not heard is that along with this growth and prosperity, there are also rising numbers of violent crimes being perpetrated, record numbers of theft, fraud and vandalism occurring all across the Imperium. The numbers of those living in quiet desperation are increasing and afraid they will be forgotten and abandoned. These things concern me greatly.

"I'm telling you the truth of the numbers. We all must work together at all levels to see why these things are happening in the midst of abundance.

"I can't fix these concerns alone. Not even the reach of my government can do this. It requires each of you, armed with Truth, to look around and see what you can do locally, with your family, friends and neighbors.

"One thing I can do, is effect change where there is a clear solution. There will be accountability at all levels of government. Over time the idea of getting timely service and a fair shake from government has become a joke. I'm letting you all know this is going to change from this night on.

"Just as Vance will have my full support in cleaning up the problems I have seen in the military, I will be empowering others to make the necessary changes in my government. Those who have acted with dishonesty and graft will be summarily dismissed and where appropriate, answer to the law. Those who have strived to serve with diligence and honor will be rewarded and promoted.

"I also warn those of you who are not in the government or military. You should look to your own houses. My government will not do business with companies or organizations who have a reputation for dishonesty and graft."

Serena stopped speaking, letting her words sink in. Vance continued to gauge the crowd. They were in shock and still confused. They didn't know how to react. Should they clap? Then

Serena spoke again, but this time not to those in the room. She spoke to the most important audience of the evening.

"To those in the home audience, I hope you have heard what I said. I pledge to you that my government will strive to be your servants, not your masters. If my government is not serving you as you think we should, please message my representatives at the link provided for in the screen you see now. This link will be quickly scanned, and each message will be taken seriously and investigated. Please be patient as I'm sure you realize this is a large undertaking. I have diverted funds and people whom I trust with this task.

"I also encourage you to listen carefully to any who would try to persuade you about anything. Make sure you can verify the *truth* of their words before you give them your *trust*. I pledge to each of you, you will always be able to verify the truth of my words. I will also level with you and tell you when I'm sharing an opinion.

"Beware of those who speak opinion and offer it to you as Truth. They are trying to sell you something for which they stand to gain, and you will probably lose."

With that the Empress smiled brilliantly and nodded her head to the audience in the room and, most importantly, to those at home.

She held out her hand and Vance took it. The message had been delivered.

"Come, Vance," Serena said, still aware that her voice was still being amplified. She was pointedly ignoring the still gaping audience. "Let's see if they taught you how to dance properly at the military academy."

The audience still didn't know whether to clap or not, and there was a small smattering of applause. The rest just watched, not quite sure what had happened.

Vance chuckled and guided Serena down off the dais and onto the dance floor as the musicians took the cue and started in on the music they had ordered for their first public dance. He could tell from Serena's grasp of his hand that, although she was outwardly calm, she was trembling. This announcement had truly laid down the gauntlet. It had been more direct and pointed than they had discussed in their meetings, but apparently, she had decided to take it all the way rather than go with any half measures.

Vance fervently hoped he had not encouraged her wrongly. For good or ill, they were both deep in it together. That made him feel strangely . . . good . . . and terrified at the same time. It was one thing to stick his own neck out. He was prepared for that and had done it often. But for Serena to trust his advice and take such a risk . . . well. He knew he loved her for that.

Love? He had no further time to consider that thought as they swung into a more intricate dance move.

They swooshed around in their practiced dance. They had worked on more than hand-to-hand combat in their morning sessions. As they moved about the floor, he caught sight of the Chamberlain. He had a strange look on his face, as if he, too, were astonished and confused. Apparently, Serena had not cleared the precision attack of her speech with him. Well he'd had concerns about this course all along. He was just doing his job to try and protect the Empress.

Then he swung back into a move where Serena was close in his arms, and she was looking directly at him, smiling radiantly and he had no other thoughts than her beautiful gaze.

Chapter 18

The night became a blur. Vance danced with Serena a number of times as others came onto the floor and danced around them. Then after a suitable time, Vance escorted Serena back to the dais and she sat while refreshment was brought to them both.

A parade of dignitaries started to flow by, offering their congratulations, the Chamberlain standing by to announce each one. Vance couldn't for the life of him figure out Jules got all their names straight, until he caught sight of the Chamberlain's earpiece and realized he was getting fed the information. He didn't feel so bad then.

There were those in the military who he knew, and in turn, knew Vance. Most gave Vance a hearty congratulations. These were in the higher ranks, just under the Joint Chiefs. Some were those Vance trusted, others were just looking to get in good with the new boss.

The chilly receptions came from the admirals making up the Joint Chiefs. These were stiff and a couple condescending in their congratulations. They knew the gauntlet had been thrown down and they were getting a measure of an enemy they thought they'd gotten rid of.

Vance enjoyed playing it up a bit. He was being influenced by the Empress and Mycal in their perverse sense of humor as Vance laid it on a bit thick in his assurances that he was looking forward to meeting with each and every one of them soon. Very soon. They thought they'd beaten him. Vance was just attacking from a new direction, and with a lot more power behind him this time.

Then the evening got interesting.

Next in line was someone Vance already recognized, notwithstanding Jules making the announcement.

"Count Henri Wallach, First Minister of Parliament."

Vance knew him by reputation. He'd also met him once, briefly, during a military inspection done on a luxury world so Count Wallach could punch his ticket and have his *vacation* paid for by the taxpayers. It was a small garrison, still it had demanded someone of high rank to accompany Wallach on the inspection, and true to form, the Joint Chiefs, seeking to keep Vance out of the way, had sent him as their representative.

"My most hearty congratulations, Admiral Vance," Wallach spoke smoothly and with a brief nod rather than shaking hands as most others had done.

Vance returned the nod with precise declination and deference as befitting his and Wallach's respective status. He didn't like the man. Didn't trust the man.

Having conducted the formality, Wallach moved forward and turned, pointedly ignoring Vance and bowed low to the Empress. "And to you, Empress Serena. May your union be fruitful and productive."

Here was a subtle dig, Vance realized, at the arranged nature of their marriage. Vance considered what he could do without causing a political incident. He found he was becoming very protective of Serena, though quickly he realized he needn't have been.

"Why thank you, Count Wallach," Serena said sweetly, completely ignoring the jibe and instead embraced it. "I'm hoping it may be so," she said, smiling, without a touch of irony.

This shocked Vance. Truly he was not used to court intrigue and hoped he could continue to ignore it while he was off doing concrete things with the military. Much simpler, he thought.

"I trust your union will bear fruit shortly as well." Serena again smiled and nodded her head. Then Vance realized Serena had just delivered a riposte that would wound Wallach deeply for he realized that Count Wallach and his latest paramour had no children and hence, no heir to the Wallach estate. A point which Vance noticed visibly disturbed Count Wallach."

"Thank you, Empress." He bowed again and moved on. Vance gave himself the pleasure of a small smirk. Not large enough to cause offense when the vids were reviewed, which undoubtedly, they would be by all the pundits in the Imperium seeking any sign of news, or more importantly, scandal.

It was then, Vance's attention was drawn back to Jules, who had hesitated, looking at the military officer standing next in line to greet Vance. He was a navy commander by the insignia on his lapels.

"I'm afraid . . ." Jules began clearly waiting for the name to be spoken into his earpiece.

"Permit me to introduce myself," the man said, stepping forward. There was something familiar about the man Vance couldn't place.

"I am commander Volus Pratt, formerly *captain* of the Bainbridge. You disabled me above the planet Hemsley with unfair tactics as I was seeking to arrest you on a proper warrant. I demand satisfaction."

Then it hit Vance where he'd seen him before. This was the pompous captain who'd tried to waylay and destroy the Lula as Mycal and his crew had taken him off planet and saved him from bounty hunters with a price on his head. Vance also recognized this as a set up. The first salvo, probably from the Joint Chiefs, Vance concluded. Then the commander continued.

"You have insulted me and my family, the Aristotle Pratts of Vandermere, as well as causing a blemish on my military career."

So, this is more than it seems, Vance thought quickly. When he mentioned his family as well as the military? This might go deeper . . . and higher . . . as Vance realized who he'd been preceded by in the reception line. And since the man clearly hadn't been on the guest list, the only way he could have gained entrance was as the guest of someone very highly placed . . .

The man continued and Vance was only half listening ". . . As I was carrying out lawful orders to detain you on the charge of vandalism and destruction of private property and engaging in public brawling. You further carried out an unprovoked attack on my vessel, endangering innocent lives of the proud men and women of the fleet with your recklessness."

The audience grew silent and the music which had been droning on for the dancers on the floor below suddenly ceased as all the dancers seemed to know, instinctively something was going on.

Vance saw several security members moving cautiously forward, trying not to look conspicuous.

Jules also started to move forward, "This is highly . . ." but Vance cut him off with a raised hand. He had a better idea on how to deal with this. Since he had held military rank, and the man before him held military rank, although reduced, they should settle this in the military fashion.

It was obvious the man was playing for the vids and spouting a well-rehearsed speech, notwithstanding the courts had already reviewed the matter and the bar owner well compensated for his losses. This was being done to impugn his reputation and make him appear reckless and callous in his regard for others.

Vance turned to the Empress, bowed and asked, "Empress, if I may handle this? As the man is military, after all."

"You may, Admiral," Serena nodded her head in acquiescence and slightly emphasizing his former military rank.

"Thank you," Vance bowed slightly again then turned back to the man who was waiting, a haughty look of satisfaction on his face.

Vance hadn't known the man before, but from his obvious arrogance he must be an accomplished dueler. "I accept your challenge," Vance said. "And as the one being challenged, I believe

I have the right to state the time and weapons? We are following military protocol, are we not?"

The commander nodded and a slight look of unease crossed his face. It was clear this wasn't what he had expected. Instead, Vance surmised the commander and his *handlers* were hoping for scandal. An arrest and a challenge gone unanswered, so it would appear Vance would not deign to recognize anyone of lower rank, or he was fearful of being injured or killed. This reason the vids and certainly the Joint Chiefs and Politicos would circulate.

Well, Vance had made a career out of not doing what was expected. He had already formulated his plan and hoped the Empress and Jules would concur later.

"Commander, you have alleged I acted unlawfully and conducted an unprovoked attack on your vessel. The vids made available have proven your allegations patently false. The record clearly showed it was you who acted illegally and first fired upon the vessel in which I was a lawful passenger.

"Rather than debate an issue which has already been confirmed by the appropriate courts, I agree we should settle this like men of the military, and have our contest be an end to the dispute. The winner will be concluded as 'in the right.' Do you agree?"

The commander nodded. It was clear his nervousness was growing though he hid it well. He knew he was playing for an Imperium wide audience. Vance knew it too and was turning their own weapon back on itself.

"Thank you, commander," Vance said. "I am always of the mind any business to be done, especially important business such as ours, must be done swiftly and directly. Therefore, as the challenged party, I see no reason to delay.

"The time and place I declare to be here, and now."

The commander's eyes widened in astonishment. There was a gasp in the audience. Vance sensed, behind him the Empress seeming startled and Jules standing up straighter, though he tried to hide his reaction. He was playing his part now and was determined to play it well.

"The method of our combat will be hand-to-hand. The winner will be the man who causes the incapacitation of the other such that he can no longer stand and fight. Or do you feel this insult rises to the level of a death?" Vance was staring straight at the commander. "In the which, I shall be happy to accommodate you, though because of the venue, I would still prefer it to be hand-to-hand. We don't want to bloody the floor."

Another gasp circulated among the crowd. Vance was making his point to those who'd sent this measly messenger. It would also set a precedent for his intended ruthlessness in cleaning up the service. Everyone would know he meant business.

"I . . ." the commander stammered. "I agree," he said with more forcefulness, clearly resigning himself to what he had gotten himself into. Then he smiled, realizing he was about to be in a fight and was confident in his abilities.

Well, Vance thought. So am I.

"Shall we?" Vance indicated the dance floor below the dais. "Lord Chamberlain, would you clear a space for us please? About ten spans square should suffice. Do you concur, commander?"

"I do," the commander said as he stepped down the dais with Vance and entering into the area being rapidly cleared by security men the Chamberlain had motioned to. They left a clear area in front of the dais so the Empress would have an unimpeded view. Vance chanced to look back at her. Surprisingly the Empress was smiling serenely. Either she had great confidence in Vance or was hiding well any trepidation she felt.

He realized she saw what he was doing, and her slight nod indicated her agreement and encouragement. From this, Vance realized Serena had wanted him to know of her support as she was capable of masking any emotional indication of what she was thinking. The Chamberlain was less readable. His face was a mask of studied indifference.

They moved out onto the floor. Vance removed his uniform medals, citations and insignia and handed them to the nearest observer, a woman dressed in a fine, shimmering gown who, startled, grasped hold of the items and held them to her breast.

Commander Pratt had done the same, though handing his to – and Vance watched this carefully – Count Wallach. So, it was he who was behind this, Vance confirmed. It was an unconscious error on the part of the commander, but a telling one.

Then Wallach, seeing Vance gazing at him, quickly realized the error as well and thrust the items into the hands of an ever-present minion, disgusted at his being so easily outed.

It was then Vance fully appreciated his new uniform. It was formal and comfortable, though made of an expansive fabric that breathed and stretched giving full range of motion without tearing or constricting. Ingenious, Vance realized. The uniform was also a security measure. Earlier he had detected, when he'd first put it on tonight, the very subtle shielding sewn into the fabric over vital areas. It would absorb and deflect slug rounds, energy weapons, and very easily fists. He didn't like having so great an edge, especially in something like a duel but rather than strip naked he had to just go with what he was given.

Vance and Captain Pratt faced one another, bowed as was tradition, then the match began.

Vance stood, poised, watching. He'd decided he would give the commander the first move so it wouldn't be said he was the aggressor. And now he was glad of the sparring matches with Mycal and Serena. It left him at the peak of his hand-to-hand training with a bit of the new fighting style thrown in.

The commander started to move sideways. Vance adjusted, following his movement, seeming at ease, though every muscle was poised, ready to respond.

Suddenly, the commander darted in with a swing. It was far from clumsy, but Vance could tell this person's dueling was primarily with weapons. Clearly, fighting hand-to-hand was not something he'd expected nor had practiced.

Vance swayed back slightly allowing the swing to barely miss his face then darted forward, using the commander's own momentum, grabbing the elbow of the swinging arm to turn the commander around and with his other arm delivered a solid kidney punch to incite a great deal of pain and momentary immobilization.

Vance's fist connected solidly, and he felt a rigid surface.

Body Armor! Pratt had come prepared for a duel. He had been expecting weapons of some sort, but the armor he was wearing would also help him in a fistfight. Seems like Vance was not at an advantage after all with his new uniform.

Pratt twisted out of Vance's grip and turned to face him again, smiling as he realized Vance now knew his secret. But there was something else in his look, Vance realized. He'd have to watch this fight closely. Also, he knew he would not be able to incapacitate with any body blows. It would have to be to the face, neck or legs. Much harder and riskier. At least he had the same edge. Vance smiled back.

It was then Vance darted in, crouching and sweeping his right leg around. This would not be a fight of punches. He reasoned that if he went for face and head punches it would seem too brutal for the vids. Instead, if he could show finesse in the fight and incapacitate in another way, it would play better and give a more positive impression of being firm, direct and decisive, but also merciful and just. Much more was riding on this duel than just winning.

Vance's mind had always operated that way, spinning up to hyper-thought when he was in a critical situation, analyzing, calculating, formulating all in the midst of his acting.

Leg sweeping out, it connected with Pratt's shin. It was supposed to knock him off his feet, but it didn't. Pratt had not anticipated the move, Vance was sure, but Pratt stood solidly still on his feet, and while Vance was crouched and at a disadvantage, Pratt punched forward with a lightning right hand straight for Vance's jaw.

It connected, though Vance had already started rolling away from the punch. It was a glancing blow, still Vance felt it. It was harder than Vance knew it ordinarily should be and it sent him sprawling, his mind starting to swirl into fuzziness from the power of the punch.

Not only wearing body armor, but Pratt was also enhanced. Vance's mind was still functioning in hyper-thought through his haziness. He shook his head and struggled to his feet. It was clear he had underestimated the planning of his adversaries. He wouldn't do that again. It would be costly.

Pratt had mentioned his family history along with his military rank. So, he was of a supposed noble family. That made sense of his enhancements, from his family lineage, not from the military. Also, another reason why he'd been chosen to challenge Vance.

He had to end this quickly because he couldn't match the strength and speed of his adversary. Any lucky punch or grapple would be his undoing. He doubted Pratt would hold off from killing him, regardless of what the challenge required.

Good thing he was practiced at sparring with enhanced people, thinking of Serena and Mycal. There was a special way he had to anticipate and feint in order to defeat the enhanced speed and strength. He hadn't been able to do it often, but it could be done. He had to make any moves he had count.

Pratt was moving toward Vance again, this time more swiftly, not trying to hide his augmentation. That would provide problems later for the commander, but clearly, he wasn't worried about it now.

The commander was not into subtlety in his fighting. As he came forward, it was evident he was going to bull his way in close and pummel Vance with superior strength and speed. Pratt was determined to make this fight bloody.

Vance let him approach, using his own speed against him. Pratt was off balance when he threw the next punch with astonishing speed, but Vance was expecting it. He started to duck even as Pratt was beginning to raise his arm for the punch which flew over his head, and swerved aside, letting Pratt move past him.

That's when Vance made his counter move, coming up behind Pratt, and wrapping an arm around his neck in a vice-like choke hold and pulled back quickly forcing Pratt off his feet so he wouldn't be able to use any leverage and superior strength to defeat the move. In an ordinary person, it would have snapped his neck. But in an enhanced person it merely constricted his windpipe and blood flow. That was the point.

Vance knew from experience he had to exert extra strength to cut off breath and blood going to the commander's brain. It needed to be done quickly, before Pratt could get his feet under him and throw Vance off.

To forestall Pratt's doing this, he continued to back up, keeping Pratt from gaining any foothold. Pratt reached up with one hand, grasping Vance's arm and prying at it with vice-like fingers, pressing into Vance's forearm and threatening to break the bones.

It was also then that Vance felt a slight punch into his leg, which his uniform stiffened against. Vance looked down and saw a slim finger dagger Pratt had pulled from concealment and was trying to stab Vance in the thigh were people could plainly see.

There was a gasp from the crowd that Vance ignored and tightened his chokehold even more while thanking Mycal silently for his new uniform's security measures. Had he not had that advantage tonight, he'd surely be dead, as Pratt had unerringly aimed for a femoral artery. Vance would have bled out quickly.

Vance was getting angry and choked harder and increased his pace backing across the room and turning just before reaching the crowded border of the fighting space. He heard the slight metal clang as the dagger hit the floor and he felt the commander's body go limp. He held on just a bit longer to insure unconsciousness.

Vance would have been within his rights to kill the commander, since he had obviously violated the terms of the duel and tried to kill him. But reason returned and his hyper-thoughts told him it would be better to not, so the commander could be brought to a public trial, and Vance, true to his earlier strategy, would appear decisive, but merciful.

With a bit of reluctance, Vance eased commander Pratt to the floor, then stood facing the stunned audience. He was breathing hard from the exertion but spoke evenly.

"The commander claims I wronged him. This is a lie. You have all seen the evidence. If not, it is freely available.

"The Empress has said today she will only speak truth. As will I.

"Those who listen to lies and liars are destined to be in bondage to those who tell them. Remember this. Trust only those who tell you the truth and you can verify their words.

"It is very seductive to relinquish truth, and hence freedom in exchange for promised security. But if you give up your ability to *act* then you surely will be *acted upon* and no longer have the freedom to choose your own outcomes. You will have sold your freedom for a mirage.

"Former Captain Pratt has just learned the consequences of allowing himself to be led around by those who would lie to him. He traded a large payoff, I'm sure, to challenge me and forsook the truth of what actually happened. Now he has lost both his freedom and security. Those who promised to support him, will surely abandon him. There is a powerful lesson in this if you choose to see it."

Vance then turned to Count Wallach. "You should collect your minion." Vance pointed to commander Pratt still laying on the floor.

Count Wallach gathered himself up in feigned outrage. "This man is hardly my minion."

Vance looked directly at the First Minister, though he was speaking not only for the audience in the room, but the whole Imperium watching on the vids. "Remember what I said about lies."

Vance then turned and collected his medals and strode up the dais to stand beside the Empress. His forearm was throbbing, and he knew a welt was rising on his jaw. "My apologies," Vance said, bowing and kissing Serena's outstretched hand. "So sorry to disrupt our engagement party."

"Not at all," the Empress said, playing her part for the vids, her voice tinkling with humor. "I don't like dull parties, and you certainly livened this one up."

There was a rumble of laughter and smattering of applause. The Empress gestured for the music to continue as the security personnel gathered up the poor, still unconscious commander. Vance noted Count Wallach had already left.

They had just angered a very powerful enemy. At least they knew who this enemy was. The signs were evident Wallach was behind this little fiasco. He had been outed and made to look foolish.

Maybe this political stuff wasn't hard after all, Vance thought. Then Jules moved closer. "You two are quite the pair," he said, turning off their mics so it wouldn't be carried on the vids.

"Yes, we are, aren't we," Serena said, smiling up at Vance. His heart swelled, and he didn't quite understand why.

Chapter 19

Mycal stood still, listening for any signs of life in the dark and vacant lower-level hallway of the main government building in Metronome, the capital city of the Obdure 4 Cluster. The small planet of Gothway held the government seat of the cluster and on their way into the system, Mycal had tried to jack into the government data feeds. It hadn't worked.

Usually, his clearances granted him access to any and all government feeds. This didn't work for some reason. The only way that could happen was for the feeds to be sealed off from back door incursions from the Gothway side. That raised a red flag that Serena's supposition was correct. Something hinky was going on.

The rest of the journey in, they played it more casual, only accessing the regular feeds for news, entertainment, business. They all seemed normal, but as they watched the live broadcasts, the entire crew had felt something was off, not quite right. Like the presenters were a bit subdued, even a bit lethargic. There was nothing specific, just the general feeling.

"Malaise." Mycal had finally said aloud and his whole crew had agreed. "A strange description, but accurate," Cassie had said. And they proceeded with even more caution to the capital world, setting down in a remote section outside the main city.

They had argued with Mycal when he ordered them to all stay aboard and monitor the situation, especially Gomy. Mycal had insisted, and made it a specific order, reasoning that one person could infiltrate much better, and he was holding them in reserve in case he had to push the panic button. However, if for some reason he got caught, they were to remain on station with the ship because he may be a while, and not to rush in if he didn't check in at the regular intervals.

What Mycal hadn't told them is he had a plan of his own, and here he was just outside the main data room door ready to put it into motion.

Seeing no one about, which he thought was extremely odd given the nature of the building, Mycal pulled out his tiny smart box and applied it to the locking mechanism, waiting for it to assimilate the type of security and subvert it. This little box worked in every government facility and had been designed specifically for Mycal's branch of the Service.

Not only could it hack all government facilities, it would also work on the majority of private mechanisms as well. The red blinking light switched to a solid green and the door snicked open. Mycal put the tiny box back into his pocket and slid inside the room, pulling the door closed behind him.

Inside, the room was filled with stacks of computer servers. Mycal moved into the center of the room where sat the master console from which he planned to access the whole shebang.

He sat and pulled out another small device and inserted it into the desktop slot and spoke the number "four." The voice-activated data crystal began its infiltration and transmission work. Mycal tapped the small bud in his ear.

"Prepare for incoming data." Mycal heard two clicks in acknowledgement inside his ear. The best way to not get caught on Comms was not to speak except when absolutely necessary. His crew was used to that.

The data crystal had been configured to reach out and grab a wide array of data, most seeming innocuous, but when combined provided an absolutely accurate picture of what was going on in an area.

This wasn't the first time Mycal had done this. The data crystal was still blinking red. Mycal watched the screen flash bits of pictures, photos, lines of code, text and geometric images as the crystal did its work. It's built in, subsonic frequency would be virtually undetected by any regular means, sending data in powerful micro surges back to the Lula where Cassie, the com officer, was picking it up and making sure it was stored in Lula's secure registers. It would then be burst back through subspace to Imperium headquarters for unpacking and review.

Normally with this type of mission, data mining is all that would be required. Mycal had other ideas, though.

He continued watching until the data crystal turned solid green, indicating its work had been completed. He pulled it from the slot, then rather than tucking it back into his pocket, casually threw it into the waste bin next to the desk. It had already wiped itself when it was pulled out and would chemically dissolve in seconds, leaving only traces of normal electronic goo.

His primary mission having been accomplished Mycal again tapped his ear bud indicating all data had been sent. Then he chanced some quick words. "Remember orders. Might be offline for undetermined period. Remain on station. Wait for contact."

Mycal waited for the two audible clicks in his ear, then pulled the ear bud out, put it on the floor and stepped on it with his heel, crushing it. I may regret doing that Mycal thought to himself, but he didn't want anyone being able to triangulate where the Lula was hidden by backtracking any comm signatures from his earpiece.

Mycal moved through the server stacks back to the door, he started to open it a crack to peer out and was only slightly startled when it was flung open and he stood staring down the barrels of four blasters leveled at his chest.

He slowly raised his hands and nodded at the guards. "I guess you got me," he said. Time for phase two of the plan, Mycal thought to himself.

Chapter 20

Mycal had been marched by the armed guard, not up into the executive suits of the office building, but further downstairs, down toward the utility rooms he knew were there. This didn't bode well, he thought. However, his contingency plan was working as it should. The best way to get at the heart of any conspiracy, if there was one, was to get captured and taken to the heart of it by those who were part of it.

He didn't know for sure, but knew if he were caught, there would have been a very highly placed leak. Few people knew of his mission. The fact he'd been snared in an obvious trap meant someone had tipped off the leaders of whatever was going on. He wouldn't have been caught otherwise. He'd tripped no alarms and his equipment was calibrated to infiltrate any Imperium computers without leaving a trace. The designers of his equipment had also designed the data bases.

Chances are he would now meet with the head honchos of whatever conspiracy was going on. This was further confirmed when he was taken down into the building instead of up. If it wasn't something nefarious, he would have been taken to the security wing and the upper management would be called, not be hidden in the lower recesses. It was more than likely the data he'd sent had been scrubbed clean, since they'd allowed him to get this far.

Looks like the plan for him now, might be for him to just disappear. They didn't realize he would be missed at the highest levels. First, though, they'd want to milk him dry. Find out what he knew and then kill him.

Hopefully, he could hold out long enough to get real inside information from those interrogating him, and then be able to transmit said information through the bone induction transmitter embedded in his clavicle. It also served as a homing beacon. And with a code phrase he mumbled, inaudibly, it would activate and send an alert to his team to come in and get him, flashing their *highest-level* Imperial Credentials to take him away for questioning.

As he was being marched down the stairs – why not take the lift? he thought about what he actually knew and realized it wasn't much. What he did know, he could easily divulge because it was plainly obvious. The *government* suspected something and sent him to twig it out. End of disclosure. This might be easier than he thought. Just then they reached the lowest level of the building.

He was frog marched down a long corridor through a set of double doors to an open room. It wasn't a large room, maybe 20 spans square, but in the center lay a medical examination table. Over it hung a large spotlight flooding bright light down on to the table. The rest of the room was dim.

So, it's going to be that kind of interrogation, Mycal thought. Maybe this won't be so easy after all.

Chapter 21

"What were you thinking?" Jules asked, as Vance, Serena and Jules entered the lift and started up to Serena's private quarters.

Serena couldn't help herself and giggled. "He was doing exactly what he needed to do," She said, resting a hand on her uncle's arm. "Relax. He did well."

"Thank you, Serena," Vance said with a slight bow.

"And just what did he do well?" Jules persisted.

It was clear to Vance he was barely controlling his anger, which was confusing. Why should he be so angry? It should be obvious.

Serena interrupted Vance's thoughts.

"Jules, you should recognized what just happened," echoing Vance's very thoughts. "Vance did it for two reasons, actually three," she said. "First was to quickly and succinctly show he would brook no nonsense from anyone.

"Second, is to demonstrate how directly he's going to deal with the cleanup of the military - which I agree with."

"And the third reason?" Jules interjected.

"Think it through," Serena said. "Cool your anger so you can see it."

Vance watched as Jules tried to calm himself and processed what had happened. Still Vance was wondering why Jules, supposedly a very astute politician, hadn't seen it already. Then, he saw comprehension crossing his face. "He used it to identify our enemies."

"Yes," Serena confirmed.

"But the 1ˢᵗ Minister?" Jules protested.

"You have to admit the signs were pretty obvious, and actually quite clumsy for Henri." Serena winked at Vance. "Our dear Vance provoked him into revealing himself."

"But for Vance to have a vulgar brawl at a state event?" Jules was still miffed. "An event designed to present him formally as your fiancée and future Consort."

The lift door snicked open and they all moved through the atrium to the entrance of Serena's private quarters where they stood.

"It was that *vulgar brawl*," Serena continued, "that shocked poor Henri into revealing himself. There was no way Henri and his cronies expected Vance to first, except the challenge and second, to finish it right then and there.

"That was brilliant." Serena rested a hand on Vance's arm and squeezed it, her eyes gazing up into his. It gave Vance an unaccountable thrill - which he immediately tamped down.

She was either teasing him or … he couldn't let himself go there. He mustn't presume.

Serena was still looking into his eyes, Vance thought she might be expecting something, could it be . . .? She was smiling, humor gleaming in her eyes as if she was enjoying Vance's obvious discomfiture.

He was about to stammer something when Jules's communicator beeped.

Jules pulled it out, scanned it quick, put a hand to his ear as if listening through his earpiece. Serena looked at him expectantly, rarely did Jules allow himself to be interrupted like this.

"It's the latest from the crew of the little Nebula."

"Yes?" Serena asked.

Vance could tell Serena was worried. This must be out of the ordinary. He'd been wondering how Mycal's mission has been going.

"Mycal has fallen out of contact," Jules said.

Serena reached out and grasped Vance's arm tightly.

"However, the crew reports, Mycal had expected this and gave them orders to stay on station."

Serena's grip relaxed only slightly. "So Mycal expected this?"

"Apparently so, Empress," Jules said. "He told his crew he would raise the alert, if necessary, to come in and get him."

"They have the necessary security identifiers?" Serena asked.

"They do, Empress," Jules answered. "They were each given a complete set of high-level security officer credentials. We can immediately issue the highest-level warrant to go in and pull Mycal out of any facility anywhere in the Imperium."

It was then Serena let go of Vance's arm. He felt sorry she had. "Well then, as you say, best to let things play out. This isn't the first time Mycal has had his own screwy plan. They've always born fruit in the past, though." She took a deep breath to calm herself.

"Goodnight all." She turned and gave Vance a wink and a slight nod to Jules and opened the doors to her private quarters and entered.

Whatever moment they had was now gone, Vance thought to himself.

"Vance," Jules said gesturing back towards the lift.

Vance nodded and proceeded him.

Jules spoke as they were walking. "I must say your demonstration tonight . . . Was another part of it to pound home the fact you and Serena are always going to be truthful with the people? What more open and honest can you be than to do everything where everybody can see, not hidden in the background?"

"No need to answer," Jules said as Vance started to say he actually hadn't thought of that aspect.

"I can tell you're going to be stirring things up quite a bit. Probably more than anyone anticipated."

Vance agreed. "And I haven't even started yet."

Jules glanced up at him, as the door to the lift door snicked open and they got on.

"Remember," Vance continued, "this is why I was brought on, to clean up the military. Believe it or not, tonight just made it easier. People now know what to expect. And I suspect, some in the military, if they're smart, are starting to clean up their own act rather than waiting for me to do it for them.

"I see," Jules said. The lift door opened. "I believe this is your floor," Jules said.

"Goodnight Vance."

"Goodnight Jules." Vance stepped out and moved down the corridor towards his quarters, his mind quickly forgetting his conversation with Jules, instead flashing back to that moment in front of Serena's door. He felt like a teenager on prom night. Vance shook his head. "I can't believe I'm thinking this." The door to his quarter's snicked open and he went inside for the night.

Chapter 22

Mycal lay on the exam table. As expected, it was hard, sparse, utilitarian and no privacy. The room had a smell of dust and there was a small hum of electrical current constantly buzzing, as if the lights, though turned off, still had current flowing.

At least he was the only person in this particular room, so he was alone. Of course, he was being monitored electronically.

His eyes were closed, waiting. That was always the hardest part. Of course, his crew had reported Mycal going offline. He also knew, for a time yet, they would sit tight waiting for any word. It was part of his plan, such as it was.

Given how long he'd been waiting, it was getting just past 0700 hours, normal operating times for this government facility – at least for those in charge.

The sound of a heavy lock being opened, and the outer door being pushed open echoed in the sterile room.

Ah, yes, Mycal thought. Right on time. Now to get some *real* intel. The head guys in this area will want to personally inspect their prize and sate their curiosity, find out what he knows about their plans and activities.

And best yet, if something big was going on, the Chief in this area wouldn't trust an underling to get at what Mycal knows. Time to see if he was right.

Mycal opened his eyes as none other than Mon Sela, the Territorial Governor strode up to his bed side. He was attended by who Mycal supposed was his Chief of Staff.

The head guy, Mycal thought. That's pretty bad.

"Well, hello Governor," Mycal said. "I must say I'm surprised and a little concerned, getting the royal treatment from the Territorial Governor, no less."

"I was told you were a pretty glib chap," The governor said, no hint of expression on his face. "And it's funny you should mention Royal Treatment, seeing as you just came from the royal court yourself."

Bingo. Thought Mycal, as his intuition was confirmed. There was a leak at Court at the highest levels. There was no possibility the leak came from his crew. He hadn't told them where they were going until they'd almost arrived. He supposed there could have been a tracer put on his ship by someone doing maintenance.

"I also know why you're here," the governor continued, "so I'll disappoint you by saying I don't need to ask any questions."

"I see," Mycal said. The situation was looking darker, especially when he considered now who the leaker might be. Only three people knew why he was coming here. Serena wouldn't have said anything to anyone. Vance? He didn't know anyone at court. Could he have said something inadvertently, even in private? His quarters had been bugged, after all. Was that how they found out? Then there was Jules. Maybe he mentioned something to a supposedly trusted subordinate.

And for another thing, why was he was lying on an examination table if they aren't going to ask him any questions?

"I see you're a bit surprised," the governor said, misinterpreting Mycal's facial expressions.

Mycal looked at the governor and smiled.

"Oh, don't be too quick to smile. Your special status won't get you released. In fact, just the opposite. We're glad to have you as our guest. We have something special in mind, but you won't like the preparation for it. It's necessary, however.

"You see, you'll be receiving a Gift from us. And you'll either accept the gift . . . or die. Those are your only two choices.

"But for now, let me tell you a few things to prepare you for what is to come. First, if you're feeling any hope you can get word to your compatriots, rest assured this room is heavily shielded. They'll be left completely in the dark as to your whereabouts and status. In fact, we're counting on that.

"Second, we want your disappearance to be noted. Your good, conscientious friend, Admiral Hamblin will certainly, after a time, mount a rescue operation in spite of what anyone else says – or commands."

Mycal was a bit startled. His plan to gain intelligence was certainly being successful, as this was all priceless information, but his overall plan to get it back to Serena, Jules and Vance was starting to show a bit of weakness.

The governor continued. "When Admiral Hamblin arrives, we'll have a suitable reception for him. And then we'll have two guests in which we'll bestow our Gift. This will either make you both one of us, or you will both die. The governor paused for a moment. "Oh yes. There's one other thing. While the admiral and you are prisoners, just know that your sister . . ."

Mycal blanched at this.

". . . will fall into our hands. Then she'll have the same choice as the both of you," the governor completed his thought and smiled at Mycal's reaction. "She will either receive the Gift and join us or die.

"Either way, in a short while, the Imperium will be ours. Have a nice day. Enjoy your rest while you're with us. My assistant, Val Dokka will attend to you many times before Admiral Hamblin arrives. You need the proper conditioning."

With that, the governor and his minion strode back through the door. It was pushed shut with a heavy clank as the locking mechanism sank back into place.

Mycal's thoughts were racing. The governor had said Serena and Vance were to join him in the dubious choice of getting this *Gift* thing or die. A bit dramatic for his tastes, but that only left very few people who knew Serena was his sister. Ben, his navigator was one of them. Could it be him? But Mon Sela, the Territorial Governor had mentioned that once Vance was out of the way, Serena would fall into their hands. Who could deliver Serena like that?

Jules!

No. It couldn't be him, could it? But the information Mon Sela knew. It had to be Jules. Could only be Jules.

Of course, mentioning Vance and Serena could just have been a red herring – Mycal made a mental note to look up the origin of that old phrase – red herring. It's funny what your mind thinks of when you're in the worst circumstances. Then he snapped his mind back on track.

As much as it pained him, it felt right that the leak, and the head of all this . . . whatever it was, led back to Jules, he and Serena's uncle. Really a father figure since their own parents had died. He now wondered if his parents' death had really been an accident after all.

Serena and Vance were both in a great deal of danger.

Best not to go down that rabbit hole, especially when he was in a hole of his own. He'd learned what he came here to learn in spades. Now he needed to bust out and get word to Serena and Vance via ultra-secure channels before this got any further out of hand.

"Okay," Mycal said aloud, smiling at what his monitors would make of that. Then to himself he thought: Time to make a new plan.

Chapter 23

Count Henri Wallach, the 1st Minister of Parliament, was abruptly ushered into the sparse oval room he'd been brought to earlier. This time the sparse respect shown him the first time was nonexistent. He was a bit scared he could so easily be abducted from his private quarters.

His security team had been neutralized and somber armed men had dragged him out of bed and brought him to this location.

This shouldn't have been able to happen to the 1st Minister. It spoke of secret power in high places, and here he thought he was at the pinnacle of such power. This morning, in the wee hours, he was disabused of that notion.

His guard took him to the center of the room, pointed to the spot in silent command for him to stay put, then turned and left. The lights in the room were dim except for the spotlight showing directly down on him. He looked around the room at the different alcoves and suddenly they all flickered into the opaque holograms he'd seen earlier.

The same projections of individuals, identity blurred and obscured by the haziness surrounding each one. Henri turned to the head of the room, toward the largest alcove which was just now flicking into existence.

Without preamble the leader spoke. "You were told to be patient. Your clumsy actions have put the Empress and her closest allies on guard."

So, this was to be a dressing down, Henri thought, not an assassination after all. If I'm to be killed or drained of information they wouldn't start with accusations. Still he had been pulled out of bed in the middle of the night, all his security circumvented and brought here against his will. These people had incredible reach. He needed to tread lightly.

"Your imbecilic attempt to mar the reputation of Vance Hamblin has just made our work much harder – and decreased your own worth to us. If you would have been patient, you would have gotten all that is coming to you."

"Just what are your plans for me?" Count Wallach was not used to being addressed in this fashion no matter how powerful these people seemed to be.

There was silence for a time, then the leader spoke. "Your life hangs on a razor's edge. Have care how you address us. Your words will dictate whether you leave this room alive or not. Align with us and do as we bid. Or defy us and die. Those are our plans for you. Choose now."

Count Wallach quickly did the required self-analysis. A rescue in time, even if he could be traced, was unlikely. He would end up being someone important who'd disappeared.

Count Wallach swallowed, bowed his head. "I am your humble servant," though it grated him to say it. What was that old saying about the better part of valor? Though valor was not necessarily in his nature.

"Well said," the leader replied. "Make sure your actions match your words. This is your only warning. Next time you won't be brought here." He left the rest unsaid.

"Count Wallach, notwithstanding your vulgar misstep, our plan is still proceeding. We have captured one of the Empresses' inner circle. Vance Hamblin will soon be joining him. Then the Empress will be all alone to do our bidding – which, I'm reluctant to say, still involves you."

Count Wallach hesitated the merest of a moment. "Thank you. I assure you I will obey and be patient. I want to be your ally."

"You will be our servant, or you will be dead." the leader responded.

So, this is the true way of it, Count Wallach thought to himself. It galled him, but he was in their power. How had they so easily taken him? He had to figure that out. He had to learn who these people were.

Outwardly he said, "As you say. I am your humble servant."

"You may go. You will be taken back to your home and you will survive . . . for now."

Count Wallach bowed his head, turned and strolled towards the door which was opening. He really had to figure this out. Henri Wallach would be a servant to no one.

***

The oval room remained silent until Count Wallach had departed. One of the images on the left spoke up. "We should just Take him or kill him."

"I agree," one on the other side of the room said.

The image at the head of the room held up one hand. "That may yet occur. He has put our enemies on guard, but our plan is still proceeding. His bumbling may yet be a screen, a mask to our real work.

"While our enemies look in the wrong place, we have captured a Primary and will soon make him ours. Vance will shortly be ours as well – or dead. Then we can break the Empress. Her personality is strongest of them all, and with those blows, her brother and consort missing . . . We will Take her or kill her. Either way the path will be open for the Crossing in mass.

"You all have played your parts well. Continue with the plan. Our time is coming. This meeting is adjourned." The figures in the alcoves winked out one by one, led by the one at the head. Then the room fell into darkness.

Chapter 24

The gathering was on the commons, outside in the bright afternoon sunshine on the planet Papal 2, which was known for its temperate weather. It was close to the capital world and the first official speech the Empress was going to make after the gala announcing her engagement. As she'd thought, there'd been some pushback on her Truth Initiative from members of her cabinet. They were getting some questions and concerns from their workers wondering what was going on.

Serena had been prepared. In that cabinet meeting she'd laid out the planning she, Jules and Vance had organized, complete with oversight and contact procedures as she'd promised. Furthermore, she'd let them know no one was immune.

The cabinet members had been startled speechless, which was good. It was also rare. Serena had assured them she meant what she'd said and was enacting the reforms as of now.

That had been a week ago. The contact department was functioning and already she had several cases in process to show she meant business. It felt good to be doing something. Today, she would continue to move forward.

Serena stood at the podium facing the crowd of graduates from Candor University, a public school that she'd long ago taken under her wing and made sure was always available to the ordinary citizen rather than being a place for only the rich and privileged. This would be a friendly audience. Behind her sat the usual school officials and her security contingent. Vance was also seated just behind her. It felt good to have him here. The afternoon air was stirring only slightly, and the temperature was perfect, not too hot, not to cold.

Off to the side of the commons where the 1,000 students and parents were seated in folding chairs, she noted a group of protestors gathered on the lawn intermixed with the trees, standing behind stanchions and security. They held signs and placards, shouting, though they were far enough away, she couldn't hear what they were saying, or to which group they belonged. That wasn't unusual in these times. It was part of the political process. This time, however, considering the topic she was going to address, she wondered if it was more targeted. It had that feeling.

She delivered her speech, keeping an eye on the protestors, who were being held back by additional security from her group as well as the university's. The crowd had loved her speech, and she could feel their energy. Not surprising, considering the crowd's makeup, but to her, it still felt like the message was resonating. It resonated with her, too. I just *felt* right.

Then the trouble started.

A few of the protestors had broken through the security cardon and were running closer to the gathering. Serena then heard what they had been shouting.

"Her Truth is a lie!"

It became obvious this was a direct counter to her Truth Initiative.

The protestors continued to surge forward, trying to disrupt the gathering. As they came closer, Serena noted some of the security standing aside, allowing it to happen. This was odd and spoke of a deeper organization than just a spontaneous protest.

The calls and chants grew louder, and then a group from the student section surged forward and stood toe to toe with the protestors so they couldn't advance any further.

"Truth is Truth!" they called back, and their side of the crowd grew louder. It was clear they were not having her speech be marred by this protest. The students continued to flood over to block the protesters, and they were joined by their parents, who also took up the chant, "Truth is Truth!"

Shocked by the response the protesters stepped back, and then back again as the students continued to surge forward. Serena was about to speak out, to urge calm. The last thing she wanted was a riot to break out.

She didn't have to, however, as first one protester dropped her sign, turned and ran. Then another, and another. Soon they all fled, as security finally got between the protesters and the crowd and kept them from chasing after.

The crowd erupted in cheers and applause and turned back to Serena, waiving to her. She waived back, and Vance came to stand beside her, grasping her hand. It felt warm and good. She would also need to investigate those security standing aside.

***

"Monsor Dooer," Serena began as the Education Cabinet Secretary sat across from her desk. Jules was seated to her right. "I have evidence you have taken bribes to grant curriculum programming to favored vendors. I further have evidence you have directed supplies and resources from public schools to private institutions of which you have received payment or other favors. These are just two allegations in a long list I've been given."

Serena watched the woman fidget in her seat. Serena was angry and let it show. "You are hereby released of your cabinet position. Further, the evidence has been forwarded to the authorities for criminal investigation." She nodded to Jules who pushed a link on his ever-present tablet computer.

Immediately the office door opened, and two men came in and stood behind Monsor Dooer. She looked back, startled, shaking her head in disbelief.

"Wait. What is this? You can't . . ."

"I can, and am." Serena said. "There is no discussion, you will have your chance to dispute the charges at your trial." She nodded and the two men stood Monsor on her feet, but before they could bind her, Monsor pulled something from the buckle of her belt, and dove forward across the desk toward Serena.

It was a knife! Aimed at Serena's throat!

Serena pushed back out of reach, using a small bit of augmentation. Monsor sprawled across the desk as the security guards grabbed her and held her flailing knife wielding arm.

Someone had failed in her security scan. Was it on purpose? Serena realized she was getting a bit paranoid.

"You'll regret this!" Dooer shouted as they started to take her from the office. "Others won't stand for this! You'll see."

"Others," Serena said calmly, "don't have anything to worry about if they are honest. Those who aren't should be worried." She watched her being escorted from the room. She noted the normally unflappable Jules looked started by this attempt. Well, she was surprised too. That type of reaction wasn't what one would expect. Way out of proportion from what she knew and experienced with Monsor before.

There were two others, not cabinet members, but at levels just below, waiting to come in. She could only imagine what they were thinking as Monsor was marched out. They had heard her screaming. Hopefully they'd be a bit more docile.

Should she postpone the remaining meetings? Serena thought a moment, running it through her mind. Word would certainly get out. But she didn't want to prevent that. Indeed, she would show what happened through official channels. Each of the meetings were being video recorded. She'd release this with the rest. And she would continue.

Serena would state the allegations then release and remanded each for criminal prosecution. But she would be more on her guard. There would be no discussion, no negotiation, no pleading allowed. The populace needed to see her doing this.

"This will have serious repercussions," Jules said, quietly.
Serena nodded.

"We just have to hope there are more good guys than bad guys
or government services are going to get very thin."

***

The security escorted hovercar pulled up to the 57 story
Mercantile Trade Association building on the planet Baulron. It
stopped as several security men scrambled from vehicles fore and aft
of the heavily armored black vehicle and surrounded it facing
outward, looking for any sign of threat. Satisfied, Commander Marc
Withers spoke into his throat mic. "All clear."

The designated security woman opened the door of the
hovercar, and Serena exited on the side nearest the building entrance.

A large crowd of the planet's populous had gathered to greet
their Empress. They cheered and shouted as Serena watched across
the 20-meter security cordon established since the last incident.
Vance exited the other side of the hovercar, came around and Serena
took his arm. They were immediately surrounded by their security
detail, increased to fifteen from the normal five in her immediate
vicinity. Of course, there were more security personnel interspersed
in the crowd, some incognito.

They had swept the area thoroughly with weapons detectors and
lots of paid informants, as well as DNA scanners to see if any

watchlist individuals were in the crowd. Everything was clear or her hovercar would never have stopped.

Serena paused and turned back to the crowd. Her security detail opened a bit at her nod so she and Vance could wave to those who'd waited hours just to catch a glimpse.

It was then she noticed a commotion from several points along the security line.

Men and women erupted forward pushing through the line brandishing what looked like ceramic or plastic clubs. The weapons detectors had missed them.

Serena didn't have time to count, but a quick estimate put more than 30 armed assailants sprinting their way. Her security detail quickly circled she and Vance to usher them inside the building.

The entrance was blocked by three men and one woman exiting the building, brandishing the same clubs. Then the fight began, her detail having drawn their stun weapons fired as quickly as they could.

There were too many of them, and they came in too fast. Hand to hand battles erupted and Vance moved in front of Serena as a shield. In seconds their entire security detail was down while seven assailants faced them. Serena stood back-to-back with Vance so they wouldn't be rushed from a blind side.

These aren't ordinary thugs, Serena noted. They looked paramilitary or somebody's private thugs. This was specifically planned.

"Come with us and Empress and no one else will be hurt," One of the assailants spoke. It was interesting they were all dressed in dark, earth toned clothes, not tight fitting so they would have freedom of movement. Also, they wouldn't attract any undue attention until they were ready to act.

So, it was to be kidnapping and extortion, Serena thought. Vance was standing still, waiting for her order. She could tell he was loose, ready to move when she gave the nod. She would not allow herself to be taken by anyone. She touched Vance lightly on the arm, still standing back-to-back with him.

Vance darted forward as quick as she had ever seen him move, snatched the startled speaker's weapon and clocked him across the side of the head and immediately turning engaged the woman standing next.

Serena waited calmly. She was wearing a flowing gown of state, but underneath she was wearing the shielded body suit of the same flexible material as Vance's uniform. And she was also enhanced. Vance had taken on the three in front. Two were down with one left. The four others ignored Serena and started moving in on Vance, which gave her an opportunity. She caught them by surprise.

Serena remembered to measure her response, knowing this would be filmed and dissected later. But why let Vance have all the fun? She saw other security personnel sprinting in from the crowd, yet they would arrive too late to help. Vance would quickly be overpowered, or worse, hurt. She moved forward, grasped hold of a raised club aimed at the back of Vance's head, jerked it from the assailant's hand, and swung it to connect with his ribs. He went down grasping his side and groaning. Ribs were surely broken. Next was a woman who hadn't seen her come into the fray. Serena hit her on the side of the knee, avoiding a head strike for fear she would kill, and she wanted them alive for questioning. There was satisfying snap, leaving two. Even odds, though Vance was in the process of taking his man down.

That left one more staring at Serena in surprise. He was tackled by a security man, born to the ground with a heavy thud.

Vance looked at her with a quirky smile.

"Shall we go inside?" Serena asked in calm, even tones as if noting the weather. "Security knows what to do from here."

He held out an arm and she took it as if they were out for a casual stroll, Vance pivoted toward the door and suddenly pulled her in front of him just as she saw a flash and heard a muffled grunt from Vance. She felt him stiffen against her, surrounding her with his arms.

"Inside quickly," he hissed through grit teeth.

There was another flash and she saw a blaster bolt strike the entrance to her right. Serena heard Vance talk into his throat mic. He was speaking to her security. They were supposed to have searched the surrounding buildings. "The shot came from no higher than the second floor. We were standing under the awning. A shot wouldn't be possible from any higher." Then Serena was ushered inside, surrounded again by those security who were supposed to have secured this lobby area. Seems not only the military has gotten sloppy, she thought to herself.

She turned to Vance, looked at him closely. His eyes were crinkled in pain, yet he smiled at her.

"You were hit." She spoke.

"A glancing blow," Vance answered. "My uniform's shielding blocked it I think."

"Let me see." She leaned to glance at Vance's back. There was a scorch mark on his uniform just above and behind his left kidney. It hadn't penetrated the uniform, but it was burned. No doubt Vance was also burned from the heat if nothing else. He hid it well, though she was sure he was in pain. "Do you need a medic?"

"No, not here. Not now. I'm bruised, but I'm all right. Remember you have a speech to give and you can't let them disrupt us."

Vance was right. Duty first, yet she stared into his deep blue eyes and realized he'd put himself in front of her. Took the blast that was meant for her. She knew he was pledged to do just that and wasn't even surprised when he'd done it. But now, the fact that he'd actually put his life on the line to protect her . . .

Just then Mal Frowther, president of the Mercantile Trade Association came forward.

"Empress, are you all right? I'm so sorry for this." His anxious tones seemed sincere.

Serena waved her hand. "Pay it no mind. Our Truth Initiative is gaining enemies. It seems they are getting desperate; however, I have an address to give and I'll not let this petty disturbance stop me from being about the Imperium's business."

Mal Frowther was startled she wanted to proceed but bowed and led them into the banquet hall where they were greeted by people standing, murmuring. They'd heard a disturbance but didn't know what it was.

Serena delivered her speech and ad-libbed to tie in today's attack. There were more murmurs from the crowd when they understood what had happened. And they'd definitely noticed the scorched blaster burn on Vance's uniform. If her enemies were going to attack her and Vance, she would give as good as she got.

The whole time, Vance was standing at her side, scanning the audience. She didn't allow security to stand in front of her. It was a calculated show of defiance.

The applause was thunderous at the end. Her message had resonated even with these jaded merchants and business beings. Most importantly, this event would resonate Imperium wide as would her forceful ad-libbed remarks.

As they made their way back out from the gathering, she kept her arm through Vance's, which felt way better than it usually did. She wasn't doing it for appearance. Serena was holding his arm close because she *wanted* to.

***

The darkness of the oval council chamber flickered into a dim glow as projections flickered on in each alcove. Though no one was present, the masking technology for each projection was still in effect, blurring each image, revealing only humanoid forms, disguising voices without revealing even gender.

The last to appear in the head alcove was the leader who spoke without preamble. "Chaos continues to mount in response to the Empress' truth initiative. You all saw the latest attack. Was it any of you?"

An immediate chorus of "no's" came from around the room.

"We are adhering to the plan, but surely this chaos benefits us," a speaker on the left said.

"Yes," the leader responded, "but this Truth Initiative is garnering a significant following with the people. This hurts us."

"If not one of us, then who instigated the attack?" This came from a speaker on the opposite side of the chamber.

"It could be more than one source acting independently," said another speaker further down the alcoves.

"Won't this mask our efforts, at least," said yet another speaker.

"It does that," The leader agreed.

There was silence for a time.

"Are we sure it wasn't 1st Minister Wallach?"

"That was the first place I checked," a speaker at the far end of the room responded. "He has been uncharacteristically docile."

"As well he should be," the leader spoke. "We will hold our course for now. It is good we're at the cusp. All of you keep watch and inform me if you learn anything. Be vigilant and press forward in each of your areas. You know what to do."

The leader's image snapped off followed by the others. The room fell back into darkness.

Chapter 25

"Ouch! Remember, I'm still sore," Vance said as he was smashed against the training room mat. "What did I do to deserve that?"

Serena looked down at him, offering him a hand back up. "You're still holding back on me, not going full force in our workouts."

Vance struggled to his feet and bowed, then launched into a counter move he'd been practicing and neatly caught Serena under an arm and leveraged her forward, catching her off guard and this time throwing her to the mat.

She rolled with it and came back up quicker than Vance would have hoped.

"That's better," Serena said, smiling. "But you're still going way to slow for me." She winked at him, making him feel she meant something more than just their sparring. "I guess it'll have to be me doing the moving, then," and with that, she darted in, faster than any normal person could move.

Vance was ready. He knew what she was capable of now, since spending the last week in a daily exercise routine together. He avoided her grasp and ducked under it, moving behind her, catching her in another hold so he could lift her off her feet and take away her leverage.

He held her tight and was about ready to throw her down again when his world suddenly turned upside down and he was lying flat on his back, Serena on top of him, face to face.

How did she do that?

Her enhanced physique was still a secret. Serena had assured him they no longer had any Watchers since everyone was now certain Vance posed no threat. Even Jules was occupied elsewhere, so the security of their workouts left them totally to themselves.

Serena smiled down at Vance. He smiled back up at her, still bewildered at how she'd turned him over so easily without being grounded.

"I warned you I was going to make a move."

"What if I said, I let you do it? You know, in deference to your superior rank and all," Vance said.

"I'd say, it was high time, I took advantage of the situation, since it's obvious you never will," Serena said, and leaned further down and surprised Vance by kissing him full on the lips.

Then he relaxed and enjoyed it. It wasn't his first kiss, and he could tell it wasn't Serena's either, but it was clear neither one was very experienced. They shared that at least.

"That was nice," she said as she raised up. "So, did I take advantage of you in your weakened state?"

"Not at all," Vance assured her. "I quite enjoyed it." He smiled back up at her. "I was sort of wondering what to expect when . . ." He still lay there with Serena on top of him, still looking into each other's eyes. "But I didn't want to assume . . ."

"You talk too much," Serena said, and kissed him again. This time longer. Vance went with it.

"I can tell," Serena said, when they both came back from the kiss. "That I'm going to have to do this honesty thing between us as well. You know, tell the truth and all?"

Vance could see what was coming. "Yes. That would be good. I'll do the same. With fewer words, I promise."

Serena laughed and got up, and then extending a hand again to help Vance up, since, truly, he was a bit sore from the last throw to the mat.

She led him, still holding his hand, over to the bench at the side of the mat and grabbed a towel, handing it to Vance, then picked one up for herself and sat on the bench. Vance sat beside her.

She turned toward Vance and picked up his hand. "I want you to know that at first, I really respected you. That I needed you for your skills as a soldier and analyst. And also, for your absolute loyalty to the Imperium. But now . . ." She smiled and squeezed his hand.

"Now that I've gotten to know you better, and see you are totally genuine, I am starting to fall for you."

Vance was shocked at how frank she was being. And at her feelings. Relieved as well.

"You have been a perfect gentleman. But now, I want you to be something . . . more. And not just because we have to. But because I'm realizing this is what I want. What I want for *me* and not just for the politics of it." She paused a moment then laughed. Vance was realizing that Serena could never be serious for too long, though what she said had volumes of serious meaning. "So, what I'm asking, is . . . you want to be my steady? We can sit in the dark and neck if you want."

Vance shook his head and laughed. She had a way of making him feel at ease. And it wasn't just her practiced political training. It was who she was. And who he was falling in love with.

"Now it's my turn for honesty."

At this, Vance could tell Serena was a bit scared of what he might say. She had made herself vulnerable, as a person who was trained to never show weakness of any kind and in any situation. She was actually worried he might reject her. Not the proposed marriage, nor his duty to the Imperium. She knew he'd never reject that. But she was afraid of him rejecting *her*.

Vance didn't want her to wait any longer. "I'm yours," he said. "I'm being totally open and honest, and I always will be with you. I'm sorry I didn't say it earlier, but from the time we went to the dance and you let me get into a fight without getting mad at me . . ."

Serena busted out laughing. "Are actually making a joke?" Then Vance saw the tears start to come to her eyes.

"I didn't say it earlier because I didn't want you to feel uncomfortable. I never want you to feel that way around me. But know that I'm yours. Heart, soul and body."

"Who knew you were such a romantic?" Serena said, the tears still flowing as she laughed through them, and then pulled him close and kissed him again. And again . . . And again.

Then they pulled back. She wiped the tears from her eyes. "It will be fun saving the galaxy with you."

Chapter 26

"Did something happen during your workout I should know about?" Jules asked as he glanced from Vance to Serena and back again. They were seated at the breakfast table they always met at to discuss the governing of the Imperium.

Vance didn't necessarily need to be there, but Serena has always insisted on him attending, especially now that Mycal had gone silent and they were both working on the same problem from two different angles. Vance had always tried to be quiet unless he had something substantive to add. Jules had never shown any problem with either Vance being there or making any suggestions. But at the same time, he also didn't show any outward warmth. It was all business as usual.

This morning was different. Jules was staring at them both. Then a smile crept across his mouth and his eyes danced with a bit of humor.

"Let's just say," Serena said dismissively, though she was hiding a smile herself, "Vance and I have been practicing our own form of honesty. We have reached a closer understanding."

Jules actually chuckled at that and turned to wink at Vance. "I was wondering . . . Well, it'll be obvious to others this has become more than a *political* alliance. I suppose that's a good thing, especially since you seem to be working together on everything."

He looked up and smiled at them. A genuine smile. "I'm happy for you both."

And that was it. Jules got back to business.

"You'll note on your screens that the latest polls have shown increasing favorability for the Empress' speeches mentioning the new *Truth* initiative. And the people queried have shown quite a favorable impression of the campaign to clean up both the bureaucracy and the military. The recent disturbances have actually spiked the numbers favorably in our direction. Seems those opposing it have miscalculated the effect it would have on the people . . . and on you."

"That's encouraging, isn't it?" Serena said. Vance could tell she was concerned by Jules' seeming deadpan attitude.

"It is encouraging," Jules nodded. "But there is a corresponding drop in moral from the government sectors – the bureaucracy – you have targeted. Especially since you have recently fired the Education Secretary, among others. And I think you already know you are ruffling quite a few feathers as evidenced by the recent . . . disturbances." Jules held up his hand to forestall any complaint from Serena, which Vance could see was building up. "I know those you released had it coming, and you had all the evidence you needed. In fact, several people mentioned in the focus groups they were heartened to see you keeping your promise the night of the . . . coming out party for Vance."

Vance couldn't help himself and laughed at that. "You still not over that little tussle?" Vance asked Jules.

"Actually, that little *tussle,* followed by graphic images spattered across the vids showing your scorched uniform from the last little tussle, showed even more favorably with the surveyed populace than the Empress. Apparently, you are the current *hero* of the people."

"Of course, he is." Serena said. "And rightly so."

"Unfortunately," Vance said looking at Jules and then back to his viewscreen. "I see you haven't posted the numbers on military moral."

"I didn't see the point," Jules said. "Suffice it to say, it is very low. At least among the leadership. We haven't surveyed the enlisted ranks. But we all expected the leadership to be opposed, and remain that way until Vance has concluded his . . . purge?"

"That's as good a term as any," Vance agreed. "And you're right. No sense in measuring that until I've done my work."

"The clean-up needs to be done," Serena said, "Of course, they're all going to be worried. They've had a free-for-all for way too long. We are here to serve the people, not the bureaucracy."

"Yes," Jules said. "We are all agreed on that." Still, his body language said otherwise. It was ever so slight. Even Vance could pick it out, now he'd been around Serena longer and had learned from her.

Vance was watching Serena also. She was showing just the slightest exasperation with Jules, as if she was wondering what had gotten into him.

"I report these numbers only because you wanted to track the effects of the Truth Initiative. As you can see, the general populace supports it in a strong majority," Jules reported. "I just hope that it doesn't adversely affect the smooth running of the government. I am concerned about the escalations. Next, we may have walkouts and such by the government or the military, and the people will feel they have been left to fend for themselves when critical services are impacted. It may grow to more than just bad poll numbers."

"Yes," Serena said. "I see your concerns. It is your job to point them out. But I have to hope there are enough good people in those positions who will rise to the occasion when they see those who have abused their positions are removed from their positions."

"Or their Commands," Vance said. "There will be. I know the military from the ground up. I can speak for the rank and file and the junior cadres. They will rise to the need."

"But will the bureaucrats?" Jules looked at Serena.

"They will have to, especially if I'm willing to give bonuses for merit and extra work. They are not all corrupt. I know it."

"We will shortly find out, because you are moving rather quickly. I think that's why there is such fear amongst your government people." Jules said this to Serena. "And, of course, Vance hasn't even started yet, except for the *tussle* as you put it.

"And incidentally," Jules interjected, "so you don't think I'm a complete stick in the mud, the ratings of your speeches are very high with your target audiences."

"That's good to know," Serena said, affecting her own deadpan, directing it to Jules. Then smiling to take the sting out of her mocking him. "Come on. We know we have to do this fast. It's like tearing off a bandage. If it drags on, we'll have greater problems. We've just started, and as you say, Vance hasn't even begun his side yet."

"I was going to bring something up about that," Vance said. "Now seems to be the right time. And it will help speed things up."

"Go ahead," Serena said, and Jules nodded.

"I know I really shouldn't be doing any changes to the military until after I officially become the Consort," he winked at Serena. It wasn't lost on Jules. "But how about I start a series of inspections? You know, start going around and being seen with the military, and also coming up to speed in some of the areas I haven't been to in a while. As an admiral over the ships and yards, they thought I would just stay close to the yards, but I made it a point to get out and around a lot, just so I could stay out from under the Joint Chiefs' thumbs.

"I'm pretty well up to speed in most things, but there are a few areas I need to get to, which would allow me to survey for myself, talk with key people I trust. It would help me have a jump-start when everything is official."

"the wedding is only a month away," Jules said.

"It's a great idea." Serena said. "Jules you have to agree. It would also set the precedent of Vance being places without me – in an official capacity. My security has been sufficiently chastised and increased so I'll be safe. And Vance could deliver speeches *cast* from whatever military facility he's at."

"You are right, of course, Empress," Jules said, again, all business.

What is wrong with him? Vance thought. Jules doesn't seem like he's supporting this at all.

"Jules?" Serena prodded. "Is there something wrong? Surely you can see this is all good. It's what we're working for, and yes, we all expected that we'd have some pushback. This isn't like you. What is it?"

For a brief instant, Jules caught himself and acted . . . almost fearful . . . then he reassumed control. What was that about? Vance wondered. Then Jules spoke.

"I'm sorry, Serena. I'm just concerned about Mycal. I haven't had any further reports. His crew is getting anxious. They want to go in and find him. I'm not sure I can hold them back much longer. I'm not sure I *should* hold them back.

"As you know, he's done this before, but this seems . . . different."

Serena was quiet for a moment. "I have to admit, I've been feeling that same concern. Like you said, something feels different about this time."

"I was actually going to make the Obdure 4 Cluster part of my inspection tour," Vance put in. "Truth be told, I've been worried about Mycal myself. It's been over a week since he's gone dark. With me being out there, I can snoop around and be a distraction so the crew can go in and find him.

"You'll not find a more able bunch to do that. And I'm assuming he was fitted with a transponder that wouldn't show up under normal scans?"

"He was," Jules confirmed. "That's why we haven't been too worried until now. It's the length of time. Normally he would have used his failsafe communication method, also not visible to scans. But either he's not felt the need to communicate, which isn't likely after so long a time, he's in a place which is heavily shielded, or he's not physically able to reach out."

Vance noted Jules left out the possibility Mycal might be dead.

"I actually think Vance's plan is a good one." Jules put in. Vance was surprised at his abrupt turnaround of agreement.

"You think it safe?" Serena asked. Now she was the one concerned. Then she voiced why. "After all, it's where Mycal went missing. I don't like putting Vance out there as well. I was thinking he'd be going to different places, not right into the heart of the problem."

"It's not as if I'm donning battle armor and doing a military extraction," Vance said. "Though, you know I've done that – several times."

"No, I really agree with Vance," Jules shook his head. "Don't look so surprised," he said to Serena. "I had been wondering what we could do, but now as Vance has suggested, an inspection tour would fit perfectly. And as his tactical sense has said, it would provide good cover for Mycal's crew to do an extraction. I think we should listen to our *military adviser*. As for being safe, Vance would be surrounded by people, *his* people, to protect him.

"It would also fit perfectly with another idea I was going to suggest, lest you think I wasn't being supportive of our efforts," Jules said.

"There was an ancient custom of world-born leaders to give an annual speech with much pomp and circumstance called, 'the State of the World' address."

"I've actually heard of that," Serena said, still not convinced Vance's idea was good, and confused with the change of subject. "You're being surprising in many ways today, Jules." Serena knit her brows together in thought as Vance watched. "But it certainly sounds like it would be good."

"I was thinking we could announce it, and have it built up big, like they used to do. It would be one of those seminal events, and you could even do it annually, if you like. It fits in with what you're trying to do." Jules paused a moment as additional thoughts visibly played across his face. "And the inspection tour could culminate just in time for the State of the Imperium address."

"Okay, that sounds good," Serena agreed.

"I was also thinking, since your wedding is planned for a month away, we could time it, so it was the same day. We'd hold the State of the Imperium address just prior so it would lead up to your wedding, an even larger event for the populace to look forward to. And hopefully, we'd have Mycal back safe and sound with further information about what's going on, and what's causing it."

"I still hate the idea of Vance going there. The inspection tour is one thing but sending Vance out where Mycal went missing . . .

that's just asking for the bad guys to do something. It would be too attractive a target, especially since they weren't shy about coming after me." Serena said. Then she fell silent for a moment, thinking. Finally, she spoke. "I hate to admit it, but it does give us the opportunity to do something about Mycal." She paused; her mouth pursed in worry.

"Vance would really need to be surrounded by *his* people," Serena continued. "In fact, Vance, please pick out a company of Marines to take with you as an Honor Guard. And take the Imperator it's our newest and best capital ship."

Vance could tell if Serena had to give in to this, she was going to make sure it was completely secure. He smiled to himself at her over-concern.

"You oversaw her final fitting as I recall. The Military Leadership is definitely not going to like your poking around any sooner than necessary. I have a feeling someone is going to take this opportunity to try and do some real damage. They've already tried to kill you twice, no three times now."

"I'm sure it will all work out just fine," Jules said. And smiled at Vance.

***

Serena noted Vance and Jules seemed satisfied. She had to admit it was a good plan. Mycal had never been out of communications this way before. Those they were against were still hidden, and they had no way of knowing what this group was fully capable of. Yet, they had Mycal's disappearance and the attack on her as an indication.

It made her anxious sending Vance out into their vicinity. She had a feeling it would go badly. Still, she didn't have anything better to offer.

If she wouldn't let Vance go, it would seem she didn't trust him or his judgement. It would also seem she was getting protective and needy. It was a hard situation. There had been many such hard decisions as Empress, but this one seemed harder. They needed Mycal back, and there was no one better to do it than Vance. She just didn't want to ever risk losing him. And that honest thought surprised her.

Chapter 27

Mycal was roused from sleep, still strapped to the exam table. "Is it that time already?" he said with a fuzzy voice. He shook his head to try and regain some semblance of normal thinking. How long had he been here? He tried to remember. He'd been tortured through various means every day, though at different times by his rough calculations. His mind was clouded with a thick haze.

Not only did they use physical implements of torture, they were also using drugs. It had been more than two weeks, by his reckoning. Serena and Vance must be getting anxious by now. And were surely working on a plan to get him out. He knew his crew, knew Serena, and knew of Vance's reputation. He had to do something before Vance could be lured here. But what? They never allowed him to be unstrapped except for brief times to walk him around and use the fresher a couple of time per day. His mind was starting to get more and more bleary.

Each time they tortured him, varying between the pain and the drugs, they never asked him anything. Just kept telling him over and over that he was the *bait*. And that Vance and he would soon be joining them or die. Serena would also soon be facing the same treatment and same decision. What was their point? He got it already.

It seemed there was a purpose to all this. They were trying to wear him down, to make him despondent, to give up, break his spirit.

Well, that made him fight all the more. He wouldn't give them the satisfaction. But he needed to get word to Vance, to warn him so he wouldn't come. His drugged state made it so he couldn't rally enough to think straight, to use his enhanced strength to get loose from his table and somehow find an unshielded spot in the room to make contact and raise the warning.

"Well, Mycal," the Territorial Governor spoke to him, bringing his mind back to the present. "I have a special treat for you today."

"What?" Mycal said, trying to focus on the face floating above him. "Why are you here? I thought you'd leave the dirty work to your little Val Dokka." Mycal could see the little man who had normally been administering the torture and other chores bristling to the side of the Governor. Mycal smiled at his reaction.

The Governor slapped Mycal's face, holding his chin in one hand and forcing Mycal to look directly at him so he had his total focus.

"I just got word that Vance is nearly here. It took him a bit to get here because he's masking your *rescue* attempt under the guise of a military inspection. But that just gave us a bit more time to prepare our special welcome for him.

"It also means we'll be taking you off the drugs. We want you to be clear headed for when we bestow our Gift upon you. We don't want any drugs to inhibit a special *guest* we'll be introducing you too. We'll want to time it so Vance will be here to witness it first-hand. It will help prepare him for what is to come. To know the same will be happening to him and his beloved Serena. And there's nothing any of you can do to stop it.

"Then you'll be reunited as a happy little family again . . . or you'll be dead, and out of the way for what's to come for the rest of the Imperium."

"Just get on with the torture and stop boring me with your speeches. Politicians will be the death of me." Then Mycal laughed, aiming to incite rage in the Governor. It worked.

Mycal felt a stinging slap across his face. Even through the drug-induced haze, Mycal realized his chance was coming. Hopefully he could clear out the drugs, break free and get out the warning before Vance arrived. There was a chance.

He steeled himself for the remaining days of torture. Knowing it was nearing an end, one way or another . . .

Chapter 28

"You have the con back Captain Beck," Vice Admiral Gatez stood from the command chair and beckoned for his adjutant to follow him. "I'll be in my quarters. Please inform me when Admiral Hamblin's shuttle is about ready to dock so I'll have time to greet him."

"Yessir," Captain Beck answered and waited for Gatez to move aside so he could be seated.

Gatez took a quick look around the command bridge of Medusa Station, a space construction and repair facility he had recently toured in preparation for Admiral Hamblin's pending inspection. Everything was ready, but not in the way Vance was expecting it to be.

He remained silent as he and his adjutant rode the lift down two decks to his command quarters reserved for him whenever he visited, which this was the first time. Gatez had recently filled the position vacated by Vance Hamblin's retirement. And unlike Vance, he hadn't been out to visit the facilities he oversaw at all. Instead, he stayed close to home with the other Admirals. He'd waited too long to get the position and didn't want to squander it by traveling too much.

Gatez preferred to be close to the political action, and the glitz and glamour his new position afforded. Not to mention the *extra* perks he obtained by personally overseeing the meetings with contractors, and their extensive wining and dining.

Yet now that Vance had survived two attempts on his life, and would soon end up being his boss, it was not something Gatez could stand. That incompetent Commander Pratt hadn't been able to put him in his place either time as he or the 1st Minister had planned.

The 1st Minister now, had gone suddenly cool to the idea of taking Hamblin out. Well, *he* wouldn't hesitate. He knew he also had the tacit blessing of at least one of the other Joint Chiefs. She hadn't told him in so many words, but he got the message. Gatez looked forward to returning back home with a *mission accomplished*, report. This would gain him another promotion at the very least.

Gatez stepped out of the lift and strode the short walk down to his quarters where the door whooshed open at sensing his approach. His adjutant stepped in with him. The lights flicked on and Gatez put his cap on the counter and poured himself a drink. He offered one to his long-time aid, Commander Porthe.

"Is everything set?" Gatez asked.

"Yes, Admiral." Porthe pulled out his com screen and glanced at it. "The technician just signaled all was set and he watched the shuttle pull out of the bay of the Flagship." Porthe gave Gatez a wicked smile. "We should be hearing in just few moments that a tragic malfunction has occurred, and Admiral Hamblin's shuttle has exploded with all hands."

***

Porthe was just as anxious for this to occur as Gatez. He'd long ago hitched his star to Gatez's and knew with Hamblin out of the way, good fortune would spread to him as well. He'd have his own command and would be able to set up his own operations rather than just be tied to another's and get the trickle-down flow of the take.

He began to think about what assignments to request. Which would provide him with the most opportunity? He knew he'd need to be assigned far away from Zyzeen and Gatez, just in case the Vice Admiral got the feeling he needed to eliminate witnesses.

"You sure the technician will stay bought?"

"No, but it's taken care. I have a friend seeing to it." Porthe had a thing for not leaving witnesses himself. "There will be no one to say the shuttle was tampered with, and the explosion will be strong enough nothing will be left to analyze."

"Well done, Porthe." Gatez raised his glass to his adjutant. "Of course, foul play will be suspected and investigated. Admiral Hamblin has made enemies, and the Empress is surely ruffling feathers with her 'Truth Initiative.' She's fired some senior people and it won't be too hard to point the blame at several of them."

"We'll be in the clear, sir," Porthe raised his own glass.

***

Serena was watching the hollo as Jules sat near her at the table in the meeting room just off the audience hall. They were taking a break from formal business so Serena could tune in to watch

Vance's latest speech during the inspection tour of Medusa Station just off the primary route near the Obdure 4 Cluster.

The projection was filled with a dark matte of stars with the background of a starship sitting in space looking small next to the massive construct of Medusa Station. Many tube spokes housing various repair and construction modules stretched out from the long vertical core which housed the administrative and residential section of the station. Serena reached over and dialed up the volume as she saw Vance's shuttle emerge from the Imperator and make its slow way between the ship and the station.

"Here was see the Admiral's, I mean to say, soon to be Commander-in-Chief Hamblin's shuttle move over to Medusa Station where he'll be addressing us as part of his whirlwind inspection tour of prominent military installations."

The hollo projection zoomed in close on the shuttle where Serena could make out the official seal she'd had emblazoned on all of the ships Vance would be traveling in. At that exact moment, a brilliant flare of light flashed over the hollo projection and Serena had to quickly shield her eyes.

"What was that?" Jules exclaimed also holding his hand up to block the glare. When the screen returned to a normal, they saw only a view of space with the Imperator and station still in the background . . . and no shuttle! There was a moment of silence and then the commentator broke back in, her voice tense with uncertainty. Serena was holding her breath, staring at the screen, and observing Jules' reaction. She felt numb and continued to watch silently.

"Ladies and Gentlemen, I'm not sure, and we're waiting for confirmation, but it appears we have just witnessed an explosion of the Commander-in-Chief's shuttle. We are trying to get reports in, but it's hard to discount what we have just witnessed.

"The question first coming to our minds, especially considering the Truth campaign of the Empress and her Consort to Be, where they have riled many in top government and military positions, is whether this is an assassination or a tragic accident?"

There was a momentary silence again.

"Wait . . . What? Ladies and Gentlemen," the hollo projection flashed to a picture of the anchorwoman sitting at her desk in the studio, clearly flustered but pressing forward with her reporting. "We seem to have another feed we'll go to immediately. It's from the command deck of Medusa Station. I don't have time to explain what's happening, only that this is something the Empress wants us to see."

Serena sat forward, also watching Jules closely.

The projection changed to an image of the command deck. There was no explanation, and then voices came over the audio feed. Serena knew they were seeing and hearing a live feed on board the bridge of Medusa Station.

***

A buzzer sounded. "Admiral, please report to Command!" It was the captain speaking from his command chair on the bridge. The image shifted to a close circuit projection of another view, this time of two men in military uniform in a different room. It looked to be one of the men's quarters.

"Be right there," one of the men answered. Serena recognized him as Vice-Admiral Gatez. "Right on que," he said to the other man after clicking off the com. He grabbed his cap and together they strode out of the quarters.

The image shifted to another one showing the two men walking down a short corridor and stepping into a lift. It was clear to Serena the network had been patched into the station's security cameras. This is even more than she and Vance had discussed. She noticed that Jules was staring raptly at the projection. No indication whatsoever that Jules knew of this.

The image shifted back to the bridge as the lift doors opened. Gatez strode out and was shocked to find armed security standing there waiting, phase pistols drawn.

"Vice Admiral Gatez, you and Commander Porthe are under arrest for conspiracy and attempted murder, among other charges to be named." Soon to be Commander-in-Chief Hamblin strode up in formal uniform as the security people stepped aside after checking Gatez and Porthe for any weapons. Serena smiled as she continued to watch the projection. She and Vance had planned this, but still it was a relief to see him and know he had not actually been in the shuttle

"It pays to have made a few friends with the enlisted ranks," Vance said. "Truth, Trust and Honor are still valuable commodities, it seems," Vance said as he stood in front of the assembled bridge crew. "The technician you hired tipped me off. He is proud of his service and is an honorable man."

"You have no proof." Gatez stammered. He looked at Porthe who appeared just as stunned as he.

Vance held up a digital recorder and clicked it on.

"You are sure the technician will stay bought?" In horror Gatez recognized his own voice.

"We got it all," Vance said. "Further, this has been broadcast for the entire Imperium to see first-hand. Based on the tip by your technician, we decided to tap the security comms in your quarters. We have both of your confessions," Vance said.

He turned to the security people. "Take them to my backup shuttle. There are others waiting to take them into custody."

Gatez staggered as the two men turned him around and placed he and Porthe in restraints, then prodded them back onto the lift.

Vance turned to look directly into the video feed.

"You were all expecting a speech. Well, this speech was more of a demonstration of what the Empress and I have been speaking about. We are serious about bringing truth and trust back to all our lives. As we've said, the *truth* will make you free. Free to be safe, secure and prosperous. We continue to pledge you the truth and to enable all to have an opportunity to live your lives free of corruption and those who would undermine our society for their own gain." He swept his hand around at those standing on the bridge. "Our thanks to all of you who serve faithfully and honorably. We all depend on you in whatever capacity to always do the right thing. In the end, we all benefit."

Then Vance smiled. "That's it for the speech making. The Empress and I sincerely thank you all. One person saved my life today. He has my gratitude." With a smile, Vance ducked his head just a bit, then looked back up. "I want to also just say to the Empress, whom I know is watching, I'll speak to you soon." And then Vance blew her a kiss in front of the whole Imperium.

Serena couldn't help herself and laughed. She blew Vance a kiss back even though she knew he wouldn't see it. Somehow, she knew he would sense it.

Chapter 29

"How do you think that went?" Vance asked Serena over the secure comms they had set up prior to his leaving on the inspection tour. Jules had excused himself rather abruptly, telling Serena he had some important items to see to. Serena had been a bit relieved so she could speak with Vance alone, but she also wondered at that. It seemed he was quite miffed he was out of the loop on this particular bit of planning she and Vance had cooked up.

"I think it went about as well as it could. It furthers our campaign of truth and openness and it certainly underscores our contention that things aren't as they should be." Serena then smiled and blew a kiss to Vance. "This is because you couldn't see me blow you a kiss back when you signed off to the Imperium. That was a nice touch, by the way."

"I wasn't doing it for the vids. I was doing it for you."

"Well, it was sweet of you, if a bit corny."

"Did you like it, even if corny?"

"I loved it," Serena said. Then she got serious.

"Jules didn't like it one bit. Not that he said anything, but from his body language, I could tell he had no clue about what was happening. So, it seems he isn't part of the conspiracy, at least. He was furious about being left out of the planning. And I don't blame him."

She took a deep breath and continued.

"But with Mycal gone missing, only we knew of his mission. It stands to reason that someone within our circle may have tipped the Obdure 4 Cluster he was coming. If Jules didn't show any signs of being part of this, then maybe Mycal being caught – if that's what happened -- was just an unlucky break, though, I still don't think so.

"It was my idea to leave Jules out of the loop, and it will be my bridge to mend," Serena said. "I'm sure when I explain it to him, he'll cool down."

Serena pursed her lips. "My concern about you being out there is still valid. We were lucky that the technician came forward. If not, you would be dead."

"At least it's proof there are some loyal and trustworthy people out here, and that our promotion of Truth and Trust has a receptive audience," Vance said.

"Still, I don't want to push our luck. I think rather than finish the tour you have planned, you should go right to the Obdure 4 Cluster and put the plan in motion."

"I agree," Vance said. "I'll contact the crew of the Lula, who are still on station. We'll get Mycal out and be back well in time for your State of the Imperium address."

"You better hurry, then, because you only have a week to do it. And it takes 3 days travel just to get back from there." They were silent for a bit, neither one speaking.

Now that their plan to expose the traitors had worked well, Serena was starting to worry about the next attempt. There would surely be one. Vance was out there by himself, really, among lots of hostile military. Or minimally, as Vance had guessed, a small part of the upper leadership. Still, that was enough. They couldn't count on learning of every attempt being planned. The military leadership must surely be getting desperate, even more so now that they'd failed. The next one would surely be more subtle.

Finally, Vance broke the silence. "I better get to it, then,"

"Vance . . . I really care for you." She almost said she loved him. Well, what of it? She was realizing she did love him and couldn't imagine going forward without him. Why didn't she just say it?

"I *love* you." Vance said, and before she could respond, Vance had signed off and the projection went blank. "I love you too," she said to the empty air.

With a deep breath, and a bit of exhilaration from Vance's last words, she had flash across her mind her earlier discussion with Jules where he assured her Vance was surrounded by only the most loyal and trustworthy people he knew.

Vance had also assured her, from his standpoint, those traveling with him were loyal. It made her feel better, but not by much.

Now she had to find Jules and mend some fences.

***

Jules left the meeting alcove and strode directly to his quarters. He was sure he'd not betrayed anything during the cursed operation Serena and Vance had cooked up behind his back. After all, the shock he felt was genuine. But it was clear that they suspected him of possibly being involved. At least they hadn't come close to knowing the reality of it.

The Council, though, seeing what had just happened must know he would be contacting them. Jules didn't bother with the normal checks of his room. He was too agitated, so got right on his secure comm unit and hit the special frequency he'd installed himself. It was undetectable by any means this side of the barrier they'd passed through from their home of Isabar.

The air in front of Jules started to swirl and formulated into 11 distinctive figures, hollo projections of the Council. They waited for him to speak.

"I know you all saw," Jules said. He knew he didn't need to elaborate. "I had no knowledge of this. It means the Empress is starting to distance herself from my guidance. It goes back to Hamblin and his influence, just as I'd feared. We need to move up our timetable before she moves any farther out of my control. I believe Vance will be moving directly now to rescue Mycal. We need to be proactive in this and wait no longer."

Two of the images of the holo projection nodded their heads. "We are ready," one of them spoke.

"The rest of you, secure your positions and be ready to move on your parts. We will act on the day of the State of the Imperium Address. That will provide maximum effect on the populace. It may even be enough of a blow we can start the full migration."

Jules hesitated a moment, thinking. "I think we need to cause some further disruption. Let's make Henri Wallach disappear under mysterious circumstance. He obviously cannot control those under his sway. He must disappear completely."

"It will be done immediately," another of the projections said.

"I will also begin my part," Jules said. "I fear the Empress is suspecting too much, so I must take control now before it spins away from us. Already we are having too many independent actors causing the chaos we want, though not under our direction. It may cost us unless we take over now."

"Yes, at last." one of the other projections said. "This Truth campaign they have started is beginning to have an effect hindering my part," Jules recognized him as Bethel, his most trusted commander from the Other Side. It was still odd seeing him in the shell of the Chairman of the Joint Chiefs of the military. "We will be ready."

"Then this meeting is concluded." Jules snapped off the comm channel and the images disappeared into the air.

He sat still, thinking on what he must do next. He strode over and looked into a mirror. It was odd seeing his *face* in the mirror. In their home realm of Isabar, there were no images, indeed, no sensations but thought, attachment and communing one with another.

This physical realm they had moved to had such rich experiences and sensations, though it also restricted them because of those same physical attributes. Their embodiment limited them to verbal communion. But the sensation of taste, of light and dark, vision, of touch, hearing, smell and also such a wide range of emotions as he had never before experienced. It was a wealth of sensation that was indescribable to those back home.

Balthar could not wait to share this with his beloved Sulzar, his mate, who was waiting to be joined with a host body he was preparing. They could be together in these physical forms and share these wonderful new sensations as one.

Just then his commlink buzzed in his ear. He tapped it to answer.

"Jules," the Empress' voice came over the com bud in his ear. "Can I speak with you? I want to explain why Vance and I didn't include you in our planning on this operation."

"Of course," Balthar answered, keeping his voice neutral. He prided himself on the control he had over this pathetic mortal shell with all its memories and knowledge. "Can you come back up to my quarters? I've left the audience hall and want maximum privacy for this."

"Of course, Empress." Jules tapped the commlink off.

"And so, it begins," he said to himself as he strode from his quarters.

Chapter 30

"Jules, please come in." Serena was seated at her conference table in the anteroom off her private bed chambers. They met here often when the meetings were casual and also the setting afforded maximum privacy.

Serena hit a button on the table. "Please see we're not disturbed until I, or the Chamberlain says,"

"Yes, Empress," came the reply.

"Help yourself to some refreshment. And please pour me a glass of that fruit juice while you're at it." Serena was steeling herself for this difficult conversation. She watched as Jules nodded and went to the side table and poured drinks. His back was to her and he seemed to be taking his deliberate time in getting the drinks. He probably knew what was coming as well.

Serena and Jules had been working together long enough she felt she could speak with him about anything, but this would be hard. It was the first time she'd left him out of anything she had planned, the first time she had not sought his advice and tacit approval. But it had been the right thing to do, because she had lately been sensing something different about Jules. It wasn't something she could specifically point to, just that Jules didn't seem quite himself. It now seemed rather foolish of her to doubt him after the evident surprise he'd shown at the broadcast. He'd always been loyal to her and her interests. She'd never had any reason to doubt him before.

"Here you are, Empress," Jules placed the goblet in front of her and sat in his customary seat next to her and settled himself. He reached forward and switched on the display inset into the table and then took a deliberate sip from his goblet.

Serena noted the formal use of her title. It indicated the sense of the meeting Jules was planning on. Well, two could play that game, Serena thought.

"Thank you, Chamberlain," she said and took a sip from her own goblet. The juice was refreshing and quenched her dry mouth with just a slight aftertaste that seemed a bit sour. It matched Jules' apparent mood. Best thing to do is just get on with it, she thought.

"Look, Jules, I'm sorry I left you out of our planning. You have to know that I needed to know if you had anything to do with . . ."

To her surprise, she found she couldn't finish her sentence. Then realized she couldn't move. She tried to reach forward to steady herself at the table. It was as if she was frozen solid. Jules noticed her stillness and chuckled.

What was happening? Serena started to feel panic, and then began to feel anger at herself for leaving herself so open.

Then a look came over his Jules' features Serena had never seen before. It was a look of . . . triumph? A malevolent look. A hostile look that suddenly frightened her.

Jules spoke to her, then, and she found she couldn't even turn her head to look at him. "You've just ingested a paralytic agent I put into your drink. You will not be able to move a muscle until you've been given an antidote.

"You were right in that I had no part in planning the attempts against your precious Vance. But you were also right in not completely trusting me. You see there are many things going on here you have sensed, but not fully grasped. Now, you're going to learn everything, and it's going to be painful for you, both body and soul. In the end, though, there is nothing you can do but accept."

Serena's mind was darting. Seeking for ways of escape, seeking to grasp what Jules was talking about.

"You see, you are about to be invaded totally and completely, both you personally, and your beloved Imperium. And it is going to be *you* who helps make it happen. Vance, and Mycal too. All of you are going to help. Or you will all die."

Jules stood then and placed her goblet on the table then came around behind her. She could feel him lifting her from her chair and hefting her over his shoulder and taking her into her bed chamber where the lights came on at their presence. All the while she was shouting in her mind, screaming at him, straining with all her might to move even the slightest muscle.

Jules settled her onto her bed and turned her head, so she had to look at him. She was growing more desperate. Then caught herself. She needed to stay calm, to gain information and figure out a way to get free. In spite of the paralysis, her mind was clear. She tried again to speak, and her mouth wouldn't respond. Again, Jules chuckled.

"I can only imagine what is going on in your mind." He then reached to the nightstand and hit a toggle. "Yes, Empress," came the response.

"This is the Chamberlain. The Empress is requesting to continue her 'do not disturb' orders until I inform you. In fact, she's ordered me to cancel all appointments for the next several days so she and I can prepare for the upcoming State of the Imperium address and the meetings with officials to follow. Further, cancel all the maid service. We'll be working at all hours and I'll be bringing the meals in and out."

"Yes, Chamberlain."

The toggle went dark and Jules stared down at her.

"That's taken care of. Now, I'm going to tell you everything, one leader to another."

Jules pulled a chair close to the bedside and made himself comfortable. Serena's mind was still flashing, though she was just now realizing anyone she could truly rely on was far away. Vance, Mycal . . . and Jules. Something was wrong with Jules. She began to feel a fear greater than she'd ever experienced before. She was totally helpless.

"You see," Jules began sitting back in the chair looking at the ceiling. "Your beloved Jules is no longer who you see before you. He is still here," Jules pointed to his chest, "but he is buried deep inside where I can access his memories and knowledge at will.

"I am called Balthar and I am the leader, the *King* you would call it, of a people you can't imagine exists. We are Isabarians, and we come from within the heart of what you call the Auspic Black Hole located near the Obdure 4 Cluster."

Serena's mind struggled to grasp what Jules . . . Balthar was saying. It was hard to concentrate while struggling to get free.

"Our realm is such that we exist in a non-corporeal state. We have no bodies and no form. Because of the tremendous gravitational forces existing within the heart of the black hole we are not subject to the normal laws of physics as you, with bodies, adhere to. In fact, we are more like a mass of *intelligence* which has formed into individual entities. We have our own society and existence outside of your time and space. I know all these terms and have this knowledge all from Jules."

At least Jules – no – Balthar was talking. She could listen, gain information, bide her time. Maybe something he would say would help her escape. What was he going to do with her?

"16 of your years ago," Balthar / Jules continued. "A scientific expedition from your side sent a hyper-dense probe down into the Auspic Black Hole."

Jules hesitated a moment. Serena stared into his eyes as tears of shame and anger streamed down the side of her face into the pillow. It was the only part of her body that could respond. He nodded, seeming content she was listening and comprehending.

"We noticed the probe and traced its trajectory back from whence it came. We were shocked to discover something mechanical reach our realm. It indicated there was another intelligence outside of our existence. We had postulated and debated this among our *scientists* but until then, nothing concrete had ever been discovered.

"Not having physical forms, we had sent only limited explorations beyond our realm. We found we could not abide long outside our normal environment. It was painful to us. We began to dissipate when away from the intense gravitational forces which held us together.

"However short the time outside, though, we discovered something amazing to us. A whole universe was out here. Such wonder. Such expanse. Such light."

Serena was amazed. It was hard to believe what this creature was saying. Surely it was a lie. Something else was going on and she needed to learn what it was.

"Finally, by a fluke chance, one of our more intrepid explorers ventured further out than any of our kind had ever done before. She encountered a ship, a scientific expedition studying the black hole from whence the probe had been launched.

"Her curiosity was stronger than her sense of survival and she pushed forward and was able to slide inside the ship and was astonished at the beings she encountered. You humans. Encased in flesh, blood, bones and water in a chemical concoction we had never conceived before.

"She reached out to communicate, though the pain was growing, and she was pending dissolution from being so far outside our normal environment. The leader, the captain of the ship was the obvious choice, and though she tried, he could not *hear* her. She got closer, and closer still until she *touched* him physically.

"What she discovered overwhelmed her and before she knew it, she had slipped *inside* the man, seeing and sharing his complete consciousness. He was a competent leader, but within was a jumbled mess of pain and sorrow. Immediately she knew he was going through a breakup with a long-time mate, and his financial fortunes were riding on this expedition discovering something of significant worth.

"Another miraculous thing she discovered was that the pain of her pending dissolution was gone. Instead, she was experiencing a myriad of feelings, sights, sounds and sensations she hadn't ever imagined possible. Being from a realm of total blackness, total absence of sensation other than thought and communion with those around her, she was nearly overwhelmed until she realized she had *joined* with the man without his even knowing and immediately perceived all he perceived, knew all he knew, experienced all he experienced.

"For a while, she observed and did nothing. Slowly she realized she could exert a small degree of control, which she tested again and again, all the while, riding within Malcolm Fluer Bosno, the captain, the first of your kind to be Taken."

Serena heard all this. Her body still wasn't responding, but her mind was racing. Could it be true? Was it possible? It must be, for here she was, being held captive by someone she didn't recognize, yet the face, the body, the man was one whom she'd grown up with, had called him *uncle*.

"You don't need to know all the details," Jules continued his story, the look on his face giving evidence he was relishing the affect he knew it must be having on Serena. "Since then, hundreds of us have crossed over and Taken your people with ease. Many in top government, and yes, top military ranks have been Taken. We now control most things of consequence.

"At this moment all my people are poised to cross over and Take as many of your people as necessary. We have formed a container, a small mechanical device which holds our essence until we can be brought into close proximity to one of you, and when opened, we simply slip inside and Take the body and push aside its inhabitant, subjugating it to the small recesses of the soul. We inherit the knowledge, memory, experience and all the sensations of our new bodies."

Serena was aghast. How could she stop this? She had to stop this! Yet, here she was, at the mercy of a man she had trusted for years. How long had Jules been gone? How long had this been in the planning. Then she remembered. It was 16 years. How could they have accomplished so much in so short a time? The malaise and its affects. She had begun to notice it about 4 years ago. That must be when they had started the invasion of those in higher positions. They can't have taken over everything, no matter what Jules – Balthar – said. There still had to be some chance. Vance was still out there. Mycal, though missing, he must be able to get free and do something . . . unless he was already *Taken*. That thought made her heart freeze.

Jules had been watching her eyes as if he could read her thoughts from the micro-expressions she was still able to make through her eyes.

"Our people, when encased with the bodies we have Taken are not able to read thoughts, to *commune* like we used to, but we are still pretty empathic, and we are expert at sensing emotions. What yours are telling me is that you still haven't resigned yourself to your fate and the fate of your Imperium.

"You should know we have Mycal captive. You were right, it was me who alerted those of my people in the Obdure Cluster, who, incidentally, are in charge there. Many of my people have already crossed over and we have complete control of that sector.

"Mycal will shortly be one of us. Vance is almost there, and my people are ready for him. He will be captured and Taken. I have someone special in mind for you. It will be Vance's new host's mate. Happily, for you the marriage will still take place. You two will continue to rule, but under my guidance and direction. Well, your new masters will be under my guidance and direction.

Jules smiled. "There is no escape."

The tears continued to flow down Serena's face. Her heart was breaking.

Chapter 31

Vance snapped off his communications console. He still hadn't been able to get through on the Empress' Private Channel. That was odd. They'd been speaking at this time every day, comparing notes, planning; and yes, speaking of private matters.

This had him concerned. He thought for moment as he sat at his desk in his private quarters aboard the Imperator, the Flagship of the Imperial Navy. After a moment, he hit the communications toggle again.

This time he punched up a different channel directly to the Palace switchboard operator. He had the codes to get directly to the highest levels.

"Yes, Admiral Vance," came the reply after a moment.

"I'm calling for the Empress," Vance said. "Could you please patch me through?"

"I'm sorry Admiral. The Empress left strict instructions she was not to be disturbed until after the State of the Imperium address. Is this an emergency?"

Vance hesitated a moment. "No of course not. Please just put in her que that I called."

"Yes, Admiral. Can I connect you with anyone else?"

Again, Vance hesitated. "Perhaps the Chamberlain. Could you connect me with him?"

"One moment admiral." In a few moments the Chamberlain's face floated in the hologram in front of Vance.

"Good morning, Vance. Is everything okay?"

"Yes, Jules. Everything is fine. Just checking in." Vance had a sudden hesitation about voicing any concerns. He didn't know why but knew from experience it was best to follow his sudden hunches.

"Please tell Serena, the tour is wrapping up and our plans are moving forward. We're in orbit above Metronome City and we'll be beginning the inspection tour as planned."

"Understood, I'll pass that along." Jules paused. "And by the way, nice work on foiling the assassination attempt. You and Serena make a formidable pair."

Vance nodded. "Thanks, Jules." Had he detected a subtle undercurrent? He knew Serena had been concerned with leaving Jules out of the planning. Was he still miffed about that?

"Anything else?" Jules asked.

"No, nothing. I'll report back when I have word on Mycal. I'm starting with the government office building where Mycal went missing. Mycal's crew is ready for my word."

"Very good," Jules said. "I know everything will go well." Then Jules smiled in a way Vance had never seen before. Vance couldn't place how, it was just . . . different.

"Jules out," and his face vanished.

The connection cut and Vance said to himself, "that was interesting." First not being able to connect with Serena then Jules' odd behavior, something was not right. He sat still a moment.

Vance then tapped a button in a syncopated code on his left breast pocket. It activated a hidden communicator within his uniform. Another little present from Mycal. His coded tap established a narrow-burst channel directly to the Lula.

"Here Sir," Cassie, the communication specialist of Mycal's team answered quickly. He'd had several vid conferences with Mycal's crew and the captain of the marines on board the Imperator as they'd traveled out to the Obdure 4 Cluster. They'd planned through several contingencies for the rescue mission and were all prepped and ready to go. They would tap into and maintain tracking on Vance's implanted and undetectable homing beacon. They could find him wherever he was on the planet unless he was shielded. He reminded himself, Mycal had the same homing beacon and communications tabs implanted as well. That had failed.

"Remain on station and monitor my homing signal. Patch in the marines also. We're about to go hot. If I go dark, wait a reasonable time, then come in and get me," Vance said through the tiny mic embedded in the collar next to the left side of his chin. The flesh-colored microscopic earbud attached into his left ear gave him a clarity of reception he didn't think possible. Mycal had explained that the material of his uniform, in addition to being thinly armored, acted as an amplified antenna.

"Understood," Cassie said. Vance snapped off the channel by touching his button one more time. The communication was supposedly undetectable by any modern comms, but he didn't want to take any chances being too verbose.

Vance pushed himself away from the table, grabbed his ship's cap off the bed and went to the door. Best to get to it he thought. The doors to his quarters opened at his approach.

He was surprised to be greeted by four armed guards with weapons drawn.

One quickly moved behind him and ushered him into the hall, closing the door behind. Commodore Blaine, the Adjutant to the Joint Chiefs who had been sent to escort him on his inspection tour came forward. Vance hadn't known him and realized he didn't know any of these guards either.

"Admiral Vance," Blaine said with an air of authority. "You are hereby placed under arrest for treason and high crimes against the Imperium.

"The Chamberlain has ordered your immediate arrest on suspicion in the disappearance of Count Henry Wallach, First Minister of the Imperium Parliament."

"You realize the Chamberlain has no Authority to issue any orders in the Imperium, don't you? He's an advisor and functionary at Court with no direct authority to issue orders."

There was no answer. Then it hit Vance. It didn't matter what actual authority the Chamberlain had. He had all the authority with these people that mattered.

"So, Wallach's disappeared," Vance said. "I had no idea." Things were starting to fall into place for him.

"Come with me, sir," Blaine said. The guard behind him quickly had relieved him of his sidearm. Vance, his mind still clicking, nodded and allowed himself to be escorted down the companionway.

"Where are you taking me?" Vance asked.

"Down to the planet," Commodore Blaine said. "There you'll be held pending extradition to the Capital for official charges and trial."

"Based on what evidence?"

"I'm not privy to that sir. I only have my orders."

They must not have formulated everything yet, Vance thought as they moved him down the corridor. They must be doing this on the fly and word hasn't been put out officially yet. They're worried people won't believe it without solid proof. And they haven't quite manufactured all they need.

They got on a lift, went down four floors and down another companionway to one of the hangar bays. Vance noticed no one else around. He figured no one else knew of his arrest. Too many onboard knew Vance and would object, the captain included. Jules had planned this well even if rushed. It had to be Jules pulling these strings.

He should have seen it. But Serena had been convinced Jules was not behind the assassination plot, and she could read people better than anyone he'd ever seen. She couldn't have been wrong in that. Yet who else could it be? Who else would have known enough of the inside information to put this in motion? It jelled with Serena now being out of touch.

Vance was loaded aboard a shuttle. The commodore took the controls. The guards fastened Vance securely with restraints into a seat. The thought occurred to Vance that maybe this had a small bright side. More than likely, he'd be taken to where Mycal was being held. Surely this same group was holding Mycal.

He'd bide his time and see what happened. His biggest concern, one which he couldn't do anything about right now, was Serena being left alone with Jules. What was happening with her? He started imagining the worst.

Chapter 32

Jules/Balthar touched the button, turning off his communicator. He was seated at the console in his private chambers, just below that of the Empress. It was a lavish space, made more so since Balthar had come to inhabit Jules' body. Before, Jules had been an austere man and had shared the quarters with his wife, who had died in a tragic assassination plot which Balthar's people had contrived. It was in that tragic aftermath Balthar had come to Take Jules as part of their invasion plan.

Since then, Balthar had discreetly been enjoying the new sensations having a body provided. His former wife's - well Jules' former wife's things had been removed and replaced with other exotic comforts not seen by anyone. Balthar had to watch closely lest weight gain betray his new tastes.

He had just received confirmation Vance had been arrested and was being conveyed to the planet's surface. Though rushed, Balthar was pleased the plan was finally coming together. Perhaps this would work out better.

He gathered the implements he had prepared along with the antidote mixed with another potent drug and placed them in his satchel and left the room, making sure to set his security protocols. No one else would be admitted under any condition, no sense getting careless at the cusp of their plan.

Down the corridor and up the lift, Balthar schooled himself to the serene, composed Chamberlain, a mask he now carried easily as a literal second skin. He approached *his* two guards, a man and a woman, detailed at the entrance to the Empress' quarters. They allowed no one to enter, to reinforce the standing orders the Empress not be disturbed.

Fists across chest, each bowed and let Jules/Balthar enter. He went right into the bed chambers seeing the Empress was still lying where he'd left her a short while before to take the comm report on his own console. His sense of security had dissuaded him from using any but his own station for these sensitive communications.

"Empress, I have good news to share." He set the satchel down on the bed next to the Empress's paralyzed form. Balthar could tell the drug had settled in a bit more, diffusing into her system. Though still paralyzed, she could make simple facial expressions and blink her eyes.

All to the good, Balthar thought. He opened his satchel, pulled out the restraints and the ampoule of the drug mixture. He started fastening the restraints securely over the Empress's reclining form, talking as he did so.

"You'll be interested to hear that your beloved Vance has been arrested, charged with treason and murder in the disappearance of Henri Wallach, our beloved First Minister.

"Of course, you know Vance didn't have anything to do with it. That was me and my people. Because of that, it will be easy to plant incriminating evidence of both you and Vance, working together to subvert our government and eliminate any obstacles to your absolute rule.

"At least that's the way it'll be presented. Now, of course, that evidence hasn't yet been revealed. It's just waiting to surface as a Plan B of sorts. Just so you realize there is no hope that you or your beloved Vance will escape this."

Balthar had finished securing the restraints and testing them. He was satisfied and continued.

"Vance will shortly be joining Mycal in a secure and shielded area. At which time they will be given the little Gift I told you about. The same type of Gift I have in store for you.

"Of course, there's always death if you reject it. If you die, I have a backup to that as well. Such an unfortunate occurrence. A pact between the two of you, Serena and Vance not to be taken alive if their treason and murder were found out."

Jules then picked up the ampoule and hypo spray and held it up to where Serena could see it. He could see the fear and anger in her eyes.

"Yes, I see you are realizing the predicament you're in. This ampoule contains the antidote to your paralysis. Unfortunately, the paralytic agent hinders your receipt of the Gift. Hence, the restraints. It will take some days for the paralytic to wear off completely. But this drug is also mixed with a mild sedative to calm you enough so you won't damage yourself against the restraints. We've found it also makes you more susceptible to our Gift."

Balthar attached the ampoule to the hypo spray and flicked the top making sure the liquid had settled with no bubbles. He reached down, relishing the frightened look in the Empress's eyes. Such power in these new sensations. Deeper emotions than he had ever thought possible. Then there was the extreme satisfaction of his planning coming together. It would never grow old.

Chapter 33

Mycal felt something was up. Yesterday Governor Sena had come in personally to let him know Vance would be joining him tomorrow – which would mean today. It must be early morning by now the way he was feeling, though he had no way of really knowing what time of day it was.

His mind was much clearer, though. The time had allowed the drugs to flush from his system. The physical torture was still being done on a daily basis, but it was nothing he'd not been able to handle. It was getting to where he felt he could escape, his body more in his control and his mind much clearer. He just needed the opportunity to make the break, and then, if Vance were here, or close, he'd get word to him via his crew. They must be beside themselves by now. Surely, they'd been coordinating with Vance for the rescue.

Mycal could get out of his bonds easily enough. It was escaping the heavily secured room that would be the problem. When someone came in and the door was open, that's when he'd do it. It would be easy to overpower the small Val Dokka the governor kept sending to do the torture. Payback would be bliss, Mycal thought.

That's when he heard it. The latch to the door being opened. It was going to be now or never.

Val Dokka stepped into the room, but then held it open. Governor Sela came striding through followed by a contingent of guards, and another officer Mycal didn't recognize. Then he caught sight of Vance.

"Ah, I see you are becoming more alert," the Governor said as he strode up followed by the rest of the contingent.

Mycal ignored him and held his head up to look directly at Vance. "It's Jules."

Vance nodded. "I'd gathered that, albeit too late."

"How nice," the Governor interrupted. "A reunion. We'll let you catch up for a bit, but not too long. We have a schedule to keep after all, and we don't want to keep Balthar waiting on his report. He's anxious to let the Empress know how you both are faring after you've received your Gifts."

"There's that word again," Mycal said. "I'm sick of hearing about it."

"You don't have long to wait, I assure you." The Governor nodded to his minion who stepped forward and administered an ampule of serum into Mycal's neck. It felt cold going in and he gave an involuntary shiver as it spread through his body.

"That's a little mixture to perk you up a bit," The Governor said. "We need to flush the last of the drugs from your system. It also has a little compound we've found to make you a bit more receptive to our Gift."

The Governor moved aside as another group of technicians came in with a new medical table they put beside Mycal. The guards moved Vance over to lay down on the table and fastened his arms and legs with restraints. The minion moved forward and injected Vance in the neck with another ampule.

"Slight change in plans as we've had to move things up a bit. Vance will get the Gift first, since he doesn't have any drugs to be flushed out." To Mycal he said, "You'll have the opportunity to watch first-hand as Vance is Taken and becomes one of us. It will only take a few moments, and then it will be your turn."

Mycal turned to Vance. "You okay?"

"Look who's talking," Vance answered, a wry smile playing across his face. "I'm not the one with a bruised face. I see they haven't treated you well."

"On the contrary, they've been trying to soften me up since I was captured. I did, however, find out Jules is the one we've been looking for. And of course, the Territorial Governor and his lackey are involved."

"Don't forget some high rankers in the military," Vance said nodding to the guards and officer he'd been arrested by.

"So, this is your rescue plan?" Mycal asked, laying his head back down as his neck muscles were getting tired. He also was preparing himself to use his enhanced muscles to break free. The drug had, indeed cleared his body. He could also feel the other drug taking effect. It didn't dull his body, but it was slowing down his mind's ability to think. He had to get moving soon or it might be too late. There were still too many guards in the room to be successful though. Especially since they were armed and alert.

"You should have both realized by now that there is no rescue. We have taken this whole system. Everyone in it of any consequence is ours." The Governor then turned back to the doorway. Mycal couldn't see who he was speaking too. Probably another technician.

"Bring in the spheres and dim the lights." To the others in the room, he said, "you can return to the ship. I have everything in hand here. Secure the ship for when Vance returns."

He looked over at Vance and saw anger reddening his face. Still, he remained silent. Mycal was sure he had a plan, though. Vance always had a plan.

Mycal had a plan too. He'd break free as soon as the guards left and were far enough away they couldn't hear the screams. Surely the Governor could be *persuaded* to reveal the security code to the door so they could escape this room. He and Vance would then escape through the building and get to where he could signal his crew. With Vance here, they must be ready for the call. The Lula could set down in the front plaza if necessary, for them to board and be off. They shouldn't return to Vance's ship, seeing it was compromised.

The guards left the room, and the door remained open. That was good! Then a woman in a lab coat came in and handed two silver spheres with odd markings surrounding the outsides to Val Dokka. The hand off was deferential, like what they were handling was in some way delicate, or special.

He came forward and handed one of the spheres to Governor Sena who moved forward as the lights grew dimmer, to the point Mycal could barely make out what has happening. He still hadn't heard the door close.

Then he noticed the shadow of the Governor leaning over Vance and opening the sphere right above his chest . . .

***

Vance watched as the Mon Sena, in the darkness, held the silver sphere over his chest and opened it. At first, nothing seemed to happen, and then he could faintly see, at the same time he felt, a dark mist spill down from the sphere until it touched -- and then penetrated his chest! He felt a cold chill envelope him, suffusing his body, spreading outward, taking control of his limbs, flowing through until he felt a spark of intelligence. It was a live entity invading his body.

He steeled his mind. He would not let the entity take him over. There was no way.

Then he felt the chill rise up his neck and start to creep into the recesses of his mind. Vance tried to block it off, to somehow slam a gate down, but he didn't know how. Inexorably the entity started to seep into his consciousness and Vance felt it blending with his mind, his thoughts, his memory and his knowledge . . .

Chapter 34

If there's ever going to be a time, this is it, Mycal thought. Only two of the enemy were in the room with the lights out and the door, hopefully, still open. The guards had left. Even the lab techs had gone. He had the element of surprise. Mycal smiled to himself at how corny that sounded.

Just then he heard the muted staccato of blaster bolts. He realized the sound came from outside the building.

He knew Vance had a plan. Time to join up with the cavalry, he hoped.

Mycal gathered himself, reaching within to gather his enhanced musculature and bones for one tremendous surge, snapping the restraints on his arms. Reaching up, he ripped off the band across his chest, then sat up, wrenching off the leg and ankle restraints.

"What was that?" he heard the governor say. Mycal wasn't sure if he was referring to the sound of blaster fire or from the sound of tearing restraints. It didn't matter.

"It's your doom," Mycal said as he slid off the table, staggering a bit from being under drugs and restrained for so long. Still, he was close enough to deliver an enhanced open-handed swat across the face of Val Dokka who'd moved up to try and force him back on the table. He went down.

Next he grabbed Governor Sena by the scruff of the neck. A quick punch to the solar plexus made him double over followed by a knee to his forehead and the Governor was down.

Mycal wasn't sure he'd restrained himself enough to leave them both alive from his blows. He didn't much care. They were traitors. He stepped over to Vance, his legs now a bit more stable.

"Come on. Let's get going."

He tore free the restraints holding Vance, surprised Vance hadn't answered, hadn't spoken a word since things went dark.

"Vance?"

No answer.

"We've got to get moving."

Still nothing. The sound of blaster fire was getting closer. They needed to get out of this room before the door was shut and bolted again. He didn't want them to be used as hostages in a stand-off.

Mycal felt for Vance in the darkness, felt his face and tapped his cheek. His face was cold to the touch. "Come on, Admiral. Hup to!" Still no response.

Then he remembered the Governor leaning over Vance with the crystal sphere. Opening it up. The *Gift*. What had he done to Vance?

"No time to wonder, soldier," Mycal told himself. "Get moving." Speaking aloud helped keep him stay focused, and he realized the second drug he'd been given to make him more *receptive* was working. "Push through it," he said aloud again, not caring if anyone heard.

He grasped Vance's arms and pulled him upright and over his shoulder in one fluid move. The dim light from far down the hallway showed him the doorway that was unguarded. Apparently, they didn't think they had anything to worry about.

"Better to be lucky than good sometimes," Mycal said to the unconscious Vance as he made his way down the empty hallway with his burden.

He came to the lift right before the stairwell. Should he take the lift or use the stairs? Both would be confined spaces, easy traps. The lift was worse. The doors would be opening up blind. Still, three flights were a long climb even with an enhanced body. Mycal grit his teeth and moved to the stairwell as the sound of fighting continued to grow in intensity. His thoughts were churning.

I'll get to the main level, find a place to set Vance down then reconnoiter the main lobby. If he could obtain some weaponry from one of the guards, he could hit them from the rear. "Going to speak with Vance about eating too much at all these State Dinners."

***

Mycal arrived at the doorway to the main lobby puffing with exertion. Here was the critical part. If there was going to be trouble, this is where he'd find it.

He set Vance down gently against the wall out of line of fire from the doorway. Mycal was about to crack open the door when he noticed something – or the absence of something. The blaster fire had ceased.

Uh oh. That might not be good, Mycal thought.

The door suddenly swung outward and Mycal was face to face with a blaster pointed between his eyes.

"Gomy!" Mycal whooped and embraced the big man.

"You had us worried for a bit," Gomy said as they broke the hug.

"Naw," Mycal said. "Had everything under control. All a part of my master plan."

"Yeah, right . . . sir," Gomy said. "The building is secure except for the lower levels. Lula and the Marine's shuttle is just outside. We'll have a lot of company before too long. The Admiral?"

"Just inside the doorway here. Help me with him, will you? I secured the lower levels and brought him up."

"The lower floors are empty, then?" Gomy smiled.

"No one likes a wiseacre," Mycal said pointing to Vance and helping Gomy get him over his shoulder.

"The fighting to get in here was pretty easy, like the defenders didn't know quite what to do. It was a bit odd. All the same, I'm glad of it." Gomy said, moving out into the main lobby where all the access points were covered by armed marines. The marine Captain came forward.

"Captain Zander at your service," he said to Mycal. "Captain Petrs I presume? Is the Admiral okay? Does he need medical attention?"

"He'll be fine, I think. We have advanced medical units on the Lula. I'd prefer Vance stays with me. I'm afraid your command ship might be compromised by the same people who've taken over this system. It runs pretty high up, and I'm not sure who to trust right now."

"Understood," Captain Zander responded, though he looked uncertain he wanted to trust Mycal with the care of Vance. It was clear his objective was to rescue Vance. He didn't want to let him out of his sight.

"Is your shuttle hyper-speed capable?" Mycal spoke, taking charge.

"It is. We're fully self-contained for missions of this sort. Our ship is home base for us."

"Good. You have now been commandeered to be part of the Admiral's new fleet. I'd show you my authorization, but it's been taken from me."

"No need. Commander Petrov showed me his. And you outrank him. I'll go on faith for now. I know the Admiral came out here to rescue you, so you must be pretty important."

"I'm not important. It's what I know that's important. And we need to get it back to the Empress and those still loyal to her – including Vance – Admiral Hamblin, I mean."

"Shall we be off, then?" Captain Zander gestured to the main doorway. A lieutenant came up.

"Sirs, we have reinforcements inbound with heavier guns this time."

"Here is a rendezvous point. Get there and make contact with us and we'll discuss our options then," Mycal said as Gomy handed Zander a small crystal data chip. It was standard procedure for them in these types of missions to have an RV point ready. They made their way out the door.

Outside sitting on the main plaza where they'd crushed several benches and ornamental shrubs sat two ships. The larger marine shuttle took up the bulk of plaza. Closer by sat the Little Nebula. Mycal had never been so glad to see his little ship. They ascended the ramp and Mycal watched as the Marines all doubled aboard their ship and closed the hatch.

At the top of his steps, Mycal hit the comm. "Ben, take us up and out. You know where. Don't be seen."

"Aye sir." came Ben's voice over the comm. "Good to have you back, sir."

Gomy was standing bye, still holding Vance over his shoulder.

"I'll take him to his quarters, get him bedded down and start the medical scanning. You get back to the bridge and make sure all stays well."

"Aye, Captain," Gomy said transferring Vance to Mycal's shoulder and turned for the front of the ship.

Chapter 35

Mycal got Vance situated comfortably on his bed. He still wasn't stirring. He was breathing, his pulse was strong though his body seemed cold.

"Come on Vance," Mycal said as he patted his cheek. "Wake up. We're in the thick of things and you're needed."

He got a med scanner and held it over Vance. The readouts confirmed what he already knew. All vital signs were within normal ranges. Body temperature was cool, barely above the dangerous zone.

Time passed.

The comm tweeted. "Captain, we're at the rendezvous point and the Marines are hailing us."

"Be right there," Mycal answered and glanced at Vance. He didn't want to leave him, but there were things to do. He was worried about Serena. And there was Adriana, though she'd be relatively safe for now. Now they knew that Jules, her step-father, was behind it all. It would break her heart. It made Mycal angry. What had gotten into Jules? What had caused him to do this?

Mycal left Vance's room, hesitated a moment, then keyed in the lock code. If Vance woke up and wasn't who he was supposed to be, it was best to be prepared. Things were going crazy.

***

The bridge was its normal controlled efficiency with an underlying tension Mycal could detect. That probably came from him being gone so long, and them having received orders to invade and attack a Territorial Governor's headquarters to save their captain and new Commander-in-Chief. That would tend to make a soldier a bit nervous.

"Put Captain Zander on the screen," Mycal said and took his command chair.

"How's the Admiral?" Captain Zander asked as soon as his face appeared on the forward viewscreen.

"Still snoozing, but otherwise okay. I ran a med scan, and everything is normal. They just drugged him. He'll come out of it," Mycal said, hoping he wasn't going to be a liar.

"You should know that I got a bulletin across the combined military channels that Vance has been charged with Treason and suspicion of murder in the disappearance of 1st Minister Wallach."

Mycal looked at Cassie at comms who nodded back in confirmation. She'd seen it too but hadn't had a chance to say anything. Mycal hesitated a moment then looked back at Captain Zander.

"And what are you proposing to do about it?" Mycal said, his tone even and minutely quieter.

"We just attacked the Obdure 4 Governor's Office. I think that should tell you something," Captain Zander said. "I, and my unit don't believe it, especially when the local guards opened up on us when we showed them our authority, so we know something isn't right.

"We know Admiral Hamblin. Served with him on Portus 7 when he went against orders and kept us from getting killed. He's been telling the truth about things, he and the Empress. I know who to trust and so do my people." There was a chorus of 'BuYahs!' sounding behind Captain Zander.

"Orders?" the Captain said with a smile. "We'll listen to you until the Admiral wakes from his nap. Figure you've been closer to what's really going on than anyone back at the Capital. By the way, you were right about the Imperator. She broke orbit and headed back for the Capital before we broke atmosphere. Not a word to us. Guess they already figured we were on the right side of things. Feel sorry for the innocents aboard though. There were a lot of loyal crew there who'll be angry when they learn what's what.

"And by the way, are you having problems with long range comms?"

Mycal looked at Cassie. "No joy on any frequency, even the most secure lines," she said.

Mycal nodded, not surprised. "I think those setting things up to fall don't want their nefarious scheme to be let out of the bag too soon – meaning, they don't want us screaming the truth to anyone who'll listen."

"That's the way I see it. Your call."

"Set course for the Capital. We'll be going into stealth mode, and I'm sure we're faster. I need to get to the Capital and . . ." He almost said *check in* with the Empress but very few outside his immediate crew knew he had close contact with the Empress, and only Ben, his pilot knew he was her brother. ". . . Get Vance where he can set things straight."

"Roger that," Captain Zander said. "In the meantime, when we get closer in, I'll put some feelers out and connect with others I know who won't believe the news. I think this goes high up, and the Admiral will need allies. I can tell them what I saw here and have them pass it along. I hope this doesn't get ugly, but if it does . . ." the Captain didn't finish.

"Good idea," Mycal said. Not because he knew it was a good idea. He'd never really been in the larger chain of command, so didn't have a clue as to what Vance would be dealing with, but it surely wouldn't be good. He'd need all the support he could get. Mycal's mind was racing.

"We'll catch you on the other side, then. And thanks for the rescue." Mycal meant it.

"Anytime, Captain. And good luck." The viewscreen switched to a field of stars.

"Course laid in and stealth mode engaged," Ben interrupted Mycal's thoughts.

"Engage at maximum speed."

Ben nodded. Mycal turned to Cassie.

"Is our secure band to the Capital still operable?"

"Sorry, Sir. All channels are dead. It's as if the whole communications system has been shut down. There's not even a carrier wave to show it's live. Someone at the head-end in the Capital has disabled the entire network. The only comms we have are local radio frequencies. Nothing on the hyper-light bands at all."

"So, we'll be going in blind," Mycal said.

His crew looked at him, saying nothing. He knew they were with him, come what may.

"I need to look in on Vance. He needs to wake up and be the strategist we need right now." Mycal stood and left the bridge.

Chapter 36

Vance was floating in darkness. He had no sensation, no feeling, a disembodied consciousness with no connection to anything physical. It would be terrifying if he had not clamped down on his fear and reasoned out what was actually happening.

Intellectually, he knew he was still connected to his body, though cut off from any of his senses by the entity which had taken control. His focus was to regain control and take back what was his.

Several attempts by force of will had not been successful. The problem was that he didn't know what he could do? What power had he? All he had were his thoughts. There was nothing he could mentally, even, grasp hold of, to apply any leverage to.

He went back over his memory of what had happened. The chill spreading through his body, and the sense of another *being* seizing control of his body and pushing his . . . mind? aside like it was less than a feather.

Such mental power. He remembered feeling that then everything went dark, and he found himself floating . . . inside himself, he guessed.

How can I fight this? Vance wondered. If there were a barrier of some sort, he could press against it.

If you have your thoughts, then use them, Vance told himself. Go through what you know. He was forcing his mind to stay on track, to do something productive, to not yield to the terror he was only barely suppressing.

You know Jules is at the head of what was happening. Why? Jules already had as much power as any man needed or could want. Serena listened to him in everything, and even though he wasn't the absolute ruler, he was right there.

How did that relate to what he'd just experienced? The answer came quickly. Jules probably wasn't who he appeared to be.

Jules must have been taken over, like Vance had been. So, this is an invasion. By beings he couldn't comprehend, who didn't have physical bodies, and who could possess the bodies of others, and take control.

Thinking about Jules, he realized that whatever entity must be inhabiting Jules had all his knowledge, memories and experiences to fool even Serena so completely.

Vance hadn't known him long, so wouldn't have recognized any differences, and it was only recently that Serena started having her doubts. Yet this invasion must have been going on for some time, to have grown to the scope it was, taking over the Obdure 4 cluster and penetrating as high up in government.

Vance realized that must have been what had happened with the military also. Some of the top leadership was affected and he hadn't seen it. Well, he had seen it, just not recognized what it was.

Was he even now being drained of all his memories, his experiences, and abilities? Completely taken over by this . . . whatever it was?

Then another thought occurred to him. The Governor had mentioned Serena was going to suffer the same fate. Was she even now experiencing the same thing as he? The thought made him shudder, inwardly, since he couldn't feel his body.

His mind darted back realizing he was missing something critical. He was sure of it. If the entities taking over people had complete access to memories, knowledge, and experiences, how do they do that if they walled off the consciousness like he was being walled off from anything and everything?

Wasn't it the consciousness where all the cognitive functions lay? The memories, the experiences, the knowledge, and the wisdom that came along with all those? Why then was he being cut off rather than just being subdued and drained?

There was so much about this he didn't know. It was then he felt it. A slight presence sharing the inner space with him, like a peephole had been opened and he was being observed.

"Oh yes," a voice intoned inside his mind / consciousness. It was so very close. "You are as smart as I'd been told," the voice said again.

"So here it comes," Vance spoke / thought back.

"Forgive me for leaving you unattended," the voice said. "I am known as Shazar. I am your new master. I first wanted to become familiar with your autonomic functions, your musculature, and your physical systems before I assimilated your consciousness. I wanted no distractions for one as strong-willed as you. Now it's time."

Vance felt the tiny peephole widening, expanding. The barrier of his prison falling but being replaced by an immense presence, overpoweringly strong. Felt it enveloping him, covering him, submerging him, and joining with him.

He fought it, tried to push it back, holding it at bay. It was no use.

The presence infiltrated every bit of him, subsumed him completely until he felt what the being felt, but it was *his* body, his arms, legs, could feel his heart beating, his pulse racing, and his consciousness starting to drown, to merge and mix with Shazar to become Vance / Shazar.

Then he could fight no more and he was drifting again, completely subsumed by Shazar. He heard his / Shazar's thoughts.

"You are quite an interesting man. It will be a pleasure taking your place. This body of yours, I have no words to describe it. The sensations, the feelings, the-- Again, I can't put into words.

"Now let's see what I can make of you," Shazar said, and Vance felt his consciousness being grasped and whirled back in time to an early memory.

***

A six-year-old Vance was huddled under the bed in the back room of he and his parents' dwelling on the planet Mowry Two. They had just arrived and built their prefab home as settlers on this outpost planet, rich in natural resources. His mother, a botanist, his father, a mining engineer. Production and harvest had been bountiful, and the first shipments for trade were due to be sent off, when the attack by raiders had come.

His mother had hidden Vance under the bed, then left for the comm station to call for help. His father had grabbed a laze rifle to go out with the other colonists to defend their livelihood. Vance had huddled fearfully under the bed, listening to the sounds of explosions, and zang of blaster fire. Heard shouts and screams of pain. Angry curses, loud whooshes of spaceships overhead. It had seemed to go on for hours. Then, slowly, started to taper to random blasts, shouts and laughter.

Then, came the sound of boot steps in the hallway outside his bedroom.

"Make sure you search all the rooms," a voice said. "These folks'll have little nips around we can sell off to the slavers."

Though young, Vance understood what they meant, and he held his breath while tears formed, knowing if these men had come into the house, his parents, likely, were dead. The sound of the boots entered his room. Vance clenched his eyes shut, holding as still as he possibly could.

The steps came closer, then stopped just beside his bed. He heard a rustling, then felt a rough hand grasp hold of his collar, pulling him out from under the bed.

Vance was jerked upright, staring into the grizzly face of a raider. He kicked, he clawed, he swung his arms, all to no avail.

"Got us a fighter, eh?"

"Stop playing around," came the voice from another room. "Take him out to the square with the others."

"Settle down, boy," the raider said, cuffing him across the face twice, making Vance dizzy with the blows. He sagged, and the raider picked him up, threw him over his shoulder, carrying him out into the bright sunlight.

The first sight that met Vance's eyes was the body of his mother, stretched across the threshold of their small home. She was face down; a blaster bolt burned into her back. She had been trying to get home to him.

Tears filled his eyes, blurring his vision, as the raider carried him out into the central square of their small settlement. He was dropped onto the hard-packed earth beside other children of the settlement who had also been gathered. He knew them all. Most were crying. A couple of kids were huddled, laying in the ground, inert, either knocked unconscious, or just giving up.

Other bodies, those of their parents, lay strewn around the compound, and the raiders were all coming back from the forays into the homes, jumbled together.

"Get the cargo loading," he heard someone shout. "Our informant tells us they were mining diamonds, so don't miss a clod."

Then, a large whooshing sound came from directly overhead, and Vance looked up to see the passage of a sleek-lined cruiser. He had always loved spaceships, and he instantly recognized the Imperial Fleet insignia.

Help had come! All the raiders had looked up to witness the dramatic fly-over. Then, blaster fire sounded again from all sides. Vance watched from his kneeling position, as raiders from all sides started falling, being hit by blaster fire.

Imperial troopers moved out of cover, continuing their fire. The raider who had just dropped Vance reached down and quickly grabbed him, holding him up as a human shield. Vance kicked and clawed, to no avail.

"Hold your fire or I'll drill this kid!"

Vance felt the blaster nuzzle against his head.

"Drop your weapon."

Vance saw an Imperial trooper holding his blaster rifle aimed at the raider holding him.

"You're gonna-"

At that point, the trooper squeezed off a blast, and Vance felt the beam narrowly miss the top of his head and strike its intended target. Vance was dropped, as the trooper quickly moved forward, embracing Vance in a sheltering hug.

"Don't look at him, boy. He got what he deserved. Remember that. Just sorry we didn't get here sooner."

Vance then looked up at the trooper. He'd never seen a more beautiful sight.

"We came as soon as we got word, but we were too far away. They'd set a diversion to draw us out. But that woman on the radio saved you kids, at least."

That woman had been Vance's mother.

"Come on, boy. Let's get you away from all this."

The trooper pick Vance up. The trooper was young, Vance noticed. Younger than his parents. Dark hair, clean shaven, crisp and trim. He'd saved Vance and the other children, he and the other troopers.

It was then Vance knew what he needed to do with his life. He didn't want anyone else to suffer what he had gone through. And if he could be like this trooper, he wouldn't be distracted by any diversion. He'd always get there on time, no matter what.

***

Then, Vance heard a distant voice in his mind: "Such a formative experience. And I see you've never shared it with anyone."

Vance wondered where the voice came from, what it meant.

"Let's see what else you have inside here."

And Vance felt a whirring motion inside his mind, blurring the vision, taking him to another point in his life.

***

Vance was in school, a newly minted 12-year-old, living with his grandparents on the heavily populated world of Kerrage. They were his grandparents on his father's side, older and retired and loved him even though they couldn't understand his fascination with the military and wanting to be a soldier when he grew up.

The playground was awash in children, running, shouting, playing, but Vance kept to himself. He'd come here right after his parents had been killed. Vance had made friends, acquaintances really, but none close. He'd held them all at arm's length, watching, observing remaining outside the close circles of friends he saw all around him.

Most of the kids liked him, though. Some had even invited him to their homes. And Vance had always been helpful, friendly, courteous, always ready to lend a hand with whatever anyone needed.

That's part of who he was now. He was here to serve, to help others, to keep others from getting hurt. His attention was attracted by shouts and jeers. A small group of boys was forming.

Vance wandered over to see what was going on. The group was being led by a trio of boys a year older than he. Vance had dubbed them the Bully Trio and had his share of run-ins with them.

True to form, they had found a newcomer to the school. Someone smaller, weaker they could tease and prey upon for sport. The newcomer appeared a couple of years younger than Vance, dark hair, thin, but gamely trying to ignore the jibes the Bully Trio were famous for.

Vance started to move forward as one of the boys knocked the tablet out of the young boy's hands then proceeded to kick it some distance away while the others laughed. It was then the young boy, rather than run after his tablet, pivoted and threw a punch directly into the gut of the offending bully. He doubled over in surprise. They weren't used to their victims fighting back.

The other two darted forward, grabbing the young boy by either arm as the crowd continued to shout. At this point, Trevor, the one punched, was straightening up again.

"Come on Trevor, get him back." The other two boys held the young man's arms pinned so Trevor would have a clear shot.

It was then Vance strode between, "You mess with him, you mess with me," Vance said, and indeed he had messed with them before.

The three of them had, on several occasions come against Vance. The three of them being older, larger and ganging up had beaten Vance pretty badly. But none of them had escaped cuts and bruises themselves. And still Vance defended their victims on any occasion necessary.

"Are you crazy?" Trevor said, "we beat you every time."

"It's not about the beating," Vance said. "It's about how much pain you're willing to take. I get better each time."

"And now there's two of us to fight back," the young boy said, still pinned between the other two.

Vance gazed directly into Trevor's eyes. Trevor had been hurt by the young boy's punch, saw the calculation. Yes, they'd probably beat the two of them, but as Vance had reminded him, none of them would come away unscathed.

Vance saw the decision and Trevor spoke, "Come on guys. This is getting boring." The crowd around them expressed their disappointment and started to disperse as the two other bullies released the young man and went on their way.

Vance walked over and picked up the tablet. It was scratched and a bit battered, but otherwise had been built for the indestructibility required of young kid's use. He handed it to the boy.

"Thanks," the kid said. "By the way, I'm Mycal. Mycal Peters."

"I'm Vance Hamblin." They bumped fists, as was common on this world between the kids.

"You really saved my bacon there," Mycal said. "Saved your what?" Vance asked.

"It's an archaic expression. I study them, you know. They sound pretty cool, don't they? "Cool?" Vance asked again.

"You'll get used to it if you hang around me long enough," Mycal said.

***

Vance's vision started to fade as did the images around him. "Ah, so that's how you met," a disembodied voice came into Vance's mind which was confusing him. What was happening?

Then Vance remembered. This had happened a long time ago. Mycal had become his first close friend and had gathered a small group of other friends around them.

That was Mycal's doing until his sudden disappearance at the end of their secondary school graduation. Mycal and his family had suddenly moved, but Vance knew somehow, within, that it hadn't been Mycal's real family because he was the son of the Emperor and Empress and brother to Serena.

How did he know that?

His mind began to swirl again.

***

Vance's mind reeled and he found himself in blackness again. It took him a bit to orient himself and realized he was back within his own mind. Of course, he'd never left, but the visions / memories were so real, so visceral, like he'd relived them over again.

He felt weak, drained, and then he sensed something else within his mind. It was full of other memories, or another place, dark, oppressive, closed-in and heavy, though he felt himself floating free. Thinking and experiencing . . . he couldn't describe it.

There were presences, all around him, crowding him, bumping him and jostling him, though that was the wrong word because there were no physical sensations whatsoever. Instead he felt their mental touches and bumps. There was nowhere he was alone. Nowhere he wasn't surrounded by many, thousands of others, and he could hear all their thoughts, their musings, their frustrations and their ambitions.

The noise, without any sound, was deafening, and Vance tried to raise his hands to his ears and realized he didn't have a body, no way to shut out the incredible cacophony which boomed in his mind.

And then all was silence again, and Vance shuddered and felt a single entity with him. Mercifully, it was just the one. And then he realized it was Shazar. And delving deeper, Vance realized he knew things, remembered experiences and conversations, plans and machinations which were not his.

They all belonged to Shazar. These were *his* thoughts, experiences, memories. Everything Shazar was now part of him.

"This is how it happens?"

"Yes," Shazar echoed within. "This is how we become one. Yet I am master and you the servant. In time, I will no longer have need of you, and your consciousness will fade, wither away into the abyss in which I will place you."

"I won't let you," Vance resisted the thought, strived to push it back.

Shazar chuckled. "Such a pitiful struggle. Yes, your mind is strong, but you are no match for those of us who evolved as nothing but pure intelligence. You couldn't even block out a normal few seconds of our day.

"That is who we are, and now you have given us these bodies with all your physical passions, feelings, experiences. They're so delicious. Just seeing and reliving your memories, much less experiencing new things; Balthar was right. This truly is a treasure. The Promised Land."

"No." Vance said in his mind. "We will fight you."

"You have already been defeated. You are our slaves to do with as we please. You pitiful creatures don't deserve all you have."

"The truth will get out. We will resist. We'll find a way to stop you."

"You were their best hope, Vance, and you were pathetically easy to subdue, walking right into our trap – even when you knew it was there."

"You won't win. I'll never give up." Even as he spoke this, Vance continued to struggle, to push back against the overwhelming consciousness striving to suffocate him, still, it hadn't completely enveloped him.

It was then Vance sensed a slight discordant feeling within Shazar, a bit of surprise, a tinge of uncertainty, as if he should have taken Vance over completely by now. Vance took heart from this, little as it was.

"I sense your uncertainty. This isn't going the way you planned."

"Your pathetic hope amuses me. It is only taking a little longer. Like I said, you are strong-willed."

"It's more than that," Vance said. "I can sense it. Something is wrong. Something is preventing you from completely submerging my will. Even now our merging is failing. I sense your pain, your . . . disruption. I feel it. You can't completely take me over. I won't let you. Something is preventing it. I'm not . . . compatible." Vance realized he was getting this sense from being almost completely connected with Shazar and was perceiving things through Shazar's senses / thoughts.

"No. You are wrong," Shazar said. "You're merely sensing my effort at completing what I started."

Vance knew it was a lie as Shazar tried again to encircle him. But Vance, feeling hope surge, continued to push back, to garner more room around his consciousness, feeling himself grow freer and while not completely understanding it, accepted and used it. Something inside of him, in his consciousness, was giving him power, making him incompatible with Shazar's intelligence, weakening him, and sapping Shazar's own energy.

Then Vance felt a renewed push of the darkness encroaching on him again, the heavy weight and the feeling of being surrounded, suffocated and drowned out by all that was covering him. He was starting to lose his hold . . .

Vance was starting to fade, and he felt his mind beginning to falter, to be consumed, and the small trickle of consciousness remaining to him grasped out for a final memory, one that he cherished above all others. His vision swirled, moving to that memory as if escaping to safety.

***

They were in the gymnasium off Serena's private quarters in the palace seated on a bench beside the mat.

Serena turned to Vance and picked up his hand. "I want you to know that at first, I really respected you. That I needed you for your skills as a soldier and analyst. And also, for your absolute loyalty to the Imperium. But now . . ." She smiled and squeezed his hand.

"Now that I've gotten to know you better, and see you are totally genuine, I am starting to fall for you."

Vance was shocked at how frank she was being.

"You have been a perfect gentleman. But now, I want you also to be something . . . more. And not just because we have to. But because I'm realizing this is what I want. What I want for *me* and not just for the politics of it." She paused a moment then laughed. Vance was realizing Serena could never be serious too long, though what she said had volumes of serious meaning. "So, what I'm asking, is . . . you want to be my steady? We can sit in the dark and neck if you want."

Vance shook his head and laughed. She had a way of making him feel at ease. And it wasn't just her practiced political training. It was just who she was. And who he was falling in love with.

"Now it's my turn for honesty."

At this, Vance could tell Serena was a bit scared of what he might say. She had made herself vulnerable as a person who was trained to never show weakness of any kind and in any situation. She was actually worried he might reject her. Not the proposed marriage, nor his duty to the Imperium. She knew he'd never reject that. But she was afraid of him rejecting *her*.

Vance didn't want her to wait any longer. "I'm yours," he said. "Heart, soul and body."

"Who knew you were such a romantic?" Serena said, the tears flowing as she laughed through them, and then she pulled him close and kissed him again. And again . . . And again.

Then they pulled back. She wiped the tears from her eyes. "It will be fun saving the galaxy with you."

***

There was a warmth in Vance's heart and soul, and he felt it growing, expanding . . .

Pushing back the darkness which had threatened to overwhelm him. That memory. That warmth he felt, the light of it was pushing back the dark, the suffocating presence of Shazar.

"I see you're faltering," Vance said. "Feelings of love, of happiness are antithetical to you and maybe even your kind. You cannot assimilate me when I feel these things. I refuse to be pulled down by you or anyone else, and I refuse you."

"No!" Shazar was growing in pain, a mental anguish so deep it seared Vance's consciousness. Vance ignored it and pushed harder, further widening the gap between them focusing on Serena and his love for her. Focusing on things that made his heart glad and brought light into his consciousness.

"No," Shazar groaned, this time weaker. Vance felt Shazar starting to disburse, to disassociate, to wisp away, being forced not only from his consciousness but from his body as well.

"Yes," Vance said. "Leave now. We will not be slaves. We will never surrender, and we will defeat you."

"Ohhhh," Shazar's faint mourn drifted off as Vance felt . . . truly *felt*, the return of his sensations, of his body, of a lightness returning, not a physical light but of his soul's light. And he came back to himself.

Chapter 37

Mycal was sitting by Vance's bedside. He'd been there for several hours as they were making the transit back to Zyzeen and the center of the Imperium. They still had a couple of days to go and Mycal was worried. Worried about his sister. Worried about still not being able to communicate, to let her know Jules, their uncle, was behind everything.

Mycal was worried about Adriana too, who, if they didn't get things resolved, may never have the type of life he wanted she and him to have.

Finally, there was Vance, an old and new friend, and future brother-in-law. He liked the guy, and the more he had been around him, his fondness had grown. He hadn't changed from when they were kids. A forthright do-gooder, but not in a sanctimonious way. He was humble, direct, and not puffed up with his own importance. That was the best part. He just wanted to do what was right. That's why he had risen in the ranks and had so great a following in the military. But now, here he lay comatose because he'd come to rescue Mycal . . . again.

"Come on, Vance," Mycal said. "I don't know what's going on or what they did to you, but I'm sorry. I'm sorry one of my harebrained schemes dragged you in."

It was then he noticed Vance begin to twitch ever so slightly. At first, there was a finger. Then his wrist and foot, then his head began to sway, and his eyes flickered.

"Come on, Vance, you can come out of this," Mycal said, grabbing the med scanner and holding it over Vance's chest. The readings were all still normal; respiration, heartbeat, though a bit elevated. Even his temperature had risen a little. It was as if Vance was struggling to wake up, to come out of whatever had him under. Should he give him a stimulant? Maybe slap his face a little?

Then Mycal stepped back as a black mist oozed out from Vance's mouth, eyes, nose and ears. "What on earth?" Mycal said. Then as Mycal watched, the mist started to dissipate and vanish, and Vance gave a low groan, expelling the last bit of it. Then he blinked his eyes open, taking in a huge lung-full of air.

"Vance are you all right? What happened?" Mycal leaned over.

Vance looked around the room, confused. "Where?"

"It's okay Vance," Mycal said. "You're in your cabin on the Lula. You're safe. The Marines got us out. We're headed back to the Capital."

"Serena?" Vance asked.

Mycal helped him sit up and swing his legs over the bedside.

"No word. Communications are out. Jules has everything locked down. We're headed back in stealth mode to get her now and stop whatever it is Jules has started."

Vance reached up and massaged his brow, closing his eyes and leaning forward.

"You okay, buddy?" Mycal asked.

"Yes." Vance said, "I know it. I know everything.

Mycal waited for him to continue.

"We've got to get to Serena."

"I know." Mycal said, "We're on our way. Best speed possible."

"We're being invaded," Vance said. "I don't know how deep it is yet, but it's gone very high. Jules is the leader and he's alone with Serena. We need to figure out a way to find out who has been--" Vance struggled with the words.

"Taken?" Mycal ventured.

"Yes," Vance said. "Like they almost had me."

"Is that what the mist was that came out of you?"

Vance looked up at Mycal.

"A black mist just came out of your mouth, eyes, ears and nose, then it just faded away."

"That was Shazar. A being from the middle of a black hole."

"What?" Mycal said.

"Look, please get me a drink of water," Vance said. "I need to quench a little thirst, get something to eat, and then I'll explain it all to you. We have some planning to do."

"That's the Vance we need." Mycal said. He was starting to feel a little better.

Chapter 38

Serena heard the outer door to her chambers open and close, then saw Jules enter with a tray of food and a bag. She could smell roast and mashed potatoes, her favorite, and wondered what Jules / Balthar had planned. Surely, she couldn't eat. She still couldn't move except to breath and blink her eyes. Well, she could swallow, but that's all she'd managed to do no matter how much she tried. Was Jules going to feed her?

He set the tray down on the side of her bed and the black bag next to it. Jules opened the bag and pulled out a sack of clear liquid and tubing.

"Yes, it's an IV drip. Can't have you getting dehydrated and looking too sallow for your big day," Jules / Balthar said as he went about setting up the drip system. Out of the bag came a folding stand to which he affixed the clear liquid and then she felt a slight pinch as he inserted the needle into her vein. At least she could feel that. He hung the IV sack then picked up the tray of food and sat in the chair next to her bed and began to eat.

"Forgive my rudeness. I still need to eat. I'm working quite hard you know, keeping things running in the Imperium and all. I'm also making a few changes, in your name of course, and under your seal." He paused to chew and swallow as Serena lay there, anger beginning to fester as it did each time he came in and checked on her.

It had been two days. There were only two more days until the State of the Imperium by her reckoning, and surely, she'd be missed if she didn't show up for that.

As if on cue, Jules spoke.

"We need to make sure you're completely ready. In the IV solution, I've put in more of the drug which will help you come out of your paralysis at just the right time. Of course, before then I'll come back and check your restraints, so you'll be sufficiently still both body and mind to accept your Gift.

"Speaking of Gifts, you should know that we had one each for Mycal and Vance. I told you this, I believe. Yes?"

Jules hesitated as if waiting for her reply and took another bite of food, chewing it thoughtfully and looking at her.

"This food is absolutely lovely. I have to be careful that I don't balloon out with weight, you know. Such a delight being able to taste your nourishment as you do. And then there's desert. I can't tell you what a temptation that has been."

Then Jules nodded as if remembering he'd been speaking about something specific.

"I'm sorry to say, that Mycal and Vance each resisted too much. They died."

If Serena could, she would have gasped, cried out and then tried to lunge at Jules and wrap her hands around his neck. As it was, a tear started out of the corner of her right eye and ran off the side of her face.

She watched Jules / Balthar, the hatred rising to burn in her chest. Then she noticed something slightly off. Her powers of observation noted something about Jules' expression and the inclination of his head as he watched her.

He was hiding something. Serena was sure of it. If she could speak, she'd ask him some questions. Something had not gone quite as he'd expected with Mycal and Vance.

"I'm so sorry for your loss, but I warned you it could happen," Jules said, taking another bite as if what he'd said was of no consequence. "Now if you'll just relax when it's your turn, and accept what's happening, then you'll survive, just as Jules is surviving and actually thriving within, as I guide and direct."

Did Jules really survive? Serena thought, again watching Jules / Balthar closely for any further signs she could discern. If even a bit of Jules remained, was he fighting within, trying to regain his body? Is that what killed Mycal and Vance? That they didn't give in? Well, it would be better to die than to live and be a tool for someone like Balthar.

Another thought took her then. The memory of how her mother and father had died. Jules had told her it was an accident. A one in a million malfunction in their spacecraft propulsion system.

And then, not long after, Jules' wife had also died in a bomb blast that was supposedly meant for Jules, but he was coincidentally out at meetings and escaped assassination himself.

Serena had always wondered if the two were connected, but no evidence showed any relation. With her knowledge now, she realized her parent's death was no accident. Jule's wife's death was also part of the plan. The invasion had started before then. When had Jules been possessed? He had always been in a position to control the flow of information.

Had these beings, these invaders, tried to recruit her father? Or had they simply orchestrated his death and gone directly after Jules, and through him to her? Did they think so little of her that they figured she would succumb easier to their taking her over?

They would find out differently. If Mycal and Vance had truly given their lives resisting, she could do no less. That's one way she could fight back.

"There's no use fighting this," Jules spoke, watching her carefully. "Even if you die, the succession then falls to me. So, I'll win no matter what. If you give in to the inevitable, you don't have to die. Besides, having you still here makes it possible for another of my people to cross over and have a place. Yes, a place of power, but if it doesn't work, it hasn't frustrated anything, really. Just a minor inconvenience for us."

Jules stood, then and once more checked the IV drip.

"I'll leave you to your thoughts. I've got to go write your new speech for the State of the Imperium. I have some great ideas, you know. Some of them you might even approve of.

"I plan to make use of yours and Vance's Truth initiative. You both are very trusted by the populace. Vance plan really is working marvelously. I can use that, you know. Of course, it won't be truth this time, but the people will certainly fall for it.

"I must say, I regret that we won't have Vance's uncanny ability to work with. His knowledge and analytical skills would have helped our cause a great deal. Still, we'll do fine without it. Things are too far along to be stopped now."

With that Jules picked up the bag and tray and she could hear him mumble something to the guards as he left her chambers. Serena was glad he was gone. She was afraid he might notice her lack of tears this time. Her careful observation of Jules / Bathar while he was talking about Vance had paid off. Jules / Balthar was definitely lying. Could that mean Vance and Mycal were not dead? Why was he trying so hard to make her think they were?

Her mind then turned to Vance and wondering how he was really doing. He was occupying a lot of her thoughts lately, and since she had nothing to do but think, that was a lot of time. She desperately hoped he was not dead. Maybe she was just wanting it too badly and had been seeing things in Jules' / Balthar's expressions.

No. She couldn't start doubting herself now. Either Vance and Mycal were alive and if so, then they would be coming for her if they could. If not, she still needed to fight. Either way, her actions would be the same. She would fight until an opportunity presented itself for her to escape and do something to counter this mess. If it didn't, her path was clear.

She would not cooperate. Serena would not be part of Balthar's plan.

Oh Vance. She thought. How I hope you're not dead. We barely had a chance to get started. I want to be able to finish with you.

Chapter 39

Vance had eaten and refreshed. It felt good and went a long way to restoring his strength. All the while he spoke with Mycal and recounted his experience with Shazar and what they were planning. Vance knew it all, and it amazed him this had all sprung up under all their noses. It was a full-scale invasion. The invaders weren't taking territory. They were taking everyone's bodies.

Mycal sat wide-eyed throughout the description. Then they had started in on planning what to do next.

Of course, with the Imperator heading back to the Capital before the communications were cut, they had to know Vance and Mycal would be coming. They would be flying into a trap.

There was nothing they could do about that except allow for it as much as they could, and rely on some surprises Vance had in mind.

It was determined their first and main priority was to get to Serena away from Jules and have her talk directly with the people.

Whatever was going on, Serena was no longer in control. She'd never have cut communications this way. The fact communications were still out was all the indication they needed to realize she was being held. Vance didn't say this out loud, but he also hoped it was an indication she was still her own person.

They talked and argued through many options and finally found one, and only one, which had some semblance of success. It was still a long shot.

With the planning done, Mycal excused himself to get back to the bridge and brief the crew.

Vance was left to himself and his thoughts. He was supposed to rest, still recovering from the ordeal of fighting off Shazar, but he couldn't really calm his mind.

His thoughts went to Serena. If she'd already been presented with a host how would she fare? She was as strong willed a person as Vance had ever met. If he had been able to resist, Serena certainly could. But Vance had thought of Serena and his love for her. That's what had saved him. Shazar, for some reason, was not compatible with that sort of feeling, that sort of *light* that came into his being any time he thought of Serena.

Did she feel the same about him? Not that he would expect it. It's just that she needed something powerful, something strong enough to hold onto that the host couldn't completely subdue.

Not long ago the thought of caring this much, of loving someone so deeply was completely foreign to him. Now the thought of being without that love, of living without Serena was something he couldn't bear.

All he could do is hope Serena would make it through. If anyone could, she would. If she didn't . . . And heaven help Jules and *whoever* he'd become.

Chapter 40

Vance strode onto the bridge of the Lula just before they were to drop out of hyperspace.

"Admiral on deck!" Gomy said as he came to attention at his weapons and science station.

"At ease," Vance said.

Mycal stood up from the command chair. Cassie and Ben both turned to look at Vance.

"Everything is ready," Mycal said, moving aside and allowing Vance to take the chair. "I'll head down to the torpedo deck and let you know when I'm ready. Vance nodded and Mycal strode off the bridge heading to the rear and lower deck of the ship.

"I'm assuming everyone has been briefed. Are there any question?" Vance looked around at each of the crew. Though, he didn't know any of them well, he was about to trust them all with his life. In return, they were trusting him – including Serena -- with their lives. He hoped what they'd planned, the sketchiest plan he'd ever enacted, would work. If it didn't . . . It was just the galaxy at stake.

"Weapons and shields ready," Gomy said.

"Comms programmed and ready," Cassie said.

"Navigation prepped and ready," Ben said. Then with a smile, "you'd all better buckle up. The Admiral requested the wildest evasives Lula can muster."

Vance nodded and at the same time heard Mycal over the shipboard comm. "I'm in place and ready to go. Get me as close as you can before you shoot me out."

"Will do," Vance said. "You sure the stealth package on the capsule will keep you hidden?"

"I'm sure," Mycal said over the comms. "I've used it before. The biggest risk is getting hit with a stray bolt from one of the ships gunning for you."

"We'll try not to get shot at during that time, then," Vance said. "Sit tight. You won't get a countdown. Gomy will just pull the trigger when I give the word."

Vance turned and nodded to Ben. "Bring us out of Hyper."

***

The forward viewscreen blurred with streaking stars which resolved into the resolution of normal space. Immediately a proximity claxon sounded.

Vance had asked them to emerge from hyperspace as close to Zyzeen as they possibly could, given the gravity well. There was the potential of hitting another ship, and it looked like a close thing, but true to Vance's supposition, the fleet had been pulled back within the circle of the potential entry points, except for scout ships send out further to see if they would emerge farther away and try and sneak in.

"Hit it, Ben," Vance said, and felt the acceleration pushing against the inertial dampeners of the little ship as she darted forward. The field in front of them was filled with ships, all arrayed against them. It seemed their strategy had been to pull in virtually every ship they could to block them from reaching the surface. They correctly guessed Vance would make a run at trying to land. He was sure they had a presence on the ground as well to block the way if Vance got through the fleet. One thing at a time, he thought.

"Commence firing," Vance ordered.

"Aye," Gomy said and started pressing buttons.

Vance watched as weapons exploded in front of them and on all sides. They weren't heavy weapons at all, and they wouldn't do damage to any of the ships arrayed in front of them. Instead, they were electromagnetic flashes designed to blind ship's sensors and make it harder for any of the ships around them to lock weapons. It also made it harder for them to be tracked.

"Anything with comms?" Vance asked as he felt Ben darting in among the larger ships, weaving as fast as possible in and through the mass of ships toward the planet on the other side.

"Sorry, Admiral," Cassie answered. "The frequency modulation is no longer working."

"It was too much to hope that they hadn't fixed it," Vance growled. "I didn't think we'd be able to use that more than once anyway, but it was worth a try."

They felt a jolt and a resounding boom lurched them at their stations.

"They're firing at us blindly," Gomy reported. "They're hitting their own ships, but it's close enough to throw us around a bit. Shields are at 70%. We're still moving through, though."

"Broaden the flashes by 15%. They're using the blind spot as an eyeball target. Let's make the target area larger so we don't make it easy. We've got some smart commanders out there. Probably not our enemies, but our own people who don't know any better.

"Cassie, go to plan B on the comms. Can you patch me in on fleetwide? I'll talk to the individual commanders and if nothing else, sow a bit of confusion as to who they're shooting at."

"All comms are blocked," Cassie responded. "Their comms are set to a secure intra-ship beam with heavy encryption. They also are jamming all frequencies so we can't call out to anyone, civilian or military. Apparently, they don't want you talking with anyone. They anticipated that as well."

"Not everything, I hope," Vance said, but inwardly he was cursing. He was running out of options. "Continue to see if you can hack into the network. I need to get through to all the commanders and keep them from blowing us out of space before we can get Mycal in position. Especially if they're willing to take out their own ships to do it."

Mycal was the key to everything. If he succeeded then it didn't matter about him. If all their planning had been anticipated, they just needed to hang on until Mycal could get free.

Another boom rocked the little ship.

"Shields at 40%. It took out a cruiser next to us," Gomy said, his voice incredulous. "Who would do that?"

Vance ignored him. "Ben. How far?" Vance could see the tense shoulders and cocked head of the young man as he focused on the finest flying Vance had ever seen. The viewscreen, when it wasn't obscured by the electromagnetic bursts Gomy was still sending out all around them, had ships blurring by at a speed that astonished Vance. He didn't know how Ben was avoiding some of those ships and was afraid there was as much chance of them hitting another ship as being hit by an energy blast.

"Give me another minute," Ben said through flying fingers and darting eyes. "The last two layers of ships are moving to close ranks, and some colliding as it is. They really want to keep us away from home."

Gomy spoke. "The larger ships are dumping off fighters since they can't bring weapons to bear effectively. They're inbound and will reach us in 20 seconds, max. And one more bit of good news. I'm just about out of Flashers. We'll be sitting ducks after this next volley."

"Can you still get through?" Vance asked Ben, seeing the mass of ships through a brief pause in the flashes as Gomy loaded the last of the ordinance into the tubes.

"Not without hitting something," Ben said, tilting his head briefly to a screen on his console. He'd been using part gut instinct and part directed sensors through a tunnel of the blasts he and Gomy had worked out. "They're just too close for us to fit through. They've got us totally boxed in."

Vance thought quickly. He had to get Mycal to the surface.

"Ben, spin us around with our backs to the planet and come dead in space. Face the fleet like we're going to blast back through again. Hopefully they'll consider what we're up to before the fighters start killing us.

"Gomy, get a firing solution for Mycal's capsule. Lock it in and time the last volley of Flashers to coincide with when you send Mycal off. Hopefully we're close enough he can make it to the surface. The Flashers will give him the last bit of cover we can."

"Ready," Gomy said.

"Fire him off," Vance said.

"He's gone and the last Flashers are detonating now."

Everyone waited, tensing for impact of enemy bolts striking their nearly undefended ship.

They all watched as the screens started to clear from the last Flasher blasts.

Gomy finally reported, "Sir, we're surrounded by fighters, all weapons locked. If they fire . . ."

"Can you track Mycal? Did he make it through?" Vance asked.

"I don't know, sir. The stealth package on his capsule is virtually undetectable even when I know what I'm looking for."

"Uh, the fighters?" Ben spoke from his station. "You want me to start evasive again? I don't think we want to be a stationary target."

"Signal our surrender on all emergency bands," Vance said to Cassie. She did a double take, looking at him, then quickly did as he directed.

"Surrender sent," she said.

Chapter 41

Mycal pushed open the lid of his tiny capsule from his reclining position. It had been a bumpy ride down to the planet's surface and at one point he could have sworn his capsule had hit something a glancing blow before the one-man pod had stabilized and dived for the surface of Zyzeen.

He sat up and looked around. It was pre-dawn local time and still dark enough to provide good cover. The stealth mode of the capsule was still operating, masking all heat and ER signatures from above. The programmed coordinates for the landing had set him down on the far side of the palace, just outside the regular security cordon and near the hidey hole only the royal family knew of. Of course, that included Jules, but hoped he hadn't considered that Mycal would use it to try and get back into the palace. After all, it was established as an escape route, not an entry point.

He climbed off the padded flight bed and made sure he had his blaster and comm situated and working. He didn't dare call Vance in orbit. It might be intercepted. But he'd need it locally if the small kernel of an idea he'd been mulling around in his mind started to gel a bit more. And when the mission was successful, he hoped Vance and his crew survived to pick up his call when it came.

The only other equipment he'd brought was his small accessory pouch affixed to his belt that had the tools necessary to open the backside doorway to get into the entry tunnel so he could slip into the palace undetected.

Mycal made his way through the dark to a rocky outcropping 50 meters to his north. Hidden at the base was the entryway he was looking for. It didn't take long to get it open and using a small pin light, he was able to start up the tight, shielded corridor to the palace proper.

As he moved, his mind was chewing over what Vance had described about being inhabited by the being called Shazar. What it had felt like, how it had overwhelmed Vance until he was able to catch hold thinking about Serena, and his burgeoning love for her. How it brought him light from inside and pushed back the darkness that was Shazar.

He'd been thinking about that, because no matter how much he hoped, he was fearful he might find Serena already taken by those beings from the heart of a black hole. And he needed to have some way to reach her, to bring her back.

It had got him thinking about another way to fight these beings, and his half-formed plan fell into place. It was taking a risk he didn't want to take, but he realized, if he didn't take it, the person on the other side of it would never forgive him. And he couldn't live with that even through the cost would be the highest he'd ever paid.

As he walked, Mycal keyed his comm to a secret, secure band and spoke, giving a quick explanation and then gave instructions. At the end of the conversation, he realized he'd either just done something really smart or condemned everything he held dear to the darkest abyss.

"In for a penny . . ." he said aloud as he continued to make his way in the dark tunnel. He laughed under his breath. He remembered when he'd first started using those archaic sayings which confused everyone around him. Except for one person. Adriana.

Well, Adriana had been confused too, but she thought he was cute when he used those sayings, and then he got to explain to her what they meant. That's how their relationship had begun. It warmed Mycal's heart to think of her. He knew full well what Vance meant in speaking about a light glowing from inside when thinking of someone you loved.

After this was all over, if it worked, he and Adriana could finally be together, out in the open. If not . . . nothing would ever matter again.

Chapter 42

Serena was flexing her muscles, laying in the bed trying to coerce more feeling, more movement back into her limbs. She was getting more control all the time. Soon, she'd have enough control to use her enhancements and break free. Then she'd see what she could do to take back control of her Imperium.

Jules had come in several times to replace the IV drip. It was the drug that was supposed to remove her paralysis and also make her more susceptible to whatever he was going to do to her next. By her reckoning the time was getting close, though she couldn't be sure. Along with her body starting to respond, her mind was getting fuzzier. Not to where she couldn't think, but her mind was slower, not as sharp. A bit more time and she'd be there.

Just then she heard Jules enter the outer door and came striding into the room. He'd left the lights on so she could see him clearly as he dropped his usual black bag on the bed and looked at the IV drip. He carefully squeezed the remaining fluid into the line and lifted the line so the fluid could run into Serena's arm.

"I think you're there," Jules said as he disconnected the plastic sack and put it into the bag and started folding up the metal holder and fit it into the bag also.

"You've got a big night tonight. I've got your speech all written. It will be great if I do say so myself. Tonight, you'll deliver the Imperium into our hands. Of course, you'll be part of it, albeit not willingly.

"Too bad Mycal and Vance aren't here to be part of it like we'd originally planned. It would have been so much more powerful to have your betrothed there and then have the wedding directly after. Such a storybook ending."

Jules disconnected the line from her vein and wiped her small needle wound with a cotton swab. "We all must adjust. Instead, we've had to create a different narrative about Vance being a traitor and being killed for it. It's going to be a harder sell, but it will still add to our plans. The populace will be stunned, and that works for our cause nicely. We have to get the population prepared to receive their Gifts just like you."

Jules reached into the bag and came out holding a silver sphere with slight markings etched on the surface. Serena just stared at it. She tried to speak, to say something defiant, but she couldn't. Jules chuckled as he saw her mouth move and no sound came out.

If she were going to escape, now would be the time. She strained at her bonds, but still just couldn't control her enhanced physique enough to break free.

Jules noticed her straining.

"It's no use, you know. Those bands are as secure as I could make them. And now it's time. You need to adjust to your new friend, and she to you before your big night. First let's dim the lights to get the proper atmosphere."

The lights in the room dimmed in response to the voice command.

"A bit dimmer, please," Jules added, and the lights responded to where the room was near dark with just enough light to make out Jules' form moving above her, holding the silver orb over her chest.

"Now just relax. This won't hurt a bit. Your whole existence is about to change."

***

Mycal was making his way up through the back ways of the palace, mostly in hidden corridors used by the servants and maintenance people. The palace seemed deserted, which was odd given they should all be preparing for the big State of the Imperium bash Vance had told him about while briefing him on what had happened since he'd gone missing. That seemed so long ago. Well, it would make it easier for the person he'd called for help to slip through. He'd given precise instructions, but should he wait? No, he decided. Time was of the essence, if he wasn't already too late. Ah, here was the passage.

Mycal moved to the end of a hallway and touched a carved molding in a certain way. The wall slid open and Mycal slipped inside while the panel slid back into place behind him. A dim strip of lights lined the floor so he could quickly make his way up the stairs to the residential wing of the palace. He picked up his pace.

It didn't take long to get to the hidden panel he was looking for. He put his head to the wall and heard a voice inside. It wasn't Serena's.

The lever was touched, and the panel slid open. Mycal quickly stepped into Serena's bed chamber. The wall panel was on the far side of the doorway and the lights were extremely dim. Mycal remembered when he and Vance were laying on tables and the lights were dimmed.

He saw the outline of what must be Jules hovering over Serena's bed. He could barely make her out laying there, Jules holding one of those silver orbs in his hand.

"Stop where you are!" Mycal shouted, hoping to stop what Jules was doing before it was too late.

"Lights. Maximum." Mycal called and Jules stood, squinting. Mycal started to move forward, using his enhanced abilities. He could see Jules speaking something aloud, giving orders and calling, no doubt, for help. Mycal had to do something fast or Jules' people would be here in enough force to take Mycal down, enhancements or not. But with the palace being as empty as he'd noted, maybe it would take time before a significant force arrived.

"Stop." Jules said, and Mycal stopped short. He'd crossed half the distance but what he saw made him freeze.

Jules was holding a dagger to Serena's throat. "I'll kill her. My people will be here shortly," Jules said, but Mycal was looking at Serena. The orb Jules was holding was still closed. He'd been in time. Though what he could do now, he didn't know.

"You escaped Bohera, but you won't escape me." Jules said. Mycal didn't know who Bohera was, and then it hit him. The territorial governor? But his name was Mon Sena. Bohera must be his alien hitchhiker.

"I'm speaking with Balthar, I presume?" Mycal asked. Not because he cared, but to give him time to figure something out. He just wasn't close enough to reach Jules before he could kill Serena. He didn't doubt Balthar / Jules meant what he said. Mycal looked at Serena and she was staring back at him as if she'd seen a ghost. And then a smile broke across her face as if she finally realized he was standing there.

"Where is Vance?" she asked, her voice throaty and harsh, barely loud enough to hear, but her expression was full of hope, completely ignoring the knife at her throat.

Chapter 43

Vance sat in the command chair, waiting. It had been some time. He looked at Cassie, who was still huddled over her communications console, trying to break into the encrypted tight beam communications between the ships. Somehow, he needed to get through, needed all of the military to hear his side.

Gomy was standing at his console, striving to repair the shields, now down to 30%. They were still surrounded by the smaller fighters, weapons locked on.

Ben was sitting at his station, hands in his lap. There was nothing he could do, no place for him to pilot the ship unless he was prepared to ram vessels in a play to take as many with them as they could.

What is their commander thinking? Vance wondered. Why is he waiting? He had them dead to rights. If they were going to kill them, they should have done it already.

However, the fact they hadn't lent credence to his thought that the other commander was worried at what his subordinates would think, firing on a vessel who had surrendered. At least that message had gotten through to all the ships broadcast as it was on all the emergency bands.

Well, the waiting didn't hurt. The more time he could give Mycal to get to Serena, the better. The fact he hadn't heard anything from Mycal on their own tight beam comms, was a good sign. If there had been trouble, Mycal would have let them know. He also would've let them know if he'd had success.

So, things were still pending on all fronts.

Vance had to stay focused. He desperately was worried for Serena, but there was nothing he could do for her now, except what he was doing. And that was to distract the military and somehow turn them back. He hated this waiting.

Gomy interrupted the silence, "I've got where I can return shields to full power."

"Good work, Gomy," Vance said, "but hold on that. Be ready to punch them to full power the second I give the word. We don't want to tip our hand quite yet."

"Aye, sir."

"Cassie, any luck on breaking encryption on the comms?"

"Sorry, sir," Cassie said.

"Wait," Vance said, holding up his hand. "I'm getting something coming through on my personal band. It's from the Joint Chiefs. Rear Admiral Collins putting in a personal comm call to me." Vance was astonished, then brightened.

He looked at Cassie, his eyebrows raised. She smiled, nodded and turned back to her console, fingers darting across the board.

"Admiral Collins," Vance said through his lapel mic, and hearing through his ear bud. "So good to hear from you."

"Let's dispense with the pleasantries, Hamblin. You know why I'm calling."

"Oh, do I?" Vance said. "Perhaps you can enlighten me."

"If you must insist, I'll be formal about it," Admiral Collins said. "We're here to execute a duly authorized warrant for your arrest, yours and Commander Petrs'. You're charged with treason and murder in the disappearance of 1st Minister Wallach."

"Come on Admiral," Vance said, "It's just you and me. Incidentally, I find it pretty interesting that you're calling on a private comm. It makes me wonder, do your subcommanders even know who's on this ship? Are you worried about their loyalty? And while we're at it, I really am Admiral J. Vance Hamblin, soon to be Commander-in-Chief. Now tell me who you really are."

"What?" Collins said. "I'm not sure I know what you're talking about."

"Of course, you do," Vance said, "You obviously know one of yours tried to recruit me, just as I'm sure you've been recruited. Does the name Shazar ring a bell?"

Collins was silent for a long moment. When he spoke the tone of his voice had changed.

"I'd heard Shazar was Taking you. I don't know how you resisted but rest assured Shazar will be back. Just because he couldn't possess you, doesn't mean he died. He's gone back to Isabar, our home. The process is painful, as we've learned over the years moving into your realm from ours, but he'll strengthen, regenerate and if Balthar commands -- and you survive, Shazar will have another crack at you."

"I wouldn't count on it." Vance said. He looked around his bridge crew. They were in rapt attention, listening to him speak.

"During the time Shazar was trying to take possession of my body, I learned everything, learned that you were trying to infiltrate our Imperium, coming out of the bowels of a black hole and possessing bodies of good men and women. Planning to take over our Imperium, to take over all of our bodies and enslave us. And in the end, kill us all."

"Yes," Collins said, "You must've been very deep into the Taking if you learned all that. Again, I'm shocked you were that deep and Shazar still failed. You pathetic humans are so weak. You don't deserve all you have, all these priceless sensations and feelings and the appetites. It's the natural order that superior beings should supplant you pathetic weaklings and take over your realm. Balthar's plan is foolproof. There's nothing you can do to stop it now. Your only choice, Hamblin, is to live and be taken into custody so that we can decide who, if not Shazar, should Take you. It's that or you die right here. Right now."

"Let's see," Vance said. "Not much of a choice. And by the way, when you refer to Balthar, you're speaking of Jules Mattock, the Chamberlain, are you not? And that must make you Bethel? You are second in command to Balthar from what I get from Shazar's memories?"

"I see you've figured out a great deal," Collins said, "Even now Balthar / Jules has the Empress and is giving her the Gift. Soon she'll be one of us and the Imperium will truly be in our hands. Either that, or she will die. It's exactly the same choice you have."

Vance looked at Cassie. Her eyes were wide with shock, but she nodded.

It had worked.

Vance made a victorious pumping motion with his fist. Ben smiled and echoed the motion, though Vance could tell he was clearly terrified at what he'd heard.

"Actually," Vance said, "I choose neither of those options and instead, I'm giving you an ultimatum of my own." He smiled widely. "You should know, Bethel, that our *personal* conversation has just been broadcast to all personal comms within your fleet. And all others within range, civilian or military.

"All those listening on this comm, you now have direct evidence that our Imperium is under invasion. The Chairman of the Joint Chiefs, Rear Admiral Collins, has been possessed by an alien being and using his body as host.

"All ships within this fleet are commanded to stand down. All officers on all ships, if your leadership does not comply with this order immediately, you're to take them into custody or execute them immediately. They are the enemy. They will also have been possessed.

"All officers on the command ship Imperator where the Joint Chiefs are housed," he looked at Cassie and she nodded, confirming that's where the comm had originated. "You are immediately commanded to take under arrest all of the Joint Chiefs and their party. Those who resist should be subdued with minimal force, as we're not sure who has been possessed and who has not, with the exception of Admiral Collins. If he resists, use lethal force. You will all execute my orders now!"

Vance now stood from the command chair and stared out the viewscreen at the fighters surrounding the Lula. "Those fighters surrounding this vessel, know that I'm in command. Admiral J. Vance Hamblin, soon to be Commander-in-Chief of the armed forces of the Imperium. Any fighter which begins an attack on this vessel is to be brought under fire immediately and destroyed. Any other vessel that displays hostile intent towards us is also to be taken under fire by those ships nearest.

"Each commander, or succeeding commander, will immediately broadcast surrender to this vessel and place yourself under my command."

Cassie started to smile. "They got it all," she said.

"Excellent," Vance said, "Admiral Collins, I suggest you lay down your weapons and submit yourself to arrest. Your fleet will soon be in my hands."

"This is nothing but a bluff." Collins sputtered. It was clear he was confused at the flurry of orders Vance had given.

"I have an excellent communications officer," Vance said, "as you'll soon find out."

Just then Vance heard a commotion, a sound of blaster fire, angry shouts, muffled curses. He sat back in the command chair and listened. He looked at Cassie.

"All the fighters have signaled surrender and placed themselves under our command. Apparently, if there's any invaders in the fighters, they're trying to hide in plain sight." She cocked her head, listening to the bud in her ear. "Now the other ships are reporting in."

Vance sat back, "Signal all fighters to face outward. Prepare to defend this ship and any other ships siding with us." He then nodded to Gomy. "Shields up."

"Aye sir," Gomy said together.

"And again, we wait," Vance said.

Chapter 44

"Sir, communications are opening up across the fleet," Cassie said. All local channels. The hyper relays are still down. Almost all ships have reported in. They have secured their ships and have placed themselves under your command. Three ships are breaking ranks. They haven't broadcast surrender."

"Send five ships closest to round them up," Vance ordered.

Cassie nodded, then said. "Admiral Vance, communication coming from Captain Goshen of the Imperator."

"Patch him through," Vance said.

The image of Captain Goshen flashed on the main view screen.

"Captain," Vance said, "good to see you."

"And you Admiral. I must say when I was ordered to leave you back on Metronome and make haste back to the Capital, and that you'd been arrested on charges of treason and murder I suspected something severely wrong. Then when the Joint Chiefs came aboard and set the fleet around Zyzeen *protect* it from you; I couldn't believe it. In fact, I didn't believe it."

"I'm glad you've had your disbelief confirmed, Captain." Vance smiled.

"The Imperator is secure and loyal to you and the Imperium. All the Joint Chiefs have been taken under arrest. Rear Admiral Collins sustained some injuries. The rest came quietly. I can't say as I quite know who's who and I don't know how we're going to sort it out, but we've rounded them all up. As far as I know, very few officers of other ships were involved. And by the way, Commodore Blaine, the one that escorted you down to the planet Gothway had to be killed. The guards attached to him, are under arrest."

"Good work Captain. I'm transferring command of the fleet to you. I need to get down to Zyzeen now."

"Aye sir."

"And have the fleet surround the planet in defensive posture. No one is to come or leave until I say so. We are under active invasion."

The Captain saluted on the screen and it blanked out.

Vance looked at Ben, "Get those fighters out of the way and have them escort us down to Zyzeen. We're going to the Capital and we may need covering fire."

"The fighters heard that," Cassie said, "I had the comm open just in case, more efficient that way."

"Good," Vance said, "Now let's move."

On the screen, the fighters parted, and Ben's fingers danced on his console as they dove for the planet being flanked by the fighters who minutes ago were prepared to destroy them.

"Congratulations, Admiral," Cassie said, "You saved the day once again, with a minimal body count."

"Not yet we haven't. I just thought of something. We need to keep communications from reaching the planet."

"Already done," Cassie said, "I guessed you didn't want the Chamberlain to have any notice of what was happening. Of course, when he doesn't get a report from his followers, he'll be suspicious."

"Get there faster Ben."

"Aye sir," he said from his console, as the planet grew bigger in the screen.

Vance's heart was beating faster now than when surrounded by fighters waiting to destroy them. He prayed Mycal had been able to get to Serena.

Chapter 45

Mycal stood, staring at Jules holding the dagger to Serena's throat. In his left hand, Jules still held the orb above her chest. Mycal waited, scarcely daring to move.

Just at that moment, four guards rushed through the doorway. Their weapons were drawn and leveled as they moved into a semicircle between Mycal, Jules and Serena, blocking his path.

"A valiant effort," Jules said, "At least my way you'll still live."

"You mean my body will live serving as a host to one of your people. I'd rather die."

"As would I." Serena spoke, her voice was stronger now.

Mycal looked at Serena. Their eyes met, understanding passed between them like it had since they were children.

This was the moment, and they both had made their choice.

Mycal subtly tensed, ready to go into action. Then a slight sound behind him made him pause. The panel through which he'd come had opened.

"Father?" A voice came from behind him, but he knew that voice. He watched Jules' face as his eyes widened in astonishment, but he didn't dare look back, didn't dare take his eyes from Jules holding the knife.

"Adriana?"

"Father, what are you doing?"

For just a split second, Jules lowered the dagger. The hand holding the orb, moved back. Consternation crossed his face. Then his teeth grit and a rigid look came over him, as if he was fighting within himself.

At that moment, Mycal saw Serena move almost faster than the eye could follow. She snapped her right hand from the restraint and drove her fist into Jules' solar plexus. Mycal took that as a sign to move himself. The guards surrounding him were confused momentarily. That's all it took. Mycal went into his own blinding motion.

Two guards were down in a blink. One of the remaining fired in Mycal's direction, but it went wide spattering into the wall, leaving a burn hole. Then Mycal was inside his aim. A quick slap and he was down. The remaining guard stood back a pace. The blaster leveled at Mycal's chest.

"You're not that quick," he said. Mycal glanced and Serena was now free. She was hovered over Jules, who was laying on the floor, holding him down at knife point.

"You've lost," Mycal said. "Look." And he gestured at Jules on the floor at Serena's mercy.

It was then Adriana came quietly up behind the guard and clocked him over the head with a vase she'd picked up from a nearby pedestal. Mycal laughed.

"My hero!" And he stepped forward taking Adriana into a tender embrace. "Your timing is impeccable," Mycal said. "Now let's go see how your father is doing."

"But you said he's not my father," Adriana said as Mycal took her by the hand and moved over to where Serena was kneeling above Jules, His face a rictus of anger.

"We'll still win. You can't stop us." He was growling.

"Looks like we already have," Serena said. "Adriana, you're alive?"

"A necessary subterfuge," Mycal said. "I'll tell you about it later."

"I expect you will," Serena said, casting quick glances between Mycal and Adriana. Mycal realized she'd seen what had transpired between them. And she knew him well enough to discern everything.

"Father, are you in there?" Adriana knelt next to her father, took his hand and pushed the silver orb away. It rolled across the floor and Mycal went and picked it up, holding it carefully. He didn't want it to open accidentally. He knew what was inside. Mycal turned back to watch as Jules' face wrenched as in agony.

"No!" He shouted. "You can't have him. He's mine. I took him. I'll kill him first."

"Father, it's me, Adriana. Fight him. Come back to me. You're all I have left."

Jules' body started thrashing, head moving side to side, his teeth grit, eyes clenched. Serena held him down on one side, Mycal came and held down the other side using their enhanced strength. Still, it was hard holding him.

"Please!" Adriana reached out and touched his cheek. "I need you."

"Ughhhh!" Jules' body heaved upward, then came a groan as Jules' body went limp. Adriana gasped, tears running down her cheeks.

Jules was still for a long moment. He was no longer breathing.

"Father? Father? Is he still alive?" Adriana looked imploringly at Mycal.

Jules' slackened mouth opened.

"Stand back," Mycal said, and abruptly thumped Jules on the chest sharply with his fist. Then he began to do chest compressions with both hands.

"What are you doing?" Adrianna asked. "You'll hurt him."

"It's an ancient technique," Mycal said. "I'm trying to save him."

Serena put her arm around Adrianna's shoulders.

Jules gasped, and coughed, then settled back to the floor. His eyes were still closed, and he wasn't conscious. Mycal noted the rise and fall of his chest. He was breathing again. Mycal touched Jules' neck.

"He's breathing and his heart is beating. I hope he's stable for now."

Serena glanced at Mycal. He knew what she wanted to know.

"Whoever's inside didn't come out. We would have seen it as a black smoke or mist coming out of Jules' mouth, nose and ears."

Mycal spoke to Adrianna. "I'm sorry, but at least he's alive. We'll figure out a way to get this thing out of him. You saved his life, you know. You saved all of us."

Just then there was a commotion in the outer room, a sound of many footsteps rushing to the door. Mycal stood and turned ready to fight. He looked around for his blaster, any blaster. There was not one close. He kicked himself for not grabbing one again. The sound was getting louder.

Vance burst into the room, followed by Cassie, Gomy and Ben. Behind them was Captain Zander and a detachment of marines. They stood there, taking in the scene.

Mycal smiled and relaxed.

"All secure here," Mycal said with a grin. "I take it things went well on your end?" Vance ignored him and moved forward. Mycal turned just in time to find Serena rushing past him into Vance's arms.

"I thought I'd lost you," Vance said.

"I thought I'd lost *you*." Serena answered. Then they kissed.

"Hey, brother standing here," Mycal said. He smiled again as they ignored him.

Chapter 46

Vance stood proudly in the spotlight next to Serena. She was dressed in the formal robes of office as Empress of the Imperium. Her speech was being broadcast throughout the known worlds.

The last few hours had been a whirlwind. Serena had decided to proceed with the State of the Imperium address. So much had happened, leaving the populace confused and worried.

Communications had been restored. The fleet sent to the Obdure 4 system to blockade it for now. Mycal was with Adrianna, who was attending a still comatose Jules. Vance knew of the inner struggle Jules must be having. The problem of how to identify the invaders and remove them safely from their hosts was still before them. But for now, Vance was simply accepting their first victory, Serena's victory.

She was speaking directly to her people, telling them the truth. They all, Imperium wide, had just heard the recording Cassie had made of Vance and Rear Admiral Collins' discussion. It was pretty evident to all what it meant.

Then Serena was speaking again, and Vance's attention returned.

"I've told you before, I will give you the truth and trust you with the result. We have just fought off an invasion of unprecedented proportions. People in key positions were taken and inhabited by these invaders from the heart of a black hole. Through the efforts of

Admiral Hamblin and those assisting him, that invasion has been foiled.

"We captured their leader and are holding him for interrogation to learn their plans and find out all who've been Taken. We will use all our efforts to rid our people of these beings.

"The Obdure 4 system is under quarantine. They know, from this broadcast we have discovered them. And I speak directly to those beings. We are coming for you. We will allow you to leave our people peacefully and unharmed. We will trouble you no further if you go back to your own realm and leave ours alone!

"Now you know the truth. There is danger out there from unknown sources. Our best defense is for each of us to simply be good, honorable people. Do what is right to help and serve one another. Stay vigilant. Being people of Light is our best defense against the Darkness."

Those in the audience chamber began to applaud.

Vance smiled, as did Serena looking back at him.

She winked then held her hands up as the audience slowly subsided.

"Now for the best part of this event." She smiled broadly. "It's time for me to get married!"

The audience erupted in cheers, even louder than before.

An attendant brought up an old-fashioned veil and helped Serena affix it beautifully in her hair. Chief Justice Brennr of the Imperium Court came forward. He looked a little gruff but was in good spirits.

Vance moved forward and took Serena's hand. And Serena, still speaking to the Imperium wide audience said, "And now you all know why I wanted to marry this guy. You've seen for yourselves this Commander-in-Chief is anything but honorary."

Vance was abashed as the audience cheered again, though quickly subsided as Justice Brennr began the wedding ceremony.

Vance hardly heard the words, until it came time for him to say, "I do!"

Justice Brennr made the final pronouncement, and they were officially wed.

Then Vance had Serena in his arms. He kissed her tenderly and moved back. They were inundated with thunderous cheers and applause. Vance had to lean in to speak so Serena could hear.

"We still haven't talked about the honeymoon," Vance said quietly, unaware his microphone was still on, being broadcast to the entire known worlds.

"I'm sure we'll figure it out," Serena said, "Now kiss me again." And he did.

The End of This Episode
Yet The Adventure Continues . . .

If you liked this book, you'll love "Recruit 2". Stakes get higher and action more intense. Continue the ride.

Go to Brad Stucki's Author Page and click "FOLLOW" to be notified of new adventures. Don't miss your next great read.

About the Author

Brad Stucki was born and raised in Southwestern Utah, keeping horses, cows and other assorted pets. He is the third of 6 children and survived childhood only by utilizing an active imagination. His hobbies include reading and travel. He lives in a remote mountain valley, population 150 (give or take).

Made in the USA
Middletown, DE
25 October 2023

41398813R00179